The Boyfriend Wish

The Boyfriend Wish

SWATI TEERDHALA

 KATHERINE TEGEN BOOKS
An Imprint of HarperCollins Publishers

Katherine Tegen Books is an imprint of HarperCollins Publishers.

The Boyfriend Wish

Copyright © 2024 by Swati Teerdhala

All rights reserved. Printed in the United States of America.

No part of this book may be used or reproduced in any manner
whatsoever without written permission except in the case of brief
quotations embodied in critical articles and reviews. For information
address HarperCollins Children's Books, a division of HarperCollins
Publishers, 195 Broadway, New York, NY 10007.

www.epicreads.com

Library of Congress Control Number: 2023936894

ISBN 978-0-06-327915-5

Typography by Molly Fehr

23 24 25 26 27 LBC 5 4 3 2 1

First Edition

To my husband.
You're my wish come true.

1

There are certain moments that define your life—a first date,
a gut-wrenching breakup, making the winning goal.

Today would determine my entire junior year.

I had gotten up at 6:30 a.m. on the dot, giving me thirty
minutes of a head start before either of my sisters woke
up to shower. Three girls in one house are no joke on the
water bill, as my dad likes to remind us often. By 7:00 a.m.
I was dressed and wrestling my hair into submission as the
house woke, which would leave me just enough time to zip
over to Mimi's Bubble Tea before first period to grab the
classic with a double shot, the way Jake likes it.

Seems like a lot of effort, I know. But today I was going
to ask Jake Nakamura to the homecoming dance—on the
last day of the time-honored Edison High asking week.
I had planned it carefully, from what I would wear to what
I would say and, of course, the exact timing of it all. It was
step one in my ultimate plan. Steps two to twenty were
next (and outlined in my binder), all laid out to hopefully
lead to one thing: getting the perfect boyfriend.

And finally finishing The List.

Lily, my best friend, and I had written our list—The List—after our first day at Edison High two years ago. It was the list to rule all lists, one that would tell us at graduation if we had managed to pull off the perfect Edison High School experience. Everyone always says high school is the most important four years of your life, so what better way to make sure you made the most of it than a plan?

Like my mom always said, a plan in hand was better than two opportunities in the bush. And it had worked out for her—award-winning ob-gyn, married to her high school sweetheart, three amazing girls (if I may say so). She was even halfway done with her plan to become the Dr. Sanjay Gupta of women's medicine.

I'd already crossed off the smaller things, like performing at Edison's famed International Night and getting Pete Hernandez's sweaty jersey after the Edison–South Central soccer finals, and some of the bigger ones, like getting all As on my sophomore-year report card.

Now there were only two things on The List I hadn't done, two things I had added at the last minute.

And this was the big one. This was my chance to clinch that coveted high school boyfriend, just one step away from high school sweethearts (like my parents), and three jumps and a skip from the perfect life. It had worked for my mom and dad; it would work for me too. My dad had been the first Josyula to find his true love during asking week and I would find mine too.

So, step one. Ask Jake Nakamura out to homecoming during asking week. Fingers crossed.

I smoothed my dress down and took a last look in the mirror. Hair tamed, fabulous dress on, and as a last touch, red lipstick. My aunt always said there was nothing a good red lip couldn't cure, and if it could help the fluttering swarm of butterflies in my stomach, I was game. Plus, I liked the way it made me feel like a bolder version of myself.

That energy carried me down the stairs and to the kitchen.

"Hey, hey!" My dad popped his head around the corner, a cup of steaming coffee in his hand. His hair was a messy mop of curls, so different from mine. I inherited my straight, refuses to curl, yet is infuriatingly thick hair from my mom. "Easy there. We just got those floors in."

"We got them in like a year ago, Dad," I said. "Anyway, the hardwood guy said we could tap-dance in stilettos, and it wouldn't matter."

My dad chuckled. "There's that steel trap of a mind that I wish you didn't have."

"You love it," I said. "The car salesman last weekend hated me. I'm a fabulous asset."

My dad took a long sip of his coffee. "That you are. Where's the fire? You're ahead of schedule for the day. I bet Mani hasn't even showered yet."

A bang and the sound of shuffling feet came from upstairs.

"That's Mani," I said. Then came the yelling. "And Ratna."

Cue the fighting: one, two, three . . .

"Get out of here!!" Ratna's voice carried down the steps, to the kitchen, and probably out to our neighbors as well. I ignored the chaos and tried to think, rummaging through the kitchen drawers.

Ballpoint pens, paper clips, scissors, and—ah, there we were. I pulled out the final touch I needed for my proposal, an old collector's quarter I had hidden away from my sisters. Ratna's special talent was finding anything you didn't want found and then somehow losing it. I had avoided that whole mess by hiding it in the cutlery drawer, somewhere she would never want to look.

I held out the quarter and admired it. Well, I didn't really get it, but I knew Jake had been looking for this last quarter, the 2004 Wisconsin state quarter with that squiggly little extra leaf. It was all he'd talked about during tennis warm-ups for the past six months.

We'd had pretty much the perfect meet-cute. It had been the first day of tryouts for tennis and we'd knocked heads going for the same down-the-middle ball. And when we got paired as partners for mixed doubles matches, I knew it was a sign from the universe that it was meant to be. We'd been talking for a while now and today was the day.

My mom walked into the kitchen then, white coat draped over one arm and keys in hand. She wasn't particularly tall—none of the women in our family were—but she had a presence. Everything from her short, collarbone-length haircut to her sleek shoes and precisely applied makeup screamed "I have my life together." She snapped her phone shut and sighed. "It's worse than I thought, Suraj—"

She stopped the second she saw me, her eyes going wide.

"What is?" I said, even though these days, there was only one reason my mom took secretive phone calls. And it didn't have to do with her book deal, which Ratna found out about in a day and told all of us about. She had totally stolen my mom's thunder. "How's she doing?"

My mom sighed and rubbed her temple. "Your aunt's okay. Doing well, actually. Starting a new yoga retreat, I think. Or maybe it was a meditation workshop?"

"Still on that 'finding herself' kick?" my dad said. I thought I heard him snort, but when I turned around, he looked innocently out the window.

I grabbed two slices of whole wheat bread and popped them into the toaster.

"It's not a kick, Suraj," my mom said, swatting at his shoulder. "Or not much of one. You know what the past few years did to her. It takes time after something like that to figure out what you want. To make a new plan."

A few years ago, just as I was about to enter high school, my aunt had come to stay with us out of the blue. It took a few days before I learned that my aunt's marriage of six

5

years had fallen apart, and my aunt with it. My beautiful, lively, free-spirited aunt's entire life had vanished in front of her eyes, just because she had decided to give her heart away to the wrong person.

That was a mistake I wasn't going to make.

I looked out to the garden as I prepped breakfast—tomato chutney and butter on sourdough—for my grandma. I knew she'd be gardening later. I was used to seeing her small sari-clad figure tending the flowers with a care that edged on reverential. I still remembered when my aunt's news first broke—my grandma had spent day and night out there, taking it on herself to rebuild our patchy, dying garden. Like it might fix my aunt's marriage.

It hadn't, but my grandma hadn't stopped her habit of spending the morning with her flowers and plants. Which was probably why we had a jasmine bush in our yard that was still alive after being transported from India forty years ago. I called it Maya.

"Your aunt's coming by next weekend, so taco night?" my mom said.

My mom and her sister couldn't be more different, but they were close despite their large age gap, and I adored my aunt.

"Of course," I said. "We can do Cantina Fresca. By then, I'll have clinched my best year ever. I can give her the entire play-by-play over guacamole and perfectly salted chips."

"Best year ever? Does that include the prank war?" my

dad said. "You used to always say high school wouldn't be complete till you won it once."

My mom laughed. "If that's what you're talking about, you have a hard road in front of you, what with Vik winning every year."

I flinched. I had thought it was an unspoken rule that we didn't speak of that *thing* or *anyone* related to it, especially not before breakfast.

"We were in middle school, Amma," I said. "We weren't that little."

"You'll always be my little baby," my mom said in Telugu, reaching over to pinch my cheek.

I rolled my eyes.

My mom had been feeling especially sentimental since I had started my junior year of high school a month ago. I'd be doing something totally normal, like folding my laundry, and I'd look over and she'd be sobbing. Even Superwoman needed time to just be.

My mom took a big bite out of her gluten-free blueberry waffle, somehow managing to not smudge her pink lipstick. "I ran into Reshma yesterday while taking out the trash and she was saying he's been spending all hours of the night working on his new plans," she said. "She was complaining that she never sees her son."

Maybe that was a good thing. Vik was the bane of my existence, the neighbor from hell, the nightmare I've known since I was ten.

7

I scoffed at that. "Vikram Mehta does not plan. He schemes. I'll have to warn Lily that he's ramping up," I said. "Wouldn't want her to wake up and put her foot into a bowl of peanut butter, like in seventh grade."

"Peanut butter?" my dad said. "You didn't tell us about that one."

I grabbed my toast and started spreading mango chutney and cream cheese on it. There were some things you didn't tell your parents, but I knew my dad loved hearing about the stupid prank war. Too bad it was the last thing I wanted to talk about today. Asking week could determine your entire year romantically, and for senior year too. Lines were drawn in the battle of love junior year, and if I wanted a high school boyfriend at all, this had to go well.

"Anyway, I have better things to do, especially today," I said. "Today is the first day of the rest of my life. Today I will finally get the—"

Something caught my eye through the window.

I stared out the kitchen window, our driveway in full view. The bright early-morning sun glinted like magic off the disaster in front of me.

My car was covered in pink Saran Wrap like a badly wrapped gift from a mall Santa shop. Painted on top of the Saran Wrap were the words "YOUR MOVE."

Vik had struck again.

2

Okay, so Vik's clear act of aggression wasn't totally unwarranted. The prank war in our little cul-de-sac at the end of Oceania Court Drive was legendary, talked about at every neighborhood Fourth of July block party, every annual Diwali, Hanukkah, Christmas party—every party, period. And every single year, Vik beat me and Lily.

I always thought it was kind of funny that one of my neighbors became my best friend and the other my mortal enemy. The story began with Vik putting Silly Putty in my hair the morning of sixth-grade photo day (which is a pretty good reason for a never-ending vendetta, in my opinion), but it didn't end there. Silly Putty is mild compared to some of the things we've done to each other over the years.

I took a deep breath. Closed my eyes. When I opened them, the disaster was still there.

"Oh my GOD," I said. I abandoned my breakfast and grabbed my backpack from the counter, trying not to panic. Unwrapping the Saran would take me at least a half hour, effectively trampling whatever head start I had given myself for the big day. "Didn't anyone look outside today?"

Their blank stares told me all I needed to know. I sighed and walked to the front door, my parents following close behind. I yanked the door open for the grand reveal, expecting indignation and declarations of loyalty in my impending war with our neighbor's son.

Instead, my dad burst into laughter. Even my mom couldn't contain herself.

"That's pretty good," my dad said, holding a hand to his side. He looked outside and snorted.

I had to agree, but why today of all days?

"Got to give him credit for innovation," my mom said.

A head appeared over the banister. "He is bringing his A game," Mani said, toothbrush in mouth.

Even Ratna, my baby sister, seemed pretty impressed. All of thirteen years old and way too smart for her age.

Traitors. All of them.

"I don't have time for this," I muttered, checking my watch. I was five minutes behind my schedule and I was pretty sure I'd have to nix the coffee from Mimi's Bubble Tea.

My disloyal family was now reminiscing over the best pranks that the cul-de-sac had seen.

"—good thing he hosed it down before Reshma returned," my dad said. "Though that white chalk was an improvement to the house."

"It's not that bad," my mom said. "It's a great lot. It just needs a fresh coat of paint. I've always wondered why it hasn't sold yet."

"The corner lot? I thought it was haunted," Ratna said.

"Nothing that cool would ever happen on our street," Mani said. "It was just empty because the old owners thought they might move back."

"That wasn't a prank, it was vandalism," I said, deciding I'd had enough of my family talking up the enemy.

I marched to my car. Up close, even I had to admit it was one of Vik's better pranks. The craftsmanship was pretty solid. He had clearly spent time practicing and planning all of it—from the Saran Wrap to the placement of the letters for optimal viewing.

But I didn't have time for the war this year. Prank wars were too messy, too unpredictable. I liked rules and order. And that was one thing Vik had never agreed to—no rules of engagement or terms. Just utter chaos.

And the result was in front of me.

"Deeps!"

I turned around to see Lily stepping out her front door. Her hair was streaked a new color—blue, this time—and it kept trying to escape the beanie she was wearing. Only Lily could get away with wearing a beanie in September.

She looked at my car, eyes wide.

"Whoa," she said. "That's—" Lily's growing smile stopped in its tracks when she saw my face. "That's horrible. Totally horrible. Especially today."

"Please, please tell me you can take me to school. If you speed a little, we might even be able to pick up Jake's favorite bubble tea."

I put on my ultimate "we are best friends and you love me" smile.

Lily gave me a sheepish shrug. "Sorry, Deeps, but I took my car to the shop yesterday. Remember I was telling you it kept sputtering? Nearly broke down on I-95."

I'd been telling Lily to take that hunk of junk to the shop for months and *now* she listened?

"I really need to get to school early today," I groaned.

"I have a car," a voice said.

Vik walked out of his garage and pressed his key, his car unlocking with a loud beep. He leaned his tall, lanky frame against his driver's-side door and crossed his arms, looking over at me with a smile. His full attention was on me now, all six foot two of him. I tried to make myself as tall as possible, which was hard given that I was almost a foot shorter.

"You?" I said. "This is your fault."

"Well, technically, it's not. See, if you had just been at our prank war summit at the end of summer, you would've known after Labor Day is open season. Lily was there," he said. "She knew the rules."

Lily threw up her hands. "Don't put me in the middle of this. Deepa, you told me you didn't want to hear anything about the prank war."

I didn't have time for this. I started to grab fistfuls of Saran Wrap and attempted to peel it off.

A throat cleared at my side. "Need a ride, Dee?"

I tugged at a particularly stubborn piece of wrap.

From behind, I could hear his car door opening. The ignition turned on, and still, I didn't turn around.

Lily grabbed another strand of Saran Wrap, but it became clear pretty quickly that we were going to need help, and lots of it.

"Deeps," Lily said quietly. "I don't know if we're going to get this off by ourselves, and definitely not anytime soon. And you said you wanted to start today off right. . . ."

Tires squealed against asphalt. Vik reversed out of the driveway and pulled into the street. I yanked at the Saran Wrap one more time, but Lily was correct.

I whipped around just as Vik rolled down his window and leaned out.

"Last call, Dee," he said. "You too, Lily."

Finally, my common sense won out. I ran over to the side door and yanked at it, but it was locked.

"Rule one, don't mess with my radio stations again," he said. "If you accept, I'll let you in."

"That was one time," I said. "Your music is depressing. I can't help it."

"Well, help it." He looked me up and down. "Especially if you want to get to school early. You're lucky I'm all ready to leave."

I sputtered. "I'm luck— You're the reason I'm in this mess!"

All he did was smirk at me. "Open season, Dee. Open season."

I heard the door lock click. Before he could say anything, I opened the passenger-side door, slid in, and yanked it closed.

"Ugh, I never get shotgun," Lily said as she plopped herself into the back seat.

A short, only slightly unbearable car ride later and we arrived at Edison High. The buses hadn't come in yet, so it was easy enough to zoom around the school and snag a great spot in the senior lot. I had put in a motion for randomized assigned spots during the last student council meeting, which I thought was the most fair and orderly option, but that had been shot down quickly. I guess people thought there was something fun about the free-for-all.

I didn't get it.

Nineties-era grunge music blared from the speakers as Vik made a tight right into the senior lot and squeezed between two parked SUVs.

"You couldn't have picked one of those wide-open spots over there?" I said in exasperation, pointing at the half-empty lot. Nothing Vik did made sense to me. Of course, he had been one of the loudest voices against my motion for randomized assigned spots.

"Why? I like a challenge," he said, turning off the ignition.

"What? Are you saying something?" Lily yelled from the back, just as the music went out. "Oh, sorry. That was loud."

I eyed the two SUVs we were parked between, sighed,

and checked my watch again. "I might actually be on time," I said, mostly to myself.

"I was wondering about that," Vik said. He leaned across the cup holders, getting into my personal space. "Why, exactly, did you need me to come to your rescue? Big meeting with the school counselor? Planning every second of your high school life again?"

I rolled my shoulders back. "At least some of us take things seriously."

"Oh yes, like those lists you and Lily would make? What was that one you made freshman year? The perfect boyfriend?" Vik's eyes danced. "Number twelve, he must love the same bands as me. That's how we know we're soul mates," he said in an affected, high-pitched voice.

"You're the worst," I said.

He smiled, like it was the world's best compliment.

"Deepa, the time!" Lily said from behind us. "We've got to go!"

My watch beeped at me at that moment. I threw myself out of the car and yanked my backpack on. "Lily!"

"Right behind you," she said, tumbling out of the car.

I stopped and swiveled around. "Uh, thanks, Vik," I said quickly. "For the ride. Not for the music."

We sprinted toward the doors, leaving Vik yelling after us.

"You're welcome! For both!"

"We made it," Lily said as we reached the doors. "Now it's time to get you ready."

I straightened my clothes and patted my hair down while Lily applied another coat of red lipstick to my lips. And the quarter was in my backpack.

"You ready?" Lily asked. "I know this morning was a lot."

I waved my hand. "It doesn't matter. Vik is the past and today is all about the future."

"The future?"

"The big, bright, shiny future."

But when I got to the hallway, at exactly the right time, everything was wrong.

Jake was there, looking cool and sexy and absolutely perfect. But he wasn't alone, and normally he was always alone, or I was there. Today, one of the Jennys, Jenny Porter, was chattering away next to him. She was pointing at something on her phone that they were both watching.

I had really hoped I wouldn't have an audience. That's what I had been nervous about all week and why I had waited so long. It was Edison asking week, sure, but it was also early on a Friday morning. Didn't people have alarms to sleep through?

Lily squeezed my hand. "You got this. You are a goddess. He is going to be so in awe that he will bow down in front of you and thank you for choosing him."

I hid a smile. "Unlikely, but I appreciate it."

I threw another nervous look over at Jake and Jenny. Lily caught my eye and winked.

"Hey, Jenny!" Lily walked over to the lockers and pulled

Jenny aside. "Quick question about the calculus homework. Did you—"

Best friends really were amazing.

I took a deep breath and approached Jake now that he was alone. I had to do it before I lost my cool. I reminded myself that this was the Josyula tradition, that our family went after what we wanted. My parents' twenty-year-long marriage was the result of my dad's nervous gamble during his own junior year asking week. My mom had said yes, and the rest was history.

I could do this.

"Hey, Jake!"

"Hey, Deepa." He smiled that bright white, gorgeous smile at me.

"So, um—" It was like my entire brain had flown out of my skull and launched itself into the trash can. "The weather. It's great. So great."

Jake gave me a small smile. "Sure, super nice. Sunny for almost October."

"Yeah! So sunny."

I winced. I sounded like a complete idiot.

"So, it's almost October. . . ."

"Yes," he said. It went to show how amazing he was that he didn't point out I was blabbering. "It is."

I took a deep breath and finally my body settled. "And it's been super fun being doubles partners with you for tennis for the past few months."

"Dream team!" Jake said, throwing his hand up for a high five. I high-fived him back. "You've been a great partner. And you got to love all that extra time with Coach Robertson."

I laughed, loosening up. "Yup, and learning all about his goat farm. We totally have to go check out if it's real. I have my suspicions."

"Same," he said. "It's like, after everything we've heard, I've got to see it in person. If only for the photos. Especially after that story about Milo, the Taylor Swift–obsessed goat."

We smiled at each other, and I remembered again why I was asking Jake. Jake was the nicest boy you'd ever meet. We clicked, we liked the same stuff, and it was so easy talking to him. What was better boyfriend material than that?

"Jake, I've really enjoyed getting to know you, and the goats, of course. And it's been really fun. I wanted to know, uh, will you go to the homecoming dance with me?"

I said the last bit all in one rushed exhale. He turned that gorgeous smile on me and I couldn't help it, but I had little visions of me and Jake, hand in hand at the dance. And then hand in hand at football games, and Winterfest, and—

Wait, that wasn't a smile.

My brain screamed a warning to me.

"Uh, I'm sorry," Jake said. He actually did look sorry,

and a little uncomfortable. "Jenny just asked me, like a few minutes ago . . . and I said yes."

"Oh." I blinked. "Oh! Congrats! That's . . . great. So, so great. You guys, you two—" I did finger guns, because that's what the moment really needed. "You both are . . . going together."

Jake's smile weakened. And I needed to stop talking.

"Fantastic. Great. I already said great, didn't I?"

But for some reason, I couldn't stop talking. If I stopped talking, I would have to register that I had a collector's quarter in my pocket that was now totally useless and my entire plan had gone down in flames.

"Are you okay?" Jake started. "I'm really sorry. It's just a timing thing, you know. You're great. Like really, really great. I just couldn't say n—"

"Yeah," I said brightly, pulling my backpack straps closer to me. It was a nervous habit I hadn't been able to break since I was in elementary school. I'd frayed more straps than my mom knew how to deal with. "Yeah, yeah, ye—"

"Dee," a voice said.

I whipped around, thankful for the interruption. It had somehow unlocked my body—and shut my mouth. Then I saw who it was.

Vik.

"You left this in my car," he said. Vik held up a little yellow coin purse embroidered with pink flowers.

That was not my purse. I'd never be caught dead with a

purse like that. Was it his younger sister's? I was about to ask exactly that when Vik caught my eye and stared me down.

Was he trying to save me?

"Oh, hey, Vik," Jake said, a sudden spark of interest in his eyes. "I didn't know you two knew each other."

"We're neighbors," I said, just as Vik said, "We grew up together."

"Nice," Jake said, in a tone that didn't really seem to mean it. I could see the confusion in his expression as he looked between us. Most people didn't realize that we knew each other. We were kind of on different wavelengths, maybe even entire spectrums, at Edison.

"So, your purse?" Vik said, eyebrows raised.

I blinked. "Oh, yes. Thanks, Vik!" I grabbed the yellow purse and waved goodbye at Jake as I jetted down the hallway to my locker.

Mixed doubles had just gotten a lot more complicated.

A few minutes later, I arrived at my thin blue locker. My body felt flushed, and I was so warm, like I had just run a marathon.

I noticed Vik had followed behind me. I opened my locker and hid behind it as much as I could. Vik was tall enough that my locker maneuver didn't work at all. He looked down at me over the top of the locker. He grimaced, seeming to make up his mind. "Are you all ri—"

I held up my hand. "I'll give you back the purse after school. It's Pooja's, right?"

"Yup," he said. Vik leaned against the locker next to me. I pretended to be rummaging around, taking deep breaths. "How did you figure it out? The yellow or the daisies?"

I snorted. "Both. But, uh, really. Thanks. You saved me."

The problem with Vik was that he knew me, unfortunately. He knew my buttons, he had known them since I was ten, and I was waiting, just waiting, for him to push one.

This was an ultimate coup for him. What could be better than seeing me so hideously embarrassed? But he wasn't saying anything. And he really did save me when he really didn't have to. He was being . . . nice.

"No problem, Dee," he said. He crossed his arms. "So, this is why you came early? Homecoming asking week?"

"Yeah," I said. My voice sounded unsteady, even to me. "I had it all—"

"—planned out?" Vik finished.

I rolled my eyes. "Yup. But it looks like I missed the boat narrowly. Apparently, Jenny got to it first—"

That's when it hit me. Jake had said Jenny had just asked him, which meant . . .

He seemed to figure it out too. We both knew it wasn't my fault that I had been late. I waited for that righteous anger to fill me, but I just felt tired. I shut my locker door.

Vik opened his mouth, fish-style, like he was going to say something.

But I was already halfway down the hallway.

22

* * *

The end-of-day bell rang, telling me that I was late for the after-school student council meeting. I hated being late. Not only did it set you up for a disadvantage, but it plastered a sign on your forehead that said "I can't be trusted."

Worse, today's student council meeting was the one where we would volunteer for committees for the semester. I had been hoping to get put on the Winterfest Dance planning committee, something I'd been dreaming of organizing since I had started at Edison High.

But after the Jake incident, my whole day had been off. Being late was just the cherry on top.

Vik and I arrived at the classroom door at the same time. Everyone was already seated inside and the meeting had started. Vik raised that stupid eyebrow at me and bowed, indicating I could go in first. I breezed past him.

"—and Jenny Lee and Jenny Porter for the Winterfest Dance committee. That rounds out our committee," Mr. Costa said. "Wow, didn't think that one would have so much interest."

My stomach sank. I took one of the empty seats and Vik sat down next to me. I ignored him. Pretty quickly I realized they had filled up all the other good committees already—Winterfest Catering, Talent Show, Field Day.

"Nice that you two could join us," Mr. Costa said with a sidelong glance.

I flinched and murmured an apology.

"We've almost finished with assignments," he said. "All that's left is the Junior Lock-In and Teacher Relations."

I straightened, ready to make my case for getting put on Teacher Relations, but Mr. Costa wasn't done yet.

"But Rowan and Sheila asked to be Teacher Relations, and seeing as they did such a good job last year, I'm giving that to them. Which leaves Deepa and Vik on the Junior Lock-In." Mr. Costa looked up from his notepad at us.

This was officially the worst day ever.

"Wait, Mr. Costa," I said. "Are you sure there isn't room on any other committee? *Any* other committee?"

Mr. Costa gave me a half smile. "What? And abandon poor Vik? He's going to need a good partner. Planning the Junior Lock-In is one of the hardest things every year. It requires creativity, strategy, and a little bit of magic. You'll both be great for it."

A few minutes later, Mr. Costa finished our assignments and broke us into our first committee meetings. Which meant I had to turn around and face my new partner in crime.

I glanced over at Vik and he had the audacity to grimace at me. Like I had somehow offended him.

A beat of uncomfortable silence followed.

It was all too much. The rejection from Jake, the embarrassment, the save from Vik. Being late and losing the best committees. And worst, all my plans and hopes falling to pieces.

I took a deep breath and steadied myself by pulling out my notebook and flipping through to find a blank page.

"Looks like we're partners, Dee," Vik said finally, his voice tight.

"Vikram, you know I don't like that nickname," I said.

He made a face. "You used to." His wavy hair fell into his eyes as he leaned forward to place his forearms on the table. "Just so you know, I've been working on Junior Lock-In ideas for the past two years. This is important to me."

I bristled at that but didn't say anything at first. I smoothed the notebook page down and quickly sketched out "Junior Lock-In" in broad bubble letters. And added a little doodle of a stick man with a party hat.

"Did you hear me?" Vik said.

I slowed my doodling down. "I'm offended you think I'd do anything but my best, even for a committee I absolutely, positively didn't want to be on."

"I'm just making sure I'm getting A-team Dee, not . . ."

"B-team?" I sniffed.

Vik leaned back in his chair and put his arms behind his head. "You're so unhappy it's oozing off you."

"I wonder why," I snapped back.

"I bet you wanted the Winterfest Dance," he said. "I bet you—"

He caught me glancing over at Jake and Jenny laughing together in the corner.

"Oh, man, please tell me it's not true. You even made a plan for that? What, were you hoping to get paired together?"

I huffed and crossed my arms. "It could've happened."

This was what Vik was good at—getting deep under my skin and pushing buttons like he was a five-year-old in an elevator. But I would not rise to the bait; I would remain calm and cool and collected.

"I'm so right. I can tell because you're blushing."

"I'm brown, I don't blush," I snapped back. "Look," I said with a sigh. "Let's agree to a truce. We have to work together, so let's make this the best stupid damn Junior Lock-In or whatever."

He stared at me. Like he didn't believe me.

"I have a reputation to uphold," I said. That seemed to convince him.

"Okay, you have a deal," he said.

He stuck a hand out. His skin was surprisingly warm and his fingers were calloused, which I remembered was thanks to the Fender in his room.

We shook on it just as Mr. Costa ended the meeting, bringing the day, thankfully, to a close.

4

I found myself in our home garden that night. To my eternal happiness, Mani had come home with a B in English on her report card, and that horrific travesty took up most of the dinner conversation. No one bothered to ask me how my day went.

I slipped outside after doing my chore for the week, clearing the table. There was a "discussion" brewing between my parents and Mani anyway and I really couldn't deal with it that night. Also, the freezer had been woefully devoid of any ice cream and Ratna had polished off all the leftover chocolate cake from that birthday party last weekend, so I was out of luck for a post-horrible-day sugar binge. The lack of peace and sugar led me to escape outside.

The evening air was cool, indicating that fall was truly on its way. The garden felt like it was on the precipice of turning and leaving behind its lush green for the crisp reds and oranges of autumn. A number of our flowers were already going into their mini hibernations.

I gently plucked the last few stragglers from the jasmine

bushes. Jasmine flowers normally bloomed in the summer, as they were tropical plants, but somehow my grandma had coaxed these bushes to keep offering up beautiful little white flowers well into fall. I had always wished I had inherited her green thumb.

One of the branches snapped in my fingers and I winced.

"Sorry, Maya," I said to the bush I had fondly named as a child. "Been a long day." I tried to fix the little branch as best I could, but it hung limply.

I sat back on my haunches. Tears prickled at the backs of my eyes. I blinked rapidly, trying to keep them at bay. Really, in the grand scheme of life, this was just another crappy day. It wasn't like I was the first person to be devastated by homecoming.

Also, I would not cry over a boy.

The backyard door opened, the light tinkling of a bell announcing someone else's arrival. I quickly wiped the few drops of moistures from my cheeks.

My grandma walked outside as I released a deep, pent-up sigh.

"Deepa?" she said in a worried tone, eyes skimming over the broken branch and then me. "Are you okay?"

"No, Amamma," I said. "My life is over."

I expected some huge dramatics from my grandma. Questions, denials, the whole thing.

She only laughed. "Oh, is that all?"

I couldn't help the smile that crept up my face. "Isn't that enough?"

"Lives are ending every day; that is the fate of humans." She waved her hand. "What to do?"

"Thanks, Amamma, but that's kind of depressing."

"Life is depressing."

I snorted and let her pull me to my feet. She pinched my cheek. "Don't worry, kannamma. Things will look up. Remember what that movie with that cute Dev Patel said? Everything will be okay in the end, and if it's not, then it's not the end!"

I laughed into the cool air. It felt nice.

"I guess so, Amamma. I guess so." As always, my grandmother knew how to make me feel better, even if it was in an unconventional way.

"I have something for you, Deepa," she said. My grandmother opened her hands to reveal a velvety white jasmine flower. "My mother always used to say the last bloom of jasmine is magical, that it hears your heart's greatest desire and honors it. It's a saying we've had in our family for generations."

I couldn't help my skeptical look. "Oh-kay. Why are you giving it to me?"

"It's time for you. You're of age," she said. "But more important, you seem like you need it today. You looked quite melancholy during dinner. Now, you're going to say, oh, what do you know, Amamma, you're so old," she said, mimicking Ratna's tone to a T. "What is this magic-schmagic, we live in the modern era."

"I would never say that."

She tapped me on the forehead. "But some things are better done the old way. You young people don't know. Now, here. Do not deny the gifts of our ancestors."

Welp, that sounded bad. I took the flower and held it gently. It looked so fragile.

"So, you're saying this flower is going to give me some three wishes type of thing?"

My grandmother clucked her tongue. "What nonsense. You merely tell it what you desire. Perhaps the universe will listen tonight. Perhaps it won't."

"Mhm," I said. I had just remembered that I had a physics problem set I hadn't finished. My desk upstairs beckoned.

Cool fingers lifted my chin up. My grandma's eyes were warm, her grip firm. "Tonight is the last bloom. Tonight, you ask."

I nodded, mostly to let her think I had given in, and she looked pleased. Amamma headed farther into the garden and I went back upstairs to my room, where I took out my problem set and placed the jasmine flower aside. A half hour and twenty mind-numbingly hard physics questions later, I was done.

There were no more distractions. No more things to do.

I slumped onto my bed and stared at the ceiling.

Immediately, Vik's face popped into my mind. That infuriatingly annoying mouth that was curved into a perpetual smirk, those frustrating unreadable eyes that always seemed to be judging me.

Sure, blaming Vik was as easy as pie and old as time. And he had ruined my whole homecoming proposal.

But something else caught on the edges of my mind. A thought, a feeling, one I wanted to push away the moment it fluttered along.

Junior year was going to be a failure. If I had just planned a little better, I might be on track to having a high school boyfriend, maybe even having a romance like my parents. My heart squeezed, like it always did when I thought of Urmila Pinni's heartbreak—my aunt's face, streaked with tears and mascara.

That's what a good plan did. It made sure you didn't get hurt. It made sure you got what you wanted. Now it was very likely that The List would never be finished, I would never have a high school boyfriend, and that perfect high school experience would be out of my grasp.

Jake was snatched up, and Jenny wasn't going to let go of him that easily. There was a rumor she had been crushing on him since freshman year, but I didn't give a lot of weight to most rumors. Most likely she had also identified his perfect boyfriend potential. I mean, he loved reading and preferred foreign art-house cinema. Which was exactly like me.

True, Jenny was more of a photography-and-thrillers type of girl, but Jake was also punctual, always raised his hand in class, and had never started a spitball fight that made me lose a chunk of hair (unlike Vik).

I groaned into my pillow. Thankfully, Mani was blasting music a room down, so no one heard or acknowledged my dramatics. I didn't need the entire Josyula family raining down on me with their hugs and sympathy.

How would I find another Jake on such short notice?

Out of all the boys in my high school class, he was really the only one with any potential. No, it hadn't been love, but that was the whole point of a high school boyfriend. It was a possibility. A promise. The cap to four hard years.

If my parents had found love their junior year, why couldn't I?

Amamma seemed so certain that my problems would be solved by telling the last bloom, that flower, and the universe what I wanted. Maybe that wasn't such a horrible idea. Maybe if I wished really, really hard, like I used to when I was a kid, the universe might hear me and listen. Take pity on me.

Before I could think too much about it, I grabbed the flower and cupped it in my hands. I held it up to my eyes and stared at the white petals.

"Okay, magical flower of my ancestors, I wish for the perfect high school boyfriend." I paused. "No, wait, I wish for the perfect boyfriend, period." And then I remembered Vik teasing me about the checklist Lily and I had made years ago for the perfect boyfriend. I immediately frowned. And then decided. "The perfect boyfriend, exactly like my freshman-year checklist."

Why not shoot for the moon if you were asking the universe for the stars? It's not like it was going to come true anyway.

Curled up in bed, I fell asleep with the flower cupped in my hand.

The next morning, I woke up with the imprint of my pillow creased down my face. Good thing it was a Saturday. Pancake day.

I brushed my teeth and made my way down to a bustling kitchen. Somehow, Mani and Ratna had both made it down before me and had already started the pancake and dosa stations. Pancakes for us three and my dad, dosas for my mom and my grandma.

My dad was flipping pancakes and keeping an eye on the amount of chocolate chips Ratna was plunking into every scoop of batter. Which meant he was totally missing Mani's sneaky double slices of cheese on the dosas. She caught my gaze and winked, and I stifled a laugh.

Mani's rebellious outfit of choice today was neon-green candy cane pajamas—in September. Sure to drive our mom crazy.

My aunt once called my mom a type A badass, which I thought was on the nose. She never had a hair out of place, and I've only ever heard her raise her voice once. She doesn't need to yell to be scary. That's a true boss.

Even today, on our unremarkable Saturday morning,

she wore a pristine ivory silk shirt, her hair styled in loose curls, which was a bit much, even for her. I ran my fingers through my hair in an attempt to flatten it before I walked in and tried to pick up on the conversation.

"—new neighbors," my mom said, taking a sip of her black coffee. "We should stop by later. Maybe drop off a basket?"

"New neighbors?" I settled onto one of the barstools and stole a handful of chocolate chips. "Have my prayers been answered? Has Vik finally committed some minor misdemeanor or done something so horribly embarrassing that he has to move?"

"Deepa," my dad said, warning in his voice. "The Mehtas are nice. We love them. And you love Nikhil and Pooja, even if you don't love their brother. Plus, Uncle and Auntie have been at every one of your birthday parties and always send over mango pickle the second they get their shipment from India. Would you really want them to move?"

I ducked my head, chastised. "No, okay, fine. It's not their fault they spawned a devil child."

"Deepa." My dad fixed a hard stare at me. I stared back.

"Apparently, Reshma told me about it weeks ago," my mom said. "I missed her text until this morning. Her best friend's cousin and his family are moving in for a few months on a trial basis, to see if they like the area and the schools. His dad has a short-term job with one of those big defense contractors, the ones no one can talk about."

"Wait," I said. "Didn't we just discuss this yesterday? How the lot has been so empty because the old owners weren't sure if they were coming back? You know, Ratna thought it was haunted and Mani said nothing cool like that ever happened on our street?"

I got four blank stares.

"Sounds like me, but don't remember that," Mani said.

"You guys seriously don't—okay, whatever." I shook my head and stuffed another handful of chocolate chips into my mouth.

It hadn't been a great twenty-four hours and now I was apparently having short-term memory loss. Though I was positive I remembered the conversation. I glanced at my grandma, who was happily eating the first dosa off the grill. Shrugging, I took my plate of pancakes from my dad and looked out the kitchen window.

There was a moving truck parked outside of the corner lot, which definitely didn't look so empty anymore. I peered closer and took a bite of my pancakes.

A very attractive boy popped out of the moving truck carrying a record player. He seemed to be about my age but looked like he had walked out of the pages of a high-end magazine. If jaw-dropping was an actual thing, my mouth probably would have been doing it. His perfectly sculpted chin rose into model-sharp cheekbones, which matched his strong, muscled frame.

Then it hit me. He didn't just look like he had walked

out of a magazine; he looked exactly like the photo of the guy I had in my locker freshman year, the one I had used as my inspiration for our freshman list.

He turned and walked up the path to the house and I read his T-shirt. The Flaming Moths? They had been my favorite band freshman year.

I looked down at his shoes. Practical, sensible black loafers. Exactly like my ideal man would wear. Lily had even made fun of me for including it on The List.

I dropped my fork and it clattered on the floor.

My wish.

Had it come true?

The first thing I did after realizing that I may have wished my perfect boy to life wasn't to run upstairs and confirm with that old, ratty list. Nope, that probably would have made sense. But my brain wasn't fully functioning at the moment. It was fritzing at the idea that maybe, just maybe, my wish had come true.

I threw open the door and ran outside. Mani followed me.

"Deepa, what the . . ." Mani's voice trailed off. She came to a stop behind me and then whistled. "Whoa, hot neighbor alert."

"Mani!"

"What? I have eyes."

"You're, like, twelve," I said.

Mani gave me a pitying look. "I'm fourteen, thank you very much. You should remember how old your favorite sister is if you want a good Diwali gift this year."

I rolled my eyes.

"Seriously," Mani said. We both watched as our gorgeous new neighbor lifted one of the huge boxes, muscles rippling as he moved. "It's like he's not real. Who's that hot in high school?"

"No one," I said.

She was right. He did seem unreal. I didn't mention my suspicion to Mani—that he might actually not be real.

That I might have wished him here. Maybe even to life.

She would definitely think I had lost my mind.

Nope, that revelation I would save for Lily. I looked over at her house, but her parents' car wasn't in the driveway, which normally meant that the family was at one of her younger sister's travel soccer games. Lily went to every single one and was basically the backup coach. Soccer was Lily's passion, but unfortunately, the athletic gene had passed over her (her words, not mine).

Something flickered in one of the second-story windows at the house in between ours. Vik's house. I stepped closer and peered at the window. The blinds stayed closed, but I could've sworn I had seen a pair of eyes peeking out.

I had probably imagined Vik's face at the window, but it did remind me that I was standing outside in my pajamas, with unbrushed hair and a plate of uneaten pancakes. Correction, they were now being devoured by Mani, who was going to town on them.

"Do you think he's going to Edison? He looks like an upperclassman," Mani said, mouth full of chocolate chip pancakes. She gave me a pointed look. "Maybe he'll be in your classes."

"Possibly," I said.

"You mean, you wish."

"What?" I startled. "I don't wish. I didn't wish anything."

Mani gave me a weird look. "Sure. . . ."

"I mean, yeah, that would be cool if he was in my classes." I couldn't help looking. We both craned our necks to see beyond the moving truck. The perfect boy hefted another box and I had to stop from fanning myself. "Really cool."

"Ugh, I hate having a summer birthday. Why did Amma and Nanna have to put me into school a year behind?" Mani complained.

"Dude, be grateful. You're going to be sixteen before everyone else, which means you'll be the first one to have a car, parents willing. Trust me, that's going to make your high school."

"But if I were in high school now . . ."

We watched perfect boy as he came around the corner and hefted another box as if it were paper. We both sighed.

That's when he turned around and waved.

I almost dropped my now-empty plate. I've never been very suave when it comes to boys, I'll admit. But I knew that the only response was to wave back cheerily. What I didn't expect was that he'd put his box down and come over.

I stood there, frozen in place.

"Mani, what do I do?" I whispered, trying not to show my panic.

"How should I know? I'm only fourteen!" she said. "Act cool." Mani looked me up and down. "Well, that might be hard."

I elbowed her and she laughed in my face, which was

exactly what I needed to loosen up and remind myself that I had, in fact, talked to someone I was attracted to before.

"Something funny?" the perfect boy asked. He stopped at the edge of our driveway, a foot away from us.

"Oh, no. Nothing," I said quickly. "I'm Deepa. Welcome to the neighborhood."

"Nice to meet you, Deepa," he said. "I'm Rohit." He jerked a thumb back at his house. "Your new neighbor."

"We noticed," Mani said. "I'm Mani, by the way. There are three of us Josyula girls, if you were wondering, and yes, we all do look a lot alike. I think our mom knows your mom too, in some Indian way."

"Ah, yes, the Indian way," Rohit said. "That old classic. Do you go to Edison?"

"Not me," Mani cut in. "Unfortunate timing of my birth, but my sister does. She's a junior."

"Oh, you're a junior too?" he asked, dimples cutting into a bright smile. A smile that was turned on me.

I almost melted in front of it.

"Yes, she's a junior too," Mani said, elbowing me in the side. She gave me a "get with it" look.

"Yup," I said. "Yes, yes. I'm in Mrs. Palmer's homeroom."

"Awesome," he said. "Same here."

"You'll love her. She's traveled all over the world and has the best stories about sleeping in a jungle tree house or skiing across a fjord." I pointed at his shirt. "You've got great taste, by the way. The Flaming Moths are one of my favorite bands, even though they're a bit retro now."

His eyes brightened at the mention of my once-favorite band. "Can't go wrong with British punk rock from the late aughts, right? I think they were seriously underrated after their first album."

"Right? I said. "Exactly, I feel the same way. Once Leo Striker left it was like the whole band fell apart. I mean, the new drummer was pretty good and they found their groove eventually, but those middle two albums were rough."

"You can say that again," Rohit said. "Like caught-in-a-tragic-sea-storm-with-a-giant-squid rough."

I laughed and let out a snort. Mani sighed and I slapped my hand over my mouth.

"Sorry," I mumbled.

"For what?" he said, grinning. "I take that as a compliment. I got a snort out of you."

Mani made a gagging noise next to me, but I was already halfway in love with our new neighbor. He had great taste in music and he hadn't made a big deal about my legendarily embarrassing snort? I was known in the family for it, mostly because it sounded like a cross between an elephant and a dying hyena.

"You know, I heard the Flaming Moths might be doing a reunion tour. . . . ," he said.

"What?" I gaped at him. How had I not heard about this?

"I heard it through the grapevine from a family friend who's a concert organizer. They might even come to DC," he said.

It had been a while since I had listened to the Flaming Moths, to be honest, but they still held a super tender place in my heart. They'd been the soundtrack for many a late night freshman year, as I worked on my 4.0 GPA. Those big guitar riffs had been the only thing that could keep me from falling asleep as I studied biology.

Mani kicked my foot.

"We should go!" I said in a rush, realizing I had just majorly spaced out. "I mean, if it really happens. You know these reunion tours are dicey."

"I do love a good reunion tour," he said, shoving his hands into his pockets. Rohit managed to make even that look cute. "I'm in. If it really happens. I'll tell my cousin to keep an eye out."

We grinned at each other.

Someone yelled Rohit's name and we both jumped, seeming to realize that there was still a moving truck outside his house.

"Looks like I got to go," he said apologetically. "But nice to meet you, Mani. And see you later, Deepa." Rohit shuffled away and then turned. "Love the penguins, by the way."

That's when I realized I was still in my pajamas (my penguin pajamas), without a speck of makeup on. My face started to burn, but then I replayed the conversation in my head. I hadn't totally crashed and burned, and in fact, I even got a tentative yes to hanging out.

Okay, so it was to a concert and maybe it was just as

friends, but mutual musical tastes were definitely the foundation of a soul connection.

Something warm settled into the bottom of my stomach. It was looking more and more likely that my wish had come true.

I didn't even bother to hide my smile as I walked back inside, victory in every step.

And it might have been my imagination, but I swore I saw the blinds on Vik's window move.

Lily barged into my room one hour later, blinking phone in one hand, dirt caked on her from top to bottom.

"I ran," she said.

"No kidding." I looked her up and down. "Another disagreement with the referee?"

"He tried to say the Stuart Littles had committed a foul during the last five minutes, which was a total excuse to give his favorite team, the Dragon Snouts"—Lily said the name as if it was the most disgusting name ever—"a free kick. He's been favoring them all season! I had to step in."

"And did Rose appreciate that?" I asked. I handed Lily a clean shirt and turned my back.

"No. Not at first, at least." Lily sighed. "Then she saw it was a total con from the referee and—wait, this is not what we should be talking about."

Lily plopped down on the bed, facing me. "Spill."

I did, recounting everything that had happened after

yesterday's Jake asking week disaster. The moping, my grandmother's flower, the wish, and then the utter weirdness of this morning.

Lily's eyes, which were already huge, kept getting bigger and bigger throughout the story.

"Magic is real," she whispered as I wrapped up. "I knew it. So is he a fake guy and really like a teacup or something?"

"He seemed real enough to me," I said. "His family just happened to move in, which is odd enough. We've been talking about that house on the corner for years and no one's ever wanted to move in."

"And you said he matches The List to a T?"

"I'm pretty sure," I said. "But that's why I called you here. I need a witness."

I went to my closet and tiptoed around to reach the top of the shelving. It took a few tries, but finally my hand hit what I was looking for.

The lock-and-key journal I had gotten for my thirteenth birthday.

It was old, vintage maybe, with fading blue leather and small tears from being carried around absolutely everywhere. What I had loved the most was the tiny lock attached to the side of the journal, ensuring that no one could open it without the key.

Clearly, I now knew that anyone with a wrench could have broken that bad boy open, but then, it had felt like the coolest, most secure thing in the world. A lot had changed in a few years. I didn't even bother with the key and instead jiggled the small lock in the right place until it slid open.

I flipped through the back, where I had chronicled every moment of my first semester of freshman year and then . . . nothing. Life had happened, I guess. My last entry had been the day my aunt had come to stay with us. I sometimes missed those early mornings when I would pour everything, every feeling, every hurt, every hope, into those pages. Somehow it now felt like a waste of time.

"Here it is," I said.

I smoothed out the page with the list we had put together one rainy fall evening, a few weeks into the new school year. It had been the first time we had seen high school boys, or boys we hadn't grown up with, and the possibilities had seemed infinite.

10 Steps to the Perfect Boy
(written by Deepsicle and Lilypad)

1. Music is life, so he has to love the same music as me. (The Flaming Moths!! —Deepa)
2. HOT!! Like that model on Instagram, the one who was also in that magazine? (I believe his name is Shey Kamdar —Lily)
3. Classy. Has a timeless style and knows the value of a tailored blazer and a good pair of loafers.

4. Listens. He's a great listener and doesn't argue for the sake of arguing. (Unlike someone we know in the cul-de-sac 😒 —Deepa)

5. Talented. He can sing like Harry Styles and dance like Hrithik Roshan. (How are you still obsessed with that Bollywood dude? He's like old now —Lily)

6. Romantic. He knows his roses from his carnations and always treats a girl like a queen. (Candlelit dinners and opening doors and old-fashioned stuff, minus the misogyny.

7. Evolved. We're talking hygiene and depth here. Two things most high school boys lack. No conversations about video games, please!

8. Compatible. Aka he agrees with me on most everything and lets me make decisions because I'm almost always right. (Also unlike someone we know in the cul-de-sac —Deepa) Okay, fine, some disagreements are allowed, but only minor ones. Like what's the best candy (Twix) or PB&J is disgusting or not (it is). (It is not! —Lily)

9. Organized. Because organization and planning are hot!! A guy with a two-inch binder and a highlighter cannot be matched. (This is all you, Deeps —Lily)

10. A perfect gentleman. He'll never kiss on the first date, only after three, which everyone knows is the right number.

Lily whistled. "Honestly, this is a tall order. You're saying this guy matches this list?"

I frowned, looking at The List and out the window at our new neighbors' house. Now that I looked at it, it all seemed a little far-fetched. But I was pretty sure.

I thought.

"I can check off three for sure right now," I started. "But the others . . ."

An idea pinged in my head like a firework.

"But . . . ?" Lily prompted. "Some of these would be hard to confirm."

"Exactly," I said, all in a rush. "So, step one. Let's confirm that he does fit The List. That he is the perfect boy."

"And how exactly do we do that?" Lily flopped back onto my bed and stared at me through her fringe, which had grown a bit too long. You could see her roots at the top, black against the blue. Somehow, she managed to rock it.

"I've got an idea," I said slowly, the pieces falling into place in my head.

Time for one of my mom's famous gift baskets.

6

We arrived at our new neighbors' front door with a gift basket that would have made Martha Stewart weep.

My mom had put it together with minimal input from me and Lily. I had strong feelings on the best coffee roast (medium, for sure) and Lily was a candle fanatic. My dad even threw in raspberry rhubarb jam from his latest batch of jams and jellies. Of course, my mom had topped it off with a haldi and kumkum packet, the traditional way of welcoming someone new in South India, and a huge sleeve of Good Day pistachio cookies, everyone's favorite accompaniment to afternoon chai. My mom had insisted on that. Who had chai without snacks?

I had also managed to convince my mom to let me and Lily go ahead and bring out the welcome wagon first, which meant we had some time to do a little sleuthing. A mini investigation, if you will. I was desperate to know if I really had wished Rohit to our cul-de-sac or if I was imagining it all.

I was wearing my cutest weekend outfit as well, a short but tasteful denim skirt with a flouncy silk top. Plus bright red lipstick. I was normally a jeans and a sweater type of girl, so I was really bringing out the big guns here.

Lily reached to ring the doorbell at the exact moment the door swung open. We both started a bit at the face that greeted us.

"Vik?"

Vik leaned against the door frame and looked us up and down. His hair was tousled and he looked like he had just woken up, which was very possible for him. Vik was not exactly known for being a morning person. He was outfitted in dark jeans and a somewhat wrinkled black T-shirt, which only confirmed my theory.

"This isn't your house. What are you doing here?" I said.

"Being neighborly." His eyes darted to the welcome basket in my arms and lit up. "Is that your dad's latest batch of jam? What flavor did he choose this time?"

I'd forgotten how much Vik had always loved my dad's jam experiments. Honestly, he might be the sole reason my dad even started to take his hobby seriously enough to start selling at the local farmers market. Vik was always encouraging him to try weirder and weirder flavors, which the rest of us didn't really appreciate.

"Raspberry rhubarb."

"Classic, I suppose. But I told him to try—"

"Deepa!" a musical voice called out. I couldn't help the way my face brightened up as Rohit came into view, and I was also pretty sure Lily's gasp was audible. "Thanks for answering the door, Vik. We've never had so many neighbors visit before. It's been a bit of a circus since this morning. Who knew Virginians were so friendly?" Rohit laughed and waved us in.

The house looked nothing like how I had imagined it. Mani, Ratna, and I had been making up stories about the abandoned house on our street for years and not a single one of them involved soaring ceilings and gorgeous weathered wood beams. The whole house, even in the disarray of plastic-covered furniture and cardboard boxes, looked like it was cut out of an issue of *Architectural Digest*.

The kitchen alone would make my dad drool—white counters, an eight-burner range, and a marble island. Huddled around that island was a gaggle of girls my age, all of them shooting glances over at us near the door. The moms stood around chatting with a tall, regal woman with salt-and-pepper hair who I assumed was Rohit's mom.

Ah, so this was what he meant by *neighbors*. I recognized some of the girls from other streets in our neighborhood. Seemed like word had gotten around quickly that a cute new boy had moved in, and seeing as most of us had been in school together since kindergarten, this was huge. Plus, Rohit was no average cute boy.

This was going to make things harder for my investigation. I'd have to make my questions work double time.

Vik peered over my shoulder. "And Good Day cookies? Your mom always makes the best baskets."

"It's the Josyula way. We do everything the right way."

Vik snorted at that, but I ignored him.

"So, Rohit, where did your family move from?" I asked before he even closed the door, shoving the gift basket into his arms. Normally, I would consider that rude, but I was a girl on a mission.

"Texas. So, this is a bit of a change," he said with a grin. "Not sure I've ever seen this much green before."

I laughed my practiced flirting laugh. Vik gave me a weird look from the side.

"Oh, here," Lily said, having finally snapped out of her mild coma. I had warned her that Rohit was jaw-droppingly gorgeous, but she clearly hadn't believed me. She stopped staring and handed a bouquet of flowers to Rohit. "From my mom's garden. She said they have a special meaning."

"Thank you, these are lovely," Rohit said. "Sunflowers and daisies, right? My mom is super into flowers." He squinted at them. "I think your mom wants us to be friends, Lily."

Lily and I exchanged a knowing glance. Test number one, complete.

Romantic? Check. He knew the language of flowers, which was something I had specifically put on my list. Yellow roses, sunflowers, daisies. All the flowers of friendship. He had passed with flying colors.

"Reminds me of this song my mom loves," Rohit said. His eyes fluttered closed and he sang a few bars of a song I recognized but didn't know the name of. "Carole King. 'You've Got a Friend'?"

Lily and I nodded like we had a clue, but I was secretly squeeing inside.

Musical? Also check. Proving he could dance would be harder, but Lily and I had decided we could test that one out later.

"My mom loves that song too," Vik said, his hands in his pockets. "Also, weird, I didn't know flowers could have a language."

Well, that wasn't surprising.

"It used to be this whole thing back in the 1800s," I said. "The language of flowers was huge in courtship and you could basically tell someone exactly how you felt by picking certain flower colors. Really romantic."

"Sounds exactly like something you'd like," Vik said with a small laugh.

"What does that mean?" My eyes narrowed.

"Nothing. Just that of course you're into that romantic stuff. You've always loved anything that looks perfect," Vik said.

I had no idea what that meant. Still, it hit me and I couldn't really place why. I sniffed and turned back to Rohit.

"Anyway, it's really cool you know about that. And you can sing!" I said.

"Only a little," Rohit said with an embarrassed shrug.

"That's a lie!" one of the neighborhood girls said, infiltrating our circle and tugging Rohit back over. "His mom blew up his spot. He can sing like Harry Styles and dance like Hrithik Roshan, I swear. She showed us a video."

All the girls tittered and sighed. Internally, I was screaming.

Rohit looked bashful. "Okay, so I was a bit of a performer growing up."

I thought I saw Vik roll his eyes in the corner as the girls fawned over Rohit. My time with Rohit was clearly up, but my investigation had proved successful. I was more and more sure that Rohit was my wish come true.

But I had one last question.

"Wait, how do you feel about binders?"

Rohit turned around and gave me a confused look. "I like them? Keeps me organized better than notebooks. I'm definitely a three-ring, college-lined-paper kind of guy."

I almost fainted right there.

My grin grew wide and it stayed there almost permanently for the next hour, even as Rohit was taken over by the girls and Vik and I fought over whether raspberry rhubarb was the best flavor combo for my dad's experiments. He kept insisting that my dad should push himself and differentiate from the other jam sellers at the farmers market. Maybe do a chili jam or an interesting version of a mango chutney. I was mostly worried about the experiments we'd be forced to eat for many, many dinners. But Mrs. D'Souza, Rohit's mom, chimed in with a vote for the chili jam, meaning I was outvoted.

And at the end of the afternoon, when Rohit made an effort to find and talk to me, I knew that I had found my perfect match.

"Hey," Rohit said, smiling that gorgeous smile down at me. He ran a hand through his hair. "I wish I could've spent more time with you and Lily, but—"

"Duty calls," I said. "I get it. And you and your mom are great hosts. I'm so stuffed with chai and pakoras, I'm going to waddle back home."

Rohit laughed and it made my chest puff. "My mom will be ecstatic to hear that." He leaned in, close enough that it wasn't a mistake. "Looking forward to seeing you in homeroom, Deepa."

I looked behind him at the line of girls covertly watching us. Out of all of them, Rohit was paying attention to me. Sure, he was almost 100 percent the perfect boy I had dreamed of two years ago, but most important, he was interested in me. After the Jake debacle, it warmed me up from the inside.

"Same here," I said.

I stood there for a moment after Rohit left, just basking in the glow of it all.

He was perfect and he was real and he was interested in me. Me!

I turned around to leave and noticed that Vik was standing at the doorway, his eyebrow raised. I ignored his pointed look and walked past him with my head held high.

Mission accomplished.

* * *

I found my grandma in the garden and tackled her with a hug. She returned it and gave me a quizzical look.

"What is this for?" she said in Telugu. "I have not made you any kajas today."

"No, no," I said. True, kajas were my favorite sweet treat ever (who didn't like syrupy pastries?) and my grandma's were next-level, but this was a different sort of high. "Just a hug. For being the best amamma ever. And for giving me that jasmine flower." I leaned forward conspiratorially. "It might be possible that you were correct about that wish."

"Of course I was," Amamma said, smacking me on the arm. She paused and looked at me. "What exactly was I correct about?"

"I wished for the perfect boy," I said. I pulled her over to the bench in her garden. We were surrounded by all her favorite flowers, and at the end of the bench, vines spilled over. "And it came true! He moved in next door and, Amamma, he actually likes me. Or I think he does. He asked me to hang out, maybe go to a concert."

She tsked in the back of her throat. "Of course he likes you. Any boy would be stupid not to. But, Deepa, how do you know he is what you wished for?"

I noticed she didn't comment on my wish itself. It had been in the back of my mind, that maybe I had wasted a wish on something frivolous. Maybe I should have wished to go to Harvard, for instance. But this was what I had wanted and I couldn't deny it. Plus, if I was being honest, I had never been any good at love.

This was where I needed my magic.

"Lily and I confirmed it." I gave her a quick recap of everything that had happened, from the first meeting to The List and our tests at Rohit's house.

"Hmm," Amamma said. "It does seem as if he is what you wished for. I am not surprised at all that little Deepa made a list of such things, though I do question whether Hrithik Roshan is a bit too old for you." She smiled wickedly. "He is much more appropriate for me, don't you think?"

She giggled to herself but then turned serious. "Deepa, a wish is only the beginning. It is family lore that wishes must be earned. They must be completed."

"What does that mean?"

"You must seal the deal," she said, waggling her eyebrows.

"Seal the deal? What does—"

My grandma puckered up at me, as if ready for a kiss, and winked. I'm pretty sure my blush was bright enough to be seen by a Mars rover.

"Amamma," I said, aghast.

"What, you think just because I'm old now that I was always this way? I was once a hot commodity, Deepa. The best dancer in Visakhapatnam." She struck a dancing pose and winked at me again. My grandmother had winked at me more in the past five minutes than in my entire life. It was mildly uncomfortable.

"Erm," I said, making a face. I was imagining things I really did not want to be picturing.

"Don't you erm or ew me. I was once your age, you know," she continued. "I was not always this wise old glamorous creature you now see."

I couldn't help but laugh at that, even when my grandmother gave me a stern look.

"Anyway," she said with a wave of her hand. "That is what you must do. You must seal the deal. If you wished for love, then you must convince the universe that love has found you."

"With a kiss . . . ," I said slowly.

My grandmother didn't say anything. "Convince the universe you are committed. That you have earned the blessing it has given you."

It made sense. The universe had granted my wish and I had to prove that I was serious about it to keep it. And what better way than with a kiss? Every romantic story, movie, book, whatever, ended in a kiss.

I had to kiss Rohit D'Souza.

Easier said than done. I needed a plan.

"A kiss?"

"One magical kiss." I dragged the huge whiteboard Lily had brought over into the center of my bedroom. I propped it against my closet and stepped back to peer at all that we had written on it so far, which was mostly a list of random ideas, from "milkshakes" to "dance-off." I wasn't sure how a dance-off was going to help me make my wish permanent, but I didn't want to discourage the flow of ideas. "It shouldn't be that hard. He is a teenage boy, after all."

And it wasn't like it would be my first kiss. That had happened on a bus on the way to a debate tournament. Like I said, teenage boys.

Lily made a very un-Lily-like noise. A cross between a groan and a wail. "We have a problem," she said. "You might want to take another look at that list we wrote."

She pulled out The List, smoothed out the paper on the floor, and pointed at a line farther down, her blue nails stark against the faded writing.

8. He's a perfect gentleman. He'll never kiss on the first date, only after three, which everyone knows is the right number.

Seriously, Deepa?

I groaned down at The List. Leave it to past me to make things infinitely more complicated for present me.

"Maybe you could just kiss him? A kiss blitzkrieg?" Lily said, looking down at the paper. "That could work. Element of surprise. Boom, there you go."

"I don't think planting one on him when he's least expecting it is going to work," I said, frowning. "First of all, consent. And second of all, my amamma said 'seal the deal'—"

"It's totally sealing the deal."

"—but I get the feeling it's got to come from him. I'll have to woo him," I said, slowly warming to the idea. Then

I thought of what my grandmother had said. "Like they used to do in the old times. Classic times. Remember that movie my mom was watching? That old one?"

"*The Notebook*?" Lily said, scrunching her face. "Isn't that super sad?"

"It's happy at the end! And he courts her all 1950s-style." A sigh escaped my lips as I thought of a swirling montage of cuteness that mimicked every romance movie I had ever seen. "They go out for ice cream and go to the Ferris wheel and do other super romantic—"

"Cheesy."

I threw a pillow at Lily, who ducked. "Super *romantic* stuff," I said. "So I'll court him."

Lily looked a bit skeptical, but she drew a big line on the whiteboard and wrote "Operation: Kiss the Frog" across the top.

"The frog is you, obviously," she said.

"Hey!"

Lily snickered to herself for a few seconds. I grabbed the dry-erase marker from her and circled the title, adding little stars and doodling a cute frog near the top of the title.

"It could work," Lily said. "What are you thinking?"

A plan started to form in my head, piecing itself together little by little.

It was simple, really. Three super romantic dates, planned to a T by me.

One kiss.

Hook, line, sinker.

We worked furiously for the rest of the day, fueled by my stash of chocolate truffles from my birthday and a never-ending supply of tomato chutney toast. My grandmother was the only one in the family who was clued in to the major, life-altering plan Lily and I were working on—and supported it. She kept leaving trays of chai and toast outside our door and trying to sneak peeks at our whiteboard. I shooed her away with a reminder that her favorite Indian serial TV show was on, which, unsurprisingly, worked.

I wasn't trying to be rude, but I wanted to perfect this on my own terms. Also, I was afraid my grandmother would start winking at me again, and I was not ready for more of that.

Lily and I fell backward onto my bed after a long day of hard work. We had finally cracked the code.

"Three dates, fully planned," Lily said. "You owe me."

"I owe you big-time," I agreed. I turned onto my side and propped my head up on my elbow. "Do you think this will work?"

"Honestly?" Lily said. "I think it could. Normally, I

would say it's dicey, especially knowing boys our age and your track record with them—"

"Thanks, Lily."

"—but he definitely seems made for you. And it was fairly obvious that he was into you too. And why wouldn't he be? You're gorgeous and smart and awesome."

"Mixed signals here, Lily."

Lily hit me lightly on the arm. "I'm here to gas you up and keep your head small. That's what best friends do. But yes, I think this could work. Should we review?"

My eyes drifted over to the whiteboard and the three dates we had landed on. It had taken a couple of false starts, like the dance-off, until we had decided on the right sequence and progression of dates. Wooing was hard work.

"First, a candlelit dinner, because that is as classic as it gets," I said.

"And it allows you to impress Rohit with your incredible mind and scintillating conversation," Lily added, perking up. "Like in a Jane Austen book. You know banter is a great foundation for a connection."

I made a face. Banter was not necessarily something I was looking for. And if I was, I could just walk next door and ask Vik about . . . well, anything. He'd be sure to immediately disagree with me.

"Maybe . . . ," I said. "I'm not sure I really want a Mr. Darcy. Maybe more of like a Wickham, without the shadiness. He got along so well with Lizzie."

Lily shook her head. "I feel like you missed the point of that book."

I shrugged. She knew I had weird opinions.

"Back to the candlelit dinner. I'm thinking Al Forno's. No spaghetti, obviously, but they have a ridiculous spinach manicotti and we could share a tiramisu. Italian food is the ultimate romantic food," I said.

Lily, who was lactose intolerant, frowned. "I'll take your word for it."

Maybe a candlelit dinner was kind of boring, but I thought it would be a good opportunity to get to know each other and actually talk. Maybe a movie also? It was a classic for a reason.

"So, no banter, but you're right," I said. "This date is my chance to set the romantic tone and show Rohit how interesting I am."

I whirled around. "I'm interesting, right?"

Lily only raised her eyebrow at me. "Didn't he first meet you while you were in your penguin pajamas? He definitely knows you're not boring." She munched on her toast and pointed at the next item on the whiteboard.

The county fair. The second date.

To be honest, I had always wanted to go. I'd only ever admit it to Lily, but I loved the idea of someone winning me a giant teddy bear that I would be forced to carry around all day like "oh, look at this giant display of affection right here."

"The clincher here is the Ferris wheel," Lily said.

"Agreed."

There was one every year and it always managed to get stuck for a little bit, which might actually work in my favor. I could see it already, the two of us stuck in a small little basket, waving in the crisp fall air and warm sunlight, snuggling a little closer, looking deep into each other's eyes—

I was getting ahead of myself.

"And the third date is the big finale," Lily said.

Ah, yes. The third and final date. The pièce de résistance. The coup de grâce.

A candlelit dinner, the county fair, and then the big one—Winterfest. Our kiss would happen under the canopy of twinkling lights and fake snow that made up the Edison Winterfest dance. It would be the ultimate end to my wooing.

"This is a good plan, if I may say so," Lily said.

"Why do you sound surprised?" I asked, throwing a pillow at her. She laughed, catching it.

"Look, Deeps, I've known you forever, and you've had just as many bad plans as good ones." She held up a hand as I started to protest. "Still, your percentage rate is pretty good." Her mouth twisted into a concerned expression. "But you're going to have to ask Rohit out to start all of this. Unless you want to wait for him to ask?"

My balloon deflated.

I groaned and sat up. "I hadn't thought about that," I said.

"I don't think I can wait. What if the magic runs out? I have no idea how it works, to be honest."

My cheeks burned thinking about having to ask another boy out. What if it all went utterly horrible once again? The memory of the disaster with Jake was still pretty fresh.

I took a deep, steadying breath. Thinking that way would only lead to defeat, something my mom always said.

Positive vibes only.

"I can do it," I said, trying to sound more confident than I felt.

Could I? Was this even a good plan? Suddenly, I imagined every possible thing that could go wrong.

Lily was right. I had always a planner, but there had been plenty of bad plans strewn along my path to planning greatness. The prank war had been the cause of many of those. It was half the reason I had backed away, though I would never tell Vik that.

"You can totally do it," Lily said in confirmation. She tucked a blue strand of hair behind her ear and frowned. "I don't know how you did it before. I think about asking someone for anything, even the barista at Starbucks when they mess up my order, and I want to break out in hives."

That was one thing that my parents had prepared me for well. Every Josyula kid had to be ordering their own food, picking up phone calls, and generally taking charge by the age of ten. My mom had never wanted me to be afraid to ask for what I wanted in life—but this was a whole other thing. Asking someone out? It was like handing your beating heart over to a stranger. I had no idea how my dad had done it junior year, but I knew I wanted to be more like him than not.

"I wanted to vomit when I asked Jake," I admitted.

"Sounds accurate," Lily said.

"But I'd rather try than not try," I said. I cupped my face in my palms. "You know?"

Also, I wasn't ready to leave my romantic fate up to a boy. I had always been someone to take my life by the horns, and this would be no different.

Lily nodded. "Sure."

"It'll work out," I said.

I didn't know who I was promising then, me or Lily, but either way, I had to believe it. All I had to do was ask Rohit out to start my three-step wonder plan.

Simple, right?

8

It took me at least three tries before I got the courage to speak to Rohit the next week. I had talked a big game to Lily about not being nervous, but the truth was that I was terrified. I mean, I had just had a homecoming ask go down in hot, burning flames less than a week ago, so I felt it was pretty justified.

But it all melted away when I saw Rohit standing next to his locker. His hair swooped into a prince curl (what Lily and I used to call the classic Disney prince hair curl on the forehead) and he was dressed to perfection. Plus, he hadn't been lying about the three-ring binder. He lugged one out of his locker and pushed it into his leather backpack. All of that, and he had shown interest in me.

I still couldn't believe it.

But I knew what I had to do. I marched myself up to Rohit's locker, entering his space with a quick "hey!"

"Hey there." He straightened and I noticed he had a Flaming Moths pin on his backpack. It was a sign, it had to be.

"I wanted to catch you before the school day started,"

I said. I took a deep breath to fortify myself. Here went nothing. "You know, there's a Flaming Moths concert movie playing at the old theater in Alexandria, if you're interested in going? It's the weekend after next."

"What?" Rohit froze, his hand mid-zip on his backpack. He got to his feet and put his hands on his hips. "How did I miss that?"

I shrugged, trying to look playful. I had scoured the internet for any hint of the Flaming Moths reunion tour, but I hadn't found anything. I *had* found a news article about a concert series that the old theater was putting on, which fit my purposes nicely.

"And maybe we could get dinner after? Al Forno's?" I said, trying to keep my voice casual.

"Never heard of it, but it sounds good."

"It is. Italian. Best tiramisu in the whole tristate area," I said with a definitive nod. "Trust me."

Rohit leaned against his locker casually. "I will. You sound like you know your stuff," he said, sincerity in his words.

How nice it was to talk to a boy who took me seriously, where there was no whiff of teasing in sight. Sometimes I just wanted to be understood, you know? Seen as the all-knowing goddess that I was.

"I'm in," Rohit said. He leaned in closer to me, just close enough that it was a little more than friendly. I blinked up at him. "It's a date."

I had to bite my lip to hide how big my grin was about to be at those words. *A date.* Hurrah! A group of juniors who I knew from US History walked by us, whispering. I tried to send my glow in their direction. Maybe word would spread that the new boy was already exploring his options.

"It's like you read my mind," he said. "I'm really excited to hang out more."

"Oh, great," I said, smiling. It was easy to smile at Rohit.

"Also, I got you something." He reached into his locker and pulled out a small handpicked bouquet of gardenias. "Since you love flowers so much, I thought you might like these. My mom and I picked them just this morning. She's planning on redoing the landscaping in our backyard, so the gardenia bushes might be toast by the time we get back."

"Ruthless, your mom is," I said.

"Truly," he said, shaking his head. "Especially when it comes to gardening."

"Thank you," I said, taking the little bouquet that Rohit handed to me. Our fingers brushed as he passed it to me, just light enough that it was almost nothing. Almost.

A little thrill went through me. Flowers and a little hand brush? This was positively *Pride and Prejudice.* I even wanted to swoon, like a Regency-era lady might.

"These are so lovely. Do you know what gardenias mean?" I asked.

Or did he just pick them because they were pretty?

He ran a hand through his hair and then looked up at me through his eyelashes. "A new start?" he said. It wasn't really a question, though, and we both knew it.

"And admiration," I said.

I was swooning hard.

"You know, I hadn't planned on this happening," he said. "Going to the concert together. And dinner. But I had a feeling this morning that something good was going to happen." He smiled and a small dimple curved into his cheek.

Seriously, this boy was perfection.

"Me too—"

"Hey, Rohit," a very familiar voice said. "Oh, and hey, Deepa." Vik loped over to us. I squinted at him. Didn't he have anyone else to bother in this entire school? "Ready to head out?"

"We're carpooling," Rohit explained. "Vik's been really helpful while I'm sorting out a Virginia driver's permit. And my parents are busy; you know how that goes."

"Are those gardenias?" Vik said, squinting at my flowers. "Thought you hated gardenias. Remember that time you fell into that gardenia bush and got all scratched up? And then blamed every gardenia varietal for the next year? You even made your mom change her perfume."

I flushed. Okay, so twelve-year-old me had done all of that, but I was seventeen now. Would I never live these small humiliations down? Also, I had come to a stalemate with gardenias over the years. I stayed away from them, and they would stay away from me.

But today felt like a truce.

I was annoyed that first of all, Vik was right, and second, that he had totally ruined my budding moment with Rohit. Fine, there was a small part of me that thought it was kind of nice that Vik remembered that little detail. It showed that maybe he did remember how to be a friend. I recalled that he had been a stalwart partner in my fight against gardenias that summer, but still, another moment ruined by Vikram Mehta.

"Used to. Key tense," I said. "And thanks for revealing that wonderful and so very special childhood moment to Rohit here."

Vik shrugged. "I'm sure he'd find out eventually. He's part of the cul-de-sac crew now."

"That might be true, Vikram, but maybe you should stop telling people all of my embarrassing stories." I made my expression as flat as possible, hoping he knew that my eyes were glaring holes into his.

"Maybe you should stop having so many. You make it easy."

He reached into his backpack to get his water bottle, and I could've sworn I saw a little smile flit over his face. He was enjoying this! What had happened to the chivalrous knight who had saved me from Jake?

"Ignore him," I said to Rohit, turning away from Vik.

"Someone's cranky," Vik said.

I glared at him. My mom always said physical violence wasn't the solution to conflict, but I really, really begged to differ at that moment.

"Has anyone told you guys that you bicker like an old married couple?" Rohit asked, an amused look on his face.

His words shot through me like a bad bout of stomach flu at summer camp. I resisted the urge to jump backward and deny everything. The word *couple* was not one that should ever be spoken in regard to me and Vik.

More like lifelong adversaries. Surprisingly, Vik laughed, the corners of his mouth tugging upward into what I interpreted as a devious grin.

"What?" I said, hoping that Rohit didn't think anything was going on between me and Vik.

"You guys are like my best friends from Texas. We had all been friends for so long, because we grew up together, and they were always bickering," Rohit said. His voice sounded a little wistful.

I immediately relaxed. "Oh, yeah. We've been like this since I moved into the neighborhood and Vik tied my shoelaces together at the bus stop on our first day of school."

Rohit was unable to hold in a laugh at that. I couldn't fault him. I was gullible back then. I had quickly learned my lesson with Vikram.

"It was so easy, though," Vik said. "I couldn't help myself."

"And that's when our bickering started," I said definitively. Back then we had been friends, at least. Sometimes enemies, but also friends of a kind. That had been back before Lily had moved in. When she did, everything changed. "I have gray hair from dealing with this boy for years."

"Likely," Vik said, raising an eyebrow. He poked me in the shoulder. "But don't forget, you gave it back just as hard. There's a reason why I lost that Bieber hair swoop I had so carefully cultivated for months."

I grinned at that. That had been fun.

"Why?" Rohit asked.

"Gum in his hair," I said. "Basic but effective. Also, he had done it to me earlier."

Vik and I exchanged a look then. I hadn't meant to look over, but Vik was giving me that secret grin, the one where I knew he was reminiscing about those old moments the same way I was. He had been a trooper about the gum in his hair, though. And a lot of other things.

I'd deny it if asked, but I had a lot of fun back then. I'd never been friends with a neighbor before, or even had any kids my age in my neighborhood before. My sisters were still young enough to be annoying (not that they weren't now) and I had just moved to a new town.

And then Vik had come in.

"So, wait, how did this all start?"

Both our heads swiveled back to look at Rohit. For a

second, I had almost forgotten he was there. His chiseled face curved into a heart-melting smile and I blinked rapidly. How could I have forgotten?

"All of what?" Vik said.

"This," Rohit said, waving between me and Vik, like there was something to wave about. Which I did not enjoy. "This prank war?"

Ah, okay. That made more sense.

"You mean our legendary prank war?" Vik said. "It's been going on since we were in elementary school in our cul-de-sac."

Rohit looked impressed. "That long?"

"It started the summer Lily moved in," I said.

"It started before Lily moved in," Vik corrected me.

I rolled my eyes. "That doesn't count."

"You can't just rewrite history, Dee," he said.

"Oh, you call that rewriting history? What about you Saran Wrapping my car this semester even though I clearly said I was out?" I snapped back.

Rohit burst out laughing and we both looked over, startled. "You Saran Wrapped her car?" he said between laughs. "That is amazing."

I frowned.

"Thanks, man," Vik said, looking way too pleased with himself. "It was a crowning moment. Not my best, though. That would have to be the time I spray-painted your house. Or, well, the house before it became your house."

"Dude, what?" Rohit's eyes grew wide. "How'd you do that?"

I was not enjoying this bromance.

"Anywaaay," I said. "The legendary prank war of Oceania Drive is not just because of Vikram. I'll tell you about some of my best moments later." I gave Rohit a flirtatious smile and tacked on a little eyelash flutter for good measure.

Vik frowned at me, like I was annoying him. Whatever. If he wanted to become besties with Rohit, he could do it on his own time. He was the one who had barged in on our conversation.

"Best moments? You mean your second-best moments," Vik said. He leaned conspiratorially toward Rohit. "Deepa has never won a prank war. At least not yet."

"I'm not sure anyone would be able to top Saran Wrap," Rohit said, sounding a bit more intrigued than he should. Vik took a little bow, and I swallowed an indignant snort.

"You know," Rohit said slowly, "we should start it up again. It sounds like a lot of fun, and clearly it built a lot of great memories for the cul-de-sac. Have you ever invited the rest of the neighborhood?"

"No," Vik and I said at the same time. That was the one thing we had always agreed on. The rest of the neighborhood was cool, sure, and they had great houses to trick-or-treat at, but this was an Oceania Court Drive matter only.

Rohit threw his hands up and chuckled. "Okaaay, message received. But what about us?"

I looked at Rohit, realizing what he was asking. He wanted to join the prank war . . . but why? Still, I hadn't missed the sharp expression that passed over Vik's face. I knew he was super anti-inviting other people into our prank war. That hadn't changed over the years.

So, of course I said, "Sure! You should totally join."

Rohit's entire face lit up, and the look on Vik's face was priceless, even if he tried to hide it. I had surprised him, and I lived to surprise Vikram Mehta. There was something so satisfying in proving him wrong. I was sure it wasn't healthy, but what's a girl to do? I had to be allowed some vices.

"Really? I thought you said you weren't doing it this year," Rohit said.

"What? No, I never said that," I said, blatantly lying. I ignored Vik's narrowed gaze. "I was just surprised by Vik's initial approach. I missed the prank war summit earlier."

"Awesome," Rohit said. "I don't mean to intrude or anything, but since I'm new to the cul-de-sac . . ."

"Of course," Vik said, his smile following a second later. "If you're sure you want to be part of it, you're welcome to join. Though I will warn you, we won't go easy on you just because you're new."

"Got it," Rohit said, grinning. "I better earn my spot. I can bring it." His grin faltered a little. "I think. I've never been part of a prank war before."

Had I heard correctly? Vikram had agreed to this? What about the years of denying everyone and anyone entry into our little war? I wasn't exactly sure what was happening, but I did not like it. At all.

"Wait," I said, suddenly panicking. I hadn't meant to actually restart the prank war; I was really just trying to get back at Vik for ruining what should have been a triumphant moment. This was not going the way I wanted it to. "We should ask Lily too. It's only fair that everyone gets a vote. We're a democracy on Oceania Court Drive."

A beanie came into view and Lily's blue-haired head popped up next to Vik.

"Vote for what?" Lily said. She poked Vik's arm and he scooted over to let her into our tiny circle.

"Whether we should allow a new member into our prank war," Vik said, ignoring me. "Rohit."

"What? Of course!" Lily said, though I was desperately trying to get her to look in my direction. She wouldn't turn, though, which was making my mind waves kind of hard for her to receive. What had happened to our best-friend hive mind?

"Then it's settled," Vik said, with that grin of his. "Here's to a new prank war, with all four of us." He turned and looked straight at me over Lily's head.

Lily spun around and stared at me, her eyes wide. She mouthed "What?" but I shook my head. Vik's expression was that of a fat cat who had somehow gotten into the milk—way too satisfied and happy.

I glared at him. He smirked back.

Rohit turned around and I slapped on a happy face.

I could not lose my cool in front of him. We were still in that early-impressions phase. I'd deal with Vikram later.

He wasn't why my stomach felt like the sea in a storm. There was a reason I had bowed out of the prank war before—it had been two years ago, after my aunt had come to stay with us. That was the month everything had changed. The prank war had morphed into this thing that felt frivolous, especially when I realized what real life was actually like. That everything could be pulled out from under you.

And some of the neighbors . . . well, my aunt stopped coming to our neighborhood Diwali after the first time she heard someone whispering about her. She had enough going on in her life; she didn't need to also deal with other people's judgments.

And me? I'd decided I wanted to focus on other things as I entered high school, and Vik hadn't taken it well. To be fair, I hadn't ever really explained it to him. I hadn't really known how to process it myself. Part of me thought he wouldn't understand. I loved my community, but divorce was still seen as a bad thing, a black mark, and I didn't want to deal with it all.

There had been a small part of me that had wanted to rejoin eventually, though. Maybe senior year, when I had set up my life the way I had wanted. And I was almost there. My GPA was solid, I had leadership positions in my extracurriculars. . . . The only thing missing was that high school boyfriend, but I was working on it.

The prank war had originally been my idea. It had started as retaliation for something small Vik had done, a flattened bike tire, I think. And I had always imagined myself winning it, at least once, if only to rub it in Vik's smug face.

I had never told anyone, but the day after Lily and I had finished The List, the one for having a great four years of high school, I added it on the end in a faint blue pen. An idea, just a little goal. An afterthought. But one I hadn't forgotten.

Win the prank war. Just once.

I could feel the panic rise in my chest like a fist, but I held it back.

"So, what are the rules?" Rohit said, breaking me out of my thoughts. "Should we have a new prank war summit?"

Vik clapped him on the shoulder. "Now, that's a great idea, Rohit. I'll plan something for us. Get ready, people, the prank war is back on."

I smiled broadly, like I wasn't a worried mess on the inside. But it was Vik who clinched it for me.

"You ready, Dee?" he said, raising that stupid eyebrow of his.

Nope. Nope, I was not. I did not have a plan and I had no idea how I'd win.

"As I'll ever be," I muttered.

The last school bell arrived way too quickly that Wednesday.
I made my way to the auditorium lobby, dodging the football team's warm-up indoors (it was raining) and the Model UN team loudly debating whether sanctions were the right option for an act of aggression. Honestly, I would have loved the ability to sanction Vik during our prank war, so I was inclined to agree with Melissa Liu, who was passionately championing the cause with wild hand gestures.

The auditorium lobby at Edison was huge, a stretch of linoleum tiles and very few windows, giving it the look and feel of a very long dentist's office that just happened to be lined with trophy cases. It was the main connecting point in the school, smack dab in between the auditorium and the gym entrance, and I had agreed to meet Vik there before we went off to find an empty classroom for our lock-in planning meeting.

Vik had agreed to meet me there ten minutes ago.

I checked my watch and blew out a breath of frustration. Typical.

We had barely even started and I was already wondering why I had bothered showing up on time. Vik hadn't always been like this. Or had he?

Five minutes later, I had gotten myself a bag of chips from the vending machine and taken a seat on the ground, far away from the gym entrance. The auditorium doors were open and I was watching the drama club do their acting warm-ups when Vik finally decided to make his entrance.

With Rohit in tow.

They were laughing about something, though how Rohit could find Vik funny I honestly did not know. They looked like they were old buddies, which I did not like. I had agreed to let Rohit into the prank war mostly as a way to annoy Vik, which wasn't my finest moment, but still, this? The universe was really repaying me with Vik and Rohit becoming friends? Couldn't Vik let me have this one thing?

"You're late," I said to Vik, picking up my things.

"Deepa!" Rohit said with a smile that made me smile too. I sighed internally. He was beautiful, even under the harsh fluorescent lights of the auditorium lobby. It was really unfair. "I found Vik as he was walking over to you and we ended up losing track of time, so that's my fault."

Hmph. I still narrowed my eyes at Vik. "Oh, really?"

Rohit dug out his phone from his pocket, and it buzzed. "I've got to go, my mom's here." He tugged his backpack on and grimaced at his phone, but the expression passed quickly, replaced by his normal smile. "See you both later!"

Before I could say anything, Rohit waved and headed off in the other direction. Once he was gone, I turned and stared at Vik, my arms crossed and a frown on my face.

Vik gave me an innocent look. "It's true."

"Really? You'd throw our new neighbor under the bus?"

Vik's eyes widened. "Are you encouraging me to tell lies, Deepa?"

I rolled my eyes and started down the hallway to find a classroom, leaving Vik to follow. We had fifteen less minutes to plan now.

"Hey, you know that's true," Vik said, taking two long strides to catch up. He slung his backpack over his shoulder.

I didn't say anything, though he was right. Vik was not a liar and he really wasn't a bad person, just a little chaotic. A lot chaotic.

"I'm thinking one of the chemistry classrooms. Dr. Cortez always leaves them open," I said, already moving forward on my plan for the meeting.

We arrived in the classroom and I made a beeline for my favorite desk, the one two rows from the back, near the wall. Didn't matter the classroom, that was always the perfect location. I put my bag down and started to pull out my binder and notebooks, laying them out on the table carefully.

Vik slung his backpack onto the first desk he could

find and marched over to me. He put his elbows down on the table and perched his chin on his hands, watching me as I organized. I tried to ignore him, but it was hard to. He made a funny picture there, his long limbs not quite wanting to fit into his odd position. And his eyelashes kept fluttering.

"I started a system. Research first—" I pointed to the red binder. "Then we'll go into budgeting and vendor selection—" Orange binder. "And then we'll go into logistics and a day-of project plan. That way, everyone on student council can see the logical flow of our thinking."

"Hmm," Vik said, grabbing one of the binders. He flipped through it, grimaced, and then put it down. "Is there a reason you're trying to suck the joy from this?"

I bristled. "I'm adding rigor, I'm not removing joy," I said with a wave of my hand. This was how you got things done. I wasn't known as the best planner on student council for no reason.

"I mean, I agree that we need to do research first, and then the rest. But I can see from the first few pages in the pumpkin binder—"

"Budgeting and vendor selection. And it's marigold—"

"—that you're not thinking big enough."

"Hmph" was my only response. "Look, we just agreed that research is the first step. So, I've drafted a detailed timeline for us to follow." I pulled the timeline out of one of the folders and handed it to him.

"Didn't you hear what I said?" he asked.

"I may have possibly ignored it," I said. He narrowed his eyes at me and then sat on the table, right on top of my folders and notebooks.

"You're not thinking big enough, seriously. I can already tell."

I threw up my hands. "What is that supposed to mean, Vik? And get off my binders!"

"It means you're already thinking about all the little stuff," he said. He wiggled to the side and grabbed one of the binders. He flipped to a page. "Confirm number of electrical outlets available for use in the gym."

"Very practical and something that needs to be checked in an old building like Edison," I said, nodding.

"This is our first meeting. This is the moment to get excited and dream big. Like what's our huge draw going to be?" he said. "Water balloon fight?"

"Messy."

"Laser tag?"

"Impractical."

"Funnel cake station?"

I paused. "That could work. They do those at the Harvest Fair, so there's definitely a vendor somewhere. But that's why I put together three-point criteria for all decisions. I think we should have a theme, something that ties back to different events from our time here. Or we can borrow what they did last year. We know that was successful."

"You want to copy the senior class?" Vik sounded aghast.

"It's a good plan," I said defensively. Not the most creative, I would admit, but I had been thrown for a loop. I had always hoped to be planning the Winterfest Dance. I felt out of my element with the lock-in—plus, it was just the lock-in. Right?

"A good plan?" Vik rubbed his temples, blinking rapidly and looking at me like I was an alien.

"Why won't you at least consider my plan?" I said, exasperated.

"I'm not *not* considering your plan, but you're kind of being a dictator about things already. Why are you trying to control everything?" Vik looked legitimately frustrated, his eyebrows knitted together, his jaw clenched. "This isn't just a to-do on your list to check off."

I shook my head. "This is exactly that."

Vik made a face. "It's so much more than that. We have months to plan and we should do it right. Take the time, do the research before we start to decide. And if you were wondering, I have a long list of potential ideas for the main activity, since they're letting us use the tennis courts."

"Sure," I said. "Happy to discuss them. But do they fit the three-point criteria I outlined on my timeline?"

Vik positively glowered at me. He stood up so quickly that two of my binders went flying. I frowned at them, and then frowned deeper when I realized that Vik was now standing close to me.

"Are you actually trying to ruin everything or does that

just come naturally?" I said, waving at the destruction on the table. It wasn't like I had spent hours on all of that or anything.

"That's hilarious, because out of the two of us, who has actually ruined something?" he said, his mouth twisting.

"What are you talking about?"

Vik only glared at me, his arms wrapped against his chest. "You know what I mean."

"Are you talking about the prank war? That was two years ago. And I told you I was out early on."

Seriously, was he ever going to get over that? I just said I was bowing out; I didn't murder anyone. Removing myself shouldn't have been a crime.

Maybe I should have told him the real reason why. Or that's what the annoying little voice in my mind said, the one that remembered that Vik had once been my friend. He had always been annoying, but it hadn't always been a problem. But after my aunt came . . . things had changed.

"What happened? You used to be fun once."

I snapped back to attention.

"And you used to be less . . ." I waved up and down at him. "Annoying."

His eyes crinkled in mirth. "Oh, really? You thought I wasn't annoying once? That's a big revelation right there."

"What? No," I said, not liking the way he was smiling like he had won something. I had just insulted him. "I mean you used to be more responsible."

"Ah, so you're comparing fun to responsibility. Very fun."

I threw my hands up. "What's the big deal with being fun? Does fun get you into college? Does fun build you a successful career?"

He gave me an "is that really a question?" look. "We are literally planning the lock-in, which is a night the school sponsors for us all to get together and have fun—"

"They're basically trying to make sure we're all safe after junior prom." I leaned toward Vik, enunciating my words. "Saaafe."

"Funnnn." He leaned forward too.

Suddenly, I realized Vik was a little too close. It wasn't like I hadn't looked at Vik before. I had spent all of seventh grade seated behind him in homeroom, so I was very familiar with the back of his head. But this was different.

Sometime in the past few years, it appeared that Vik had grown up. His face was lean and angular, no traces of baby fat to be seen. And that annoying, smirking smile was actually framed by full lips.

Wait, no. No, no, no. I could not be thinking about Vik in that way. I froze up inside. Could he see that I had noticed he was no longer a seventh grader? Because that was all this was. What if he thought I was checking him out?

I glanced up to see Vik looking down at me with a curious expression. It flashed in my mind for one fleeting second—had Vik just noticed the same thing?

The thought made my entire body flush and I suddenly needed to regain some control, stat. I blurted out the first thing in my head.

"We're following my plan. That's that," I said, trying to sound like my mom on one of her important business calls.

Vik tensed, his jaw tightening. His entire body language shifted too, so quickly I barely had any warning.

"You can't just be an . . . absolute monarch! We're a team here and I've actually been planning this for a while. You made it very clear you only got stuck with it, so we're definitely not deferring to you," he said, sounding a little huffy.

I wasn't sure I had ever really seen Vik get mad before, actually. He was usually the picture of chill. Not necessarily calm, but someone whose feathers rarely got ruffled. Unlike me. Which I was woman enough to admit.

But it seemed as if I, Deepa Josyula, had finally cracked through.

"Did you just call me an absolute monarch?" I said.

Vik blinked rapidly, his mouth pulling into a taut line. "I think I did."

The laugh just erupted out of me, even though I was mildly offended. "Don't think—I'm forgiving you—for that character assassination—" I said through snorts. "But maybe AP European History is getting to you."

Vik was trying to stay mad, but I could see a smile peeking through after my laughing outburst. I couldn't help myself, but something about it was so ridiculous. And I hadn't really meant to get Vik angry. I still thought I was right—I was the better planner out of the two of us and it only made sense to follow my lead.

But something told me to step back, so I did.

"Truce?" I asked. I stuck my hand out, the way we always would during our prank war summits, making deals and agreements, all sealed with a firm handshake. A gentle-person's agreement.

For a second, I wasn't sure Vik would agree. It was more and more clear that I had touched some sort of nerve here, and for that I did feel bad. Not really about anything else. But I knew he had worked hard on brainstorming ideas for the lock-in already. If I could just put some organization and planning around it all, it would go off well.

"Fine," he said after a beat.

He clasped my hand and gave it a firm shake. And then he yanked me in. I stumbled forward and Vik caught me.

"But don't think I'll give in to everything so easily," he said down to me. I flushed, mainly because I was realizing just exactly how tall Vik had become, and after my previous revelation that Vik was no longer a round-cheeked seventh grader, my body was in a heightened state. A very heightened state. Vik and I had roughhoused plenty of times before, so I wasn't unfamiliar with his touch. Not really.

But this was different.

A second later he let go. I coughed to cover up the fact that for a moment, I had lost my voice.

"Of course not," I said. "Then you wouldn't be Vik."

He only smiled at that.

10

The weekend after next, and my date with Rohit, arrived sooner than Mani the moment ice cream enters any room. I swear, it's like she is a human homing device when it comes to sweets.

I almost ran into Lily as I flitted around my bedroom, making last-minute dress changes and second-guessing my lipstick for the sixth time.

"Deeps! Slow down!" Lily tried to come after me with red lipstick. I ducked. "Seriously."

"No, I think I'm going to go with the pink, actually," I said, squinting at the pink lipstick in her hand. Why had I decided to wear a pink dress? Weren't you not supposed to mix pink and red?

"But a red lip is your signature look," Lily said. For once, her beanie was off, and her newly dyed blue roots shone in the bright lighting of my bedroom. "Don't you want to be your best Deepa self tonight? For your big night?"

"I know it's my signature," I said, a little distracted as I tried to remember where I had put that cute coat my mom had bought me last winter. "But I can't wear red with pink.

That's like a cardinal fashion sin. Rohit is sophisticated and worldly and he's, like, next-level. I have to bring my A game."

"You can do whatever you want, Deeps," Lily said.

Incorrect. I was not planning on angering the fashion or beauty gods tonight, not when I wanted to impress Rohit. This was the time to play it classic—*classy*.

"Pink. It's got to be the pink," I said.

Lily shrugged and handed it over, but not without letting me see the giant frown on her face. She was always pushing to get me to try new things—she had invited me on her blue-hair-dye expedition, for instance—so I didn't really get why she was against the pink. I always wore red.

But there wasn't much time to think about it, not when I was already running behind schedule. Rohit was supposed to arrive. . . . I looked down at my watch and saw that it was about to turn seven, when he said he would stop by, which meant I probably had another few minutes.

The doorbell rang.

"Punctual," I said, nodding in approval. Then I realized that even though Rohit was punctual, I was totally not ready.

"My hair!" I wailed, running into the bathroom. "Lily, stall, please."

She saluted. "On it."

The door closed and Lily stomped down the stairs in her combat boots. Then I heard a bright "Hi, Rohit!" Lily was a lifesaver.

If tonight didn't go well, I could kiss goodbye to . . . well, my kiss. I had tried to explain this to Lily earlier as we were getting ready, but she kept asking me if I shouldn't be more focused on finding out if I liked Rohit. Treating it like a real first date.

Given that Rohit was literally a wish come true and had every quality of the perfect boyfriend, I didn't totally understand what she meant. Rohit wasn't the problem here.

And there would be no problem if I could just make this night a success. A courtship that had to go off with expert precision.

I did my best to rush through styling the rest of my hair as quickly as I could.

Not a hair could be out of place tonight. Not a single hair.

I made my way down five minutes later, and Lily was regaling Rohit with a story of some kind, one that was resulting in a lot of laughter.

"And then, one time, we stuck toothpaste in his mail-box. That one we got in trouble for—the Mehtas were nice about it, but my mom was not happy. Deepa and I were separated and grounded for the rest of the school year. Being grounded was whatever, I'm a total homebody, but they knew how to hit us where it hurt with the separation. That was when Deepa and I developed our first window-signal language."

"So, you both are close?" Rohit's voice was warm and curious.

"Like superglue."

"Hey, guys!" I said brightly. I winked at Lily, catching her eye before Rohit turned. She winked back and mouthed "gorgeous" at me.

There was clear approval on Rohit's face. "Wow," he said. "You look amazing."

He held a bouquet of pink roses and tulips tied with a glittery ribbon—not a gardenia in sight—and when he turned, he produced a box of chocolates in his other hand. I recognized the box design; it was from that high-end chocolatier that had opened nearby in downtown Vienna. My mom had mentioned that one of her patients had brought her treats from the place as a thank-you, but Mani had gotten to them before I had a chance to try even one.

"Are those from La Jolie?" I said, unable to conceal my delight. He stuck his hand out, offering the box and the flowers to me. I took them from him carefully, making sure not to muss up that gorgeously tied ribbon. Some things were just meant to be done right, and this bouquet was perfection. Rohit had nailed it. "Thank you, Rohit. The flowers are beautiful. Someone must have told you that chocolate was the way to my heart."

"I just heard they're the best chocolatier in town," Rohit said. "You can never go wrong with bringing a gift. Plus, it's the first time I've come to your house."

"I'm tempted to open them right now," I said, eyeing the chocolates longingly. Instead, I handed them to Lily with a quick whisper about hiding them from Mani. Lily nodded, knowing the drill. "But we're running late, which is my fault."

I winced, knowing how much I hated it when others were late.

"Ah, no worries," Rohit said. "I was a bit early anyway. Lily and I were just chatting."

"What did I miss?" I said as I went to the closet. I pulled out the heels I had chosen for this outfit. They were low and blocky but had a delicate strap that fancied them up.

"Not much," he said. "Lily was just telling me some stories of your pranks so far."

"The prank war again? You must think we do nothing else," I said, wiggling my feet into my heels. I stumbled a little.

"Let me help you," Rohit said, offering me his arm to steady myself on. The wall was right there, but what was I going to do? Not take the chance to be close to him? I nodded gratefully and took his arm. And yes, he was as muscular as he looked. I snuck a peek at him, noticing that he had very nicely shaped eyebrows and that even up close, his nose was exceptionally straight.

"Thanks," I said, once my shoes were on. "Again."

"Okay now, you two. You better get a move on if you don't want to miss the movie," Lily said. She handed me my coat and shooed both of us out the door. "You be good, now! Have fun!"

I turned back to give Lily an odd look, but the door was already closed.

And like that, I was on my first date with Rohit.

The concert movie was one of those where they spliced the concert itself with a documentary about the music, and when the movie ended and we walked out, we had a lot to talk about. The October air was dipping its toes into cold, which meant that I was shivering a little in my pink sundress. The temperature had dropped rapidly once the sun had set thirty minutes ago and the streets of Old Town Alexandria were lit in a soft glow.

Old Town Alexandria was one of my favorite places to go, and I had been dying to go to Al Forno's since my mom had first talked about it. It was my parents' go-to date spot.

"Could you believe that Leo wanted to leave the band at one point?" Rohit said, shaking his head. "I have to admit, I feel kind of betrayed."

"Me too," I said. "Actually, I'm pretty pissed about it. Do you think that's why they didn't release an album for five years? It seemed like they alluded to it."

"Totally could be," he said. "You've got a point."

"Right? I know they stopped recording the documentary after the concert tour and that was when things started to get weird from them. Like their single 'Don't Fall for It.'

What if it was about Leo trying to leave?" I said, getting excited.

I realized I was sounding a little conspiracy theory there, but Rohit didn't say anything. He only nodded slowly, as if he was thinking. "Could be, could be."

"It's okay," I said. "You don't have to indulge my theories."

"No, really. I'm thinking about it and you're right, the single could be the first signs of tension. The lyrics would support it."

"Thank you," I said. "It's nice for my genius to be acknowledged."

Rohit laughed, and I laughed too. A breeze rattled by us and I held back a shiver, drawing my arms around myself.

"Do you want my jacket?" Rohit asked. He didn't wait for me to answer and took off his blazer, hanging it around my shoulders. I was instantly cocooned in warmth, and nearly swooned. Not from the warmth. From the boy.

"Seriously, how are you so sweet?" I said. "You're like candy."

Rohit shrugged but looked pleased, his cheeks turning a light pink. "My mom told me to always be a gentleman."

"Roses, chocolates, and your jacket?" I said, teasing. "It's like straight out of a movie."

"Right?" Rohit said. "I used to love romantic comedies. I mean, I still do, but they were my thing for a while."

"Wow, me too," I said. "Had a major Julia Roberts moment there in middle school. I used to watch them with my aunt a lot too. We've moved on to Marvel, but I definitely have a soft spot for them."

"Kindred spirits," he said. "It's nice to find someone else." His glance at me was appreciative. "Especially someone so cute."

I was glad that the darkness hid my expression. I searched for a topic.

"How's the move so far? Is Virginia any better than Texas?"

"Well, that's a touchy subject." Rohit's expression turned mischievous. "Y'all have a horrible football team—"

"Watch it," I said jokingly, nudging him in the shoulder. He nudged me back. "Though that is probably the first negative thing I've heard you say since you moved in."

"Oh, I'm sorry," Rohit said, blinking.

"No, no," I said quickly. "I'm just teasing."

Really, he was too cute. How could someone this unnaturally attractive be wrapped up in such a milk chocolate shell? For a fleeting moment, I wondered if it was all real. He seemed almost too good to be true.

But that was the point of a wish coming true, wasn't it?

Of course no other high school boy had matched up before. None of them had checked off everything on The List.

"But yes, Virginia is nice," he said.

Something about his tone seemed off, so I asked, "And the move here?"

"Everyone has been so welcoming," he said. "I really can't complain at all." He shrugged. "And I'm used to moving. My dad's job takes us around. It's a busy lifestyle."

"That must be hard," I said. I thought back to the comment he had made a few days earlier in the auditorium lobby, about how parents just got busy.

His eyes slid away from mine. "It's okay."

I remembered how hard moving had been for me, and I had only moved a county over. Still, it had been a whole new experience, and I empathized. I wanted to push a little, but I figured it would be rude. And this wasn't really first date conversation material, was it? Maybe he was totally fine and I was projecting onto him.

We turned the corner and the softly lit neon sign of Al Forno's loomed ahead, which I was glad for. It was getting colder and these heels were not my friends. I should've worn the more comfortable ones, but I wanted everything to be just right tonight.

All my efforts had paid off, because so far, so good.

We checked in for our reservation with the host and were led to a table for two just a few over from the windows, exactly as I had requested.

Rohit held out a hand to stop me. He stepped in front of me, blocking my view. I was confused at first, and then I saw what he was trying to do. He had pulled my chair out for me. I almost swooned again right there.

"Thank you," I said.

"You're welcome," he said, with a gallant sweep of his arms.

I sat down in the chair, only to realize that once you sat down, it was pretty awkward to scoot yourself in. I had no idea what I was supposed to do. Romantic comedies had not prepared me for this.

"Let me," Rohit said. He placed his hands on both sides of my chair and pushed me into the table, like it was no sweat.

So that's how it worked.

Double swoon.

I fidgeted to get my purse out, realizing that Rohit had pushed me in a little too tight. And I was a little stuck. I tried to move back, and the chair made a horrible squeaking sound. I had to fidget and tilt the chair back and forth to move without alerting the entire restaurant. Thankfully, only the older couple two tables down saw me.

Still, it was my first time having a chair pulled out for me and I gave it a four out of five. A little awkward, but worth it, mostly because it showed how thoughtful Rohit was. The older couple, the wife in particular, had noticed, and I positively glowed.

Once Rohit sat, the conversation turned to other things, talk of school or bands we loved, or other light topics. He also loved cinema and religiously watched the SAG Awards, and could even recite all of the winners from the past few years.

And when the time for the dessert menu came, Rohit suggested the tiramisu himself, like he had read my mind.

The rest of the date went as smooth as butter. He reached for the check and pulled out my chair. Even the air outside had warmed as we left, or maybe it felt that way because I was literally beaming from the inside out.

This entire night had been . . .

A dream date. If this was what life would be like with Rohit, I couldn't wait to kiss him and seal the deal. I hadn't had a lot of experience with dating, but even I knew that the evening probably had to be in the top ten of dates of all time.

Romantic, check.

Pulled out my chair, check.

Shared a dessert, check.

Brought me roses, check.

Pleasant, agreeable conversation, check.

What else could a girl want? I seriously tried to think of anything else, but all I could imagine was how cute Rohit had looked all night, from the top of his coiffed hair down to his polished leather loafers. And how many people had smiled at us, saying how cute we were together.

Thank you, universe.

Thank you, magical jasmine flower. I had always wanted magic to be real as a kid (and now, if I was being honest) and for the first time I felt it in the air.

And exactly as Lily and I had thought, when he dropped

me off at my doorstep, he didn't try to kiss me. Part of me was a little disappointed, but it was also the confirmation I needed.

I sighed and fell back on my pillow, ready to nod off to dreams of red roses and Rohit's swoony prince hair curl.

One date down, two more to go.

11

I basically floated through the rest of the night on the high from my date with Rohit, even dreaming of us both at Winterfest, drawing closer under the fake snow and twinkling lights. Nothing could bring me down. That was, until I woke up on Saturday morning, stumbled down the stairs, and discovered Vik sitting at my kitchen counter.

"What are *you* doing here?" I said. "The terms of a truce include space, Vikram."

"You look very comfortable," Vik said, a smirk playing at the corner of his lips as his eyes trailed down my outfit. I tucked my hair behind my ear but resisted the urge to run back upstairs and put on a different pair of pajamas, one that wasn't so ratty and old. I did not need to look good for Vik, of all people.

"This is my *home*," I said, emphasizing the last word. "You have one over there." I pointed toward his house. "Away from here."

"Oh really?" Vik said, with a fake, confused tone. "I had no idea. You should teach geography, put Mr. Corfeld out of a job."

I rolled my eyes, another retort ready. A burst of giggles rocketed into the room, followed by Ratna. I glared at my sister.

"What? It was funny," she said.

Mani appeared from the dining room. "He's helping Nanna with a new jam collection. Fair warning, I think I saw Nanna picking some green chili peppers from the garden."

"The tongue-melting ones?" I said, taking a bite out of a piece of toast that had been left near the counter. Tomato chutney and butter, which meant my grandmother had left it for me. "Good thing you're here, then, Vik; maybe the spice will shut you up for once."

Vik grinned, glancing at me from under his lashes. "I can handle spicy, Dee."

Something about the way he said it caught me unaware, snatching my body in a tight, warm grip. It went away quickly, but I wondered if I had eaten something bad last night.

"Move," I said, shooing Vik over.

He didn't budge. "I was here first."

"That's my spot." Everyone knew the end counter seat was mine.

Vik only shrugged. "Guess it's not today."

I took a deep breath. I would not let Vik ruin all the good vibes I had accumulated from my date. So, I smiled serenely, hoping he understood that it was a mask for my death stare.

"What happened to pancake morning?" Vik said.

"It's toast morning today," I said, rummaging around for food. "My mom had to go into the clinic early for a training workshop she's leading, so she requested we do pancake Saturday on Sunday."

Vik frowned. "Was hoping for some of Asha auntie's chocolate chip pancakes, to be honest."

"Is your mom back on one of her no-sugar kicks?" I asked.

"You know it."

"That sucks, man," I said. And yes, I did grab the Nutella on purpose and lick a spoonful of it, all while locking eyes with Vik.

"Evil, Dee. You're truly evil," he said.

But not that evil. I put the Nutella and a slice of toast in front of him before taking a seat at the dining table.

"You put me out of a home." I eyed my seat, which he was occupying.

"I can't believe you have your own seat," he said in turn.

"Don't tell me you don't have certain things you have to stake as your own as the eldest. I'm sure Nikhil is always taking your stuff."

"Nikhil will never win," Vik said, his mouth semi-full. Ugh, boys. "But you may have a point."

"By the way, since you're here, we should have another planning meeting," I said. Two weeks had passed since we had been assigned lock-in and most of our meetings involved us arguing. Maybe I could leverage some of this goodwill to actually move our proposal forward. "Hopefully, a more successful one."

Vik gave me a look, like the outcome was my fault.

"I can't do this week; tons of soccer practice before our next game," he said.

"And then it's homecoming," I said, sighing. Suddenly, I wondered if Vik had asked anyone. In all my asking week chaos, I hadn't noticed. I knew he had been talking to some girl over the summer, and he had a crush on one of the Jennys in ninth grade or something, but nothing since then.

"I'll see you there," Vik said. "I thought about asking Violet, I think she's been hoping I would—"

Ahh, that was her name. The girl he'd been chatting with. "Not sure why exactly she would want that."

Vik gave me a look. "—but Rohit wanted to go to homecoming; he said it was something he didn't really get to do before, so I said I'll be his wingman and—"

"Rohit's going to be there?" I said, perking up.

Vik rolled his eyes. "Try to be less obvious, Dee."

I scoffed, crossing my arms. "What's the point? It's only you." I scrunched up my nose in thought. "Should I ask him? Or is it too late since asking week is over? Or—"

"Jeez, take a breath," Vik said. "He just moved here. Give him some time to get the lay of the land."

"See, that's exactly what I'm worried about."

"He's a cool guy, but I don't know if he's right for you," Vik said, his lips quirking.

"Thanks, Vik," I said, pushing away from the table and collecting my plate. I placed it in the dishwasher and poured myself some of the chai still on the stove. "He's a dreamboat and absolutely perfect, so obviously not a match for little weirdo me."

Vik stared at me, blinking in that owlish way of his. "That's not what I meant, you pillow head."

"Pillow head?" I nearly choked on my chai. "Why am I even here? I can leave and not be insulted in my own home." Somehow Vik had made his way over to me, leaning against the stove. I sniffed into the air and made to pass him by.

He grabbed my wrist and tugged. "Stop being so melo-dramatic. That's not what I meant and you know it. And what happened to your last dreamboat? Jake? And what about Marcello?"

My cheeks burned at the mention of my eighth-grade crush, which had ended horribly. "Seriously? Vik, we prom-ised to never speak of that. You swore."

"I'm not telling anyone else," he said. "Look, it's not my fault you have such embarrassing things in your past. Like I said before, you make it too easy. It's like standing under an apple tree ripe for picking. All you want to do is reach up and—"

"Don't even start with me, Vikram. I remember middle school, I remember the day you needed help with—"

Mani's head popped up around the corner. Vik dropped my arm.

"Day he what?" Mani asked innocently. She didn't share the same enmity with Vik that I did, but she was also not the type to pass up some leverage.

Vikram glared at me. "Don't you dare, Dee."

I took a deep breath, acting like I was going to reveal all, simply to see Vik's face. It was worth it to see the way his brow creased and his jaw tensed. He had forgotten that I once knew him well too. But I let it out.

"That's between us, Manisha," I said primly. She rolled her eyes and flounced away, back on her phone.

Vik and I exchanged a look, and I knew I had done the right thing. Even if I had been so, so tempted otherwise. Vikram was my enemy, but I didn't play dirty.

"I'm back and only mildly injured from gathering the chilies," my dad said as he strode into the living room with a basketful of green chilies and a wide grin. "Oh, Deepa. Are you joining us?"

I tried to think of an excuse, any excuse, until I saw how excited my dad looked. Vik poked me in my side.

"I'll be good," he whispered to me.

I doubted it.

However, I didn't want to be the reason that smile on my dad's face changed. Plus, let's be real, I wasn't going to leave Vik around here alone to do reconnaissance for the prank war.

"Yup, I'm in. Just let me get changed," I said.

My mom came in the front door as I started to walk up the stairs. "Suraj! I brought you some extra green chilies!"

She looked at me and whispered, "How's it going so far? Better than the turmeric jam?" We both winced at that.

"Hasn't started yet," I said. "I'm changing to go help."

My mom pinched my cheek. "That's kind of you." I waved her away and mumbled something about having your nemesis in your own home and turf rights.

She didn't ask me what I meant, which was the right move. Nanna came to the foyer and grabbed one of the bags she was carrying, tilting her back into a kiss.

Okay, fine, it was sweet to have parents who loved each other and everything, but I didn't need to stay around for it. I glanced over my shoulder and into the kitchen as I took the stairs.

Vik stared back and mouthed, "Best behavior."

I rolled my eyes and made my way up to my room.

It took the next week for my stomach to recover from the chili raspberry jam that my dad and Vikram concocted, at least the first few stomach-burning versions. Still, the days flew by, and before I knew it, the dreaded week was upon us.

Homecoming.

Usually, our school got really festive about it, but an early frost had canceled the homecoming parade, and a lot of the other events, which put a damper on things. The week seemed to drag on, and all the school spirit only reminded me that I had no date. Lily caught me staking out Rohit's locker a few times, and I had to admit that I was really, really close to asking Rohit. The only thing that stopped me was Vik's voice playing in my head.

Also, I didn't want to seem that desperate.

Still, I couldn't deny I was happy that Rohit still hadn't seemed to ask anyone by the day before the dance. I overheard him and Vik talking, and while I wasn't normally an eavesdropper, it did settle the worry in my stomach. Maybe he really was still getting the lay of the land. If that was the case, it would make sense to go with friends. It was definitely less stressful.

The day of the homecoming dance arrived with minimal fanfare. Lily and I were both dateless this year and I had already found my dress over the summer, so there wasn't much preparation. We spent most of our getting-ready routine trying out new hair-curling methods from YouTube and driving around the neighborhood while screaming our hearts out to our favorite songs. It was the perfect pre-dance ritual.

We met up with a group from the student council, which happened to include the Jennys (super awkward) and some of the boys from the lacrosse team. I was surprised that Vik wasn't there too, but it seemed he had been honest about being Rohit's wingman. Jenny Porter told me Rohit was with some of the crew kids. Of course, she told me while holding Jake's hand, which only served to make me want to melt into a puddle.

No date, and stuck in a group with Jake and Jenny. I couldn't wait for homecoming to be over.

Alex Pastor was there too, Lily's co-conspirator in middle school soccer crime, and they spent a good twenty minutes discussing new offensive measures that the Stuart Littles could practice, which wasn't very fun for me. Alex's younger sister was also on the team and Alex occasionally came to practices, which Lily had mentioned. She was known for being as into soccer as Lily, if that was even possible.

I was standing there, trying not to fall asleep, and also keeping an eye out for Rohit, when I noticed a red dress that looked a lot like the one from my sweet sixteen. My eyes trailed up the dress and—

What the hell was Mani doing here?

She turned around and her eyes went wide as she saw me. And she was totally holding hands with some boy.

I marched over to her.

"Manisha," I said in a low voice. My sister looked like she wanted to bolt away, but my gaze pinned her down. "I don't remember you telling me you'd be here."

The boy next to Mani smiled at me, but I didn't return it. "Did you tell Amma and Nanna?" I said to Mani, hands on my hips.

"Roger, this is my older sister, Deepa. Give us a second, will you?" Mani said, her voice dripping with charm. He smiled nervously and left.

I grabbed her by the arm. "Mani, what the hell?"

"I'm fourteen!" she said, pouting. "And all my friends from dance were coming, so when Roger asked, I . . ."

She looked so sad that some of my anger dissipated. I remembered eighth grade, feeling like you were on the precipice of something bigger but feeling stuck where you were. I hadn't done it, but I knew quite a few kids who had snuck into this same dance in middle school.

"You know, you only turned fourteen a few months ago," I said, crossing my arms. "You're not that old yet. You still forget to brush your teeth sometimes."

"But I'm not a kid anymore," she insisted.

"Who did your hair?" I said, eyeing her loose curls. "The dress is obviously mine. Did you think you wouldn't see me?"

Mani looked sheepish. "Ask for forgiveness, not permission? And Pooja did my hair."

I let out the deepest sigh known to humankind. "I'm annoyed, but mainly because you didn't even tell me. This is my high school, Mani. And also, how can I cover for you with Amma if you don't tell me things? But your curls do look good." The last part I added a little begrudgingly.

I hated the idea that she had felt the need to go to someone else for that, instead of me. Look, I didn't love that she had used my closet as her own personal store, but I had also borrowed her sweater set last week, so . . . I wasn't one to talk.

Then the words registered. Pooja?

Loud voices filtered over and we swiveled our heads. In the corner, Vik was with Pooja, and he didn't look happy either. Sometimes it was easy to forget that Vik was the oldest, with the way he acted.

"Pooja's going to get it," Mani said, shaking her head.

"Totally," I said. "I would not want to be on the end of that."

Older brothers were a different breed than older sisters. And Vik, despite all his laid-back surfer dude vibes, could be decidedly not chill when it came to his little sister. Less so about his brother, mainly because he was a menace in his own right. But Pooja was the apple of Vik's eye.

I whirled back to Mani. "Next time, you tell me, okay? I can do your hair a lot better than Pooja and we can get ready together."

"Fine, bossy." Mani rolled her eyes, but I could tell she was pleased. "I didn't want to step on your toes, you know, in case you were going to try to get some quality time with Rohit," she said, waggling her brows at me.

"Mani, stop," I said. She was totally trying to distract me. And things were going as planned with Rohit, at least for now. "Also, Roger?" I shot her a look.

She shrugged, brushing her hair away from her neck. "He's kinda cute, I guess. But Rohit— Wait, has he asked you on the second date yet?"

I frowned. "No."

I hadn't forgotten, but I had hoped it might have happened this weekend. Another homecoming opportunity missed.

"I'm sure he will," I said. I tried to sound more confident than I felt. Leave it to Mani to zero in on the one thing that had been bugging me all week.

"Well, at least you know where he lives," Mani said, and then burst out into laughter at her own joke.

Lily appeared next to Mani out of thin air. I was so used to her stealth walking that it didn't bother me, but Mani nearly jumped out of her skin.

"Know where who lives?" Lily said, her face flushed and her eyes bright. Probably from finding some new way to defeat their archnemesis team, the Dragon Snouts.

"Rohit," we both said at the same time.

"Still hasn't asked you on the second date?" Lily said. I shook my head. "Homecoming is a weird time for that. He's with the crew kids if you want—"

"No," I said quickly. I had noticed where Rohit was already. He'd come over and said hi before being swept away by the crew boys. No date. And he had stopped by. All good signs. "It's only been a week, and we've been texting, so I'm sure it will happen soon."

I wasn't sure, but I didn't want to show it. "You seem happy," I said to Lily.

"New love interest? Crush?" Mani said, looking eager all of a sudden. "Was it that girl you were talking to before?"

Lily flushed to the roots of her hair. "No."

Mani glanced between us. "Mhm. Anyway, Roger's waiting." Roger waved, two glasses of punch in his hands.

I made sure Mani had a ride home before she left and then Lily and I wandered over to the gym entrance, watching all the students dancing their hearts out to some song that came out when Ratna was born.

"I can't believe Mani has a date to homecoming and we don't," Lily said, staring gloomily into her punch cup. "That is one thing on The List we've both majorly failed at."

I nodded in agreement. There wasn't even a point in trying to defend ourselves. "Mani's always been cool like that, though." I shot Lily a glance. "There's a girl? Alex?"

Lily blushed again. "Not really."

I'd known Lily for years, and she had two types of blushes. This was her "I might be crushing" blush and not her "I'm going to hide in a hole for the rest of my life, I'm so embarrassed" blush. I made a note to keep an eye on it. I was just glad to see her having fun again after her breakup over the summer. Plus, Alex was the total opposite of Lily's ex, Martin, so I was all for it. Martin had kind of sucked.

But I let it drop for now. Sometimes these things took time. I noticed Rohit in the corner, talking to Jenny Boateng.

Not for too long, I hoped.

Rohit and I both arrived at the door to Mrs. Palmer's home-room at the same time, like a scene from a movie. One notch further and we would've bumped heads, making it absolute rom-com fodder. Instead, he tilted his head and waved me forward, like the perfect gentleman that he was.

"What is this I hear about a cul-de-sac calendar?" Rohit asked, trailing behind me. He slung his backpack over one shoulder in that casual way that few people were able to pull off.

A number of the girls was staring at him, and I puffed my chest out a little. I wasn't typically very vain, I didn't think, but it felt good to be getting Rohit's attention, especially in front of everyone. After the disastrous Jake ask, it was a healing balm on a very, very open wound. Jake and Jenny had started dating for real after homecoming last weekend, which meant Lily had been right about Jenny having a crush on him for a while.

Yes, it was cute, and yes, I did feel bad that I hadn't picked up on those vibes. I had apologized to Jenny and she had brushed it off with a laugh, saying it had all worked out. And then she had gone off with Jake, their arms around each other. I guess I was in the clear.

I slid into my seat and Rohit slid into the one in front of me, immediately turning around. "Deepa?"

I had been so caught up in my thoughts I hadn't responded. "Oh, it's just this calendar we have for all the cul-de-sac events we plan to have aside from the neighborhood events."

"Neighborhood?" He looked intrigued.

"Yup, there are tons of block parties, especially with the holidays coming up. Oh, and Winterfest. Since the whole neighborhood feeds into Edison for high school, Winterfest is the main kickoff for the holiday parties." I peered at Rohit.

It was hard not to stress over when, and if, the second-date ask would come. Things had gone well, right? But so far, Rohit hadn't said anything.

Should I pick up the ball, even though I had been the one to ask him before? Or was that too forward? Ugh, this was why I had never dated. Everything seemed so unnecessarily complicated.

"Oh, cool. I've never had anything like that in the other places I lived," Rohit said. "Oceania Court Drive is kind of special, isn't it?"

"I never thought about it that way, but I guess it is. We're all really close."

"Huh. Real-life neighbors," he said, almost like he was in awe of the concept.

I poked him with the eraser side of my pencil. "You've never done stuff like this before? Block parties? Prank wars?"

"Prank wars, definitely not. Our neighborhood in Dallas started doing block parties, but we moved right before the first one," he said, a note of disappointment in his voice. And a hint of something else. Loneliness? But that couldn't be right. Rohit was objectively the hottest and coolest boy in our entire year. It couldn't have been that different at other schools.

"You'll have lots of opportunities with us, though," I said. "We can take you on the full circuit."

I didn't know if it was just me, but it seemed like Rohit visibly perked up at that. "Really?"

Was that an actual question? "Yes, really," I said, laughing.

"Can't wait to go to them," he said, looking at me with that easy grin.

What was that supposed to mean? Did he mean with me? Or in general? Or was he just excited for the parties or—

Why were boys so confusing?

The bell rang, startling half the class awake.

I took out my notebook and binder, lining them up next to each other. Next to it went my pencil pouch, full of multicolored highlighters and ballpoint pens, for easy reach and to switch out colors while taking notes.

Rohit pointed at my desk. "Why do you do that?"

I bristled a little.

"Nothing wrong with it, just curious," he added quickly.

"I just like things in their place," I said, relaxing, reminding myself that this wasn't Vik. "It's the most optimal way to set it up; I can easily grab anything I need." I paused. "And my aunt does it this way, so I picked it up, I guess. I used to copy everything she'd do when I was younger."

"That makes sense," Rohit said. He took out his stuff from his backpack and I noticed that his binder was tabbed up but packed with papers. "I had to learn how to be organized because I'm really bad at remembering things sometimes. I get that from my dad, my mom always says."

Interesting. I didn't know how literal the wish would be, but this was pretty spot-on. Even if the reason was a little different than I had imagined.

"I bet you were the one everyone stole notes off of at all your schools," I said.

Rohit shrugged but looked pleased. His eyelashes fluttered prettily. "Maybe."

Damn. That was really sexy.

And no, I wasn't going to think too much about why I found that so attractive. I was in the process of deciding if I should bite the bullet and ask Rohit out again, when Mrs. Palmer walked to the front of the room.

Rohit smiled at me and turned around, intent on the whiteboard. Of course Rohit would be a good student. Thwarted by my own list.

Our second date would have to wait. But a part of me wondered, how long?

12

Here's a general rule of thumb that I truly believe in—always expect problems. Case in point, when I walked downstairs on Sunday afternoon, I discovered that our entire living room was covered in glitter-adorned cardboard cutouts of the solar system. Glitter had somehow made it onto every edge of our kitchen table as well, which was where I discovered Ratna, who was working diligently on a large threefold poster board.

"Ratna," I said, my voice taking on my stern older-sister tone. "What happened to the living room?"

Ratna brushed her bangs out of her eyes and squinted up at me. There was a streak of glitter across one of her eyebrows (which looked pretty cool) and dots of pink and purple marker all over her hands. I loved my little sister, but she was not necessarily a clean artist. Or an artist.

"Science project," she said, as if that explained everything.

"All right, but why is it being constructed . . . here? Today?"

Ratna gave me a blank look. "It's due tomorrow."

I didn't even have the energy to get on her case about starting projects early and not the day before. That was my mom's job, and I only came in as cavalry support occasionally. My problem wasn't that Ratna was doing her project, but that she was doing it here, right now, in the living room.

"Didn't Amma tell you that I had the living room for the afternoon?" I said. I leaned over and pointed at the corner of her poster board. "And that's wrong. Jupiter has fifty-three named moons, not fifty-four."

"Oh, thanks, Deepu," she said, quickly leaning over to squiggle out the number four and turn it into a very confused three.

"Ratna."

"Amma never said anything," Ratna said, intensely focused on perfectly lettering her name in cursive on the board.

That was hard to believe. I marched over to our dry-erase calendar, the huge one we used to keep track of all our family commitments and appointments. It hung in a very prominent position right next to our fridge for exactly this reason. And there, in bright red (my color), it said, "DEEPA EVENT—LIVING ROOM."

"Ratna, it's right here!" I said. I looked down at my watch. The others were supposed to be arriving in fifteen minutes. "Did you even look at the calendar?"

"No."

I threw my hands up. I had never wanted to be an only

child, and I dearly loved my sisters, but good god they could be annoying sometimes. I didn't even have a good backup option, because Mani had claimed the basement for the afternoon, and unlike some people, I respected dibs on the family calendar.

With another glance at my watch, I went to the living room and began to clean. "Ratna, get your butt over here and help me get this living room ready for guests."

Ratna didn't move.

"Now! Or I'll make sure Mani knows you were the one who borrowed her sandals and broke them."

Ratna raced over. "You promised you wouldn't tell!" she said, frowning at me.

"And I won't," I said. "If you help me tidy this up."

I reached for Neptune, but Ratna swatted my hand away. "Don't! The glue is still setting."

"Ratnaaaa," I groaned into my hands. She was right, though. I had a new streak of glitter down the palm of my hand.

"What's the big stink, anyway?" She brushed her bangs off her forehead, bangs she refused to get cut but was constantly brushing aside. "Lily won't care. She actually said she'd help me with my graphic design for my history project."

"Due tomorrow also?" I said, frowning. "Ratna—" I stopped, remembering my commitment to not lecture. But then I couldn't help myself. "You have to stop doing your homework so late."

"No, it's due next week, jeez," Ratna said. "And I get my stuff done, that's all that matters. Who cares when?"

"There's a right way to do things, Ratn—I don't have time for this. And it's not just Lily, thank you very much. I do have other friends."

Ratna gave me a disbelieving look.

"Rude," I said. "That is a rude expression, missy. But if you have to know, we're having a prank war summit. And for a reason I can no longer remember, I volunteered to host it."

Her eyes lit up, just as I knew they would. She smacked her hands down on the table and leaned in, excitement dancing across her face. "Vik's coming?"

Huh, what? Who cared that Vik was coming? Rohit was coming, and that's what mattered. "And Lily and Rohit—you know, our new neighbor?"

Ratna nodded knowingly. "You mean Mr. Dreamboat?"

"Ratna, you're like ten!" Why did it feel like I was always having this conversation with my sisters?

"I'm thirteen."

"That's still young! You should still be thinking about ponies and . . . headbands."

"Toby Stilton asked me out last week," Ratna said with a shrug. "I know about boys."

I opened my mouth, ready and willing to track down this Toby figure and give him a good talking-to about leaving my baby sister alone.

"Don't worry, I told him no," Ratna said. She pushed

her bangs aside again and I resisted the urge to reach over and brush them down flat. "A boyfriend is someone who should make you feel like you could take on the world."

"Amma?" Sounded like something our mother would say.

"No, you said that," Ratna said. She reached over and touched Neptune to see if it was dry, and then prodded a few rings of Jupiter.

"I did?"

The words sounded familiar, but I hadn't thought about them in a while. Still, it warmed me to think that Ratna remembered something I'd said and had actually listened.

"Of course I did," I said. "Because it's true. So, good. No Toby. I approve."

"I think we can move them now," Ratna said, ignoring me. "Not all of them, but we can clear a little space. I didn't realize it was a prank war thing." She stopped and whirled around. "Can I be a part of it?"

I shook my head. "Nope. You know the rules."

"But Vik said—" Ratna whined.

"What? What did Vik say?"

Ratna pouted. "I'm not supposed to tell you."

What was going on? Now Vik was encouraging my sisters to keep secrets from me? Ooh, the words I would have with him when I—

"It's not a bad thing, Deepu. Stop making that face. That death face," Ratna said, poking me in the arm.

I deepened my frown on purpose. "This face is specially reserved for Vik."

"But he's so much fun," Ratna said offhandedly.

"Sometimes there's such a thing as too much fun," I said matter-of-factly. Ratna looked at me like I had lost my marbles and they were rolling across our hardwood floor.

"Can I at least eavesdrop?"

"No," I said. "But I promise to give you a play-by-play of what happens after. And you can be part of my planning team." Seeing as she was family and I assumed I could trust her, I added, "I plan to win this year."

Ratna lit up like a Fourth of July firework. "Done."

She zoomed over and helped me move another set of the cutouts, but five minutes later, the living room was still a disaster zone.

"You could have the summit in the garden? Or on the porch?" Ratna said as I looked gloomily at the living room. We could move Ratna's remaining cutouts, but I didn't want to be the reason that she got a less-than-stellar grade. Which somehow would definitely get blamed on me, being the eldest.

We both looked outside at the same time. It was raining, a light drizzle, but just enough that outside would be unpleasant. I had volunteered to host the prank war so that it would be on my turf, mostly to ease my nerves. This was not helping.

The doorbell rang at that moment, forcing my hand.

"We'll make the living room work," I said with a decisive nod. "But you're on snack duty because you totally owe me right now. I made seven-layer dip this morning and there's a bag of chips in the pantry. And paper plates in the cupboard."

"On it," Ratna said, making a beeline for the kitchen.

"Don't eat any! We're having guests!"

"I'm only going to have a bite! No one will notice," she yelled back.

"They will definitely notice one bite out of a tray of dip, Ratna." I groaned.

She ignored me and I shook my head. That girl could put away food, a fact that I usually admired. I went for the door, putting on my brightest smile.

Vik stood on the other side, lounging against the door frame.

"Hey, Dee."

"Hey yourself." My smile fell, and I didn't try to hide it. I had hoped Rohit would be the first to come and that we'd have some time alone. We had texted a bit since the date two weeks ago, and I was hoping that we'd get another one.

"What a warm welcome," Vik said, following me inside.

"What exactly were you expecting?" I fake bowed and waved my arm. "Please come inside, sir."

"Stop that," he said, his nose twitching. "It looked like you were expecting someone else." His voice was light, but there was an undercurrent I couldn't read.

"I can't imagine what you mean," I said airily.

"Right. You know I live next door to you, Deepa."

I looked up sharply at him. Vik was watching me

intently, like he was waiting for something. Of course he knew about Rohit. If it hadn't been Lily, it was because Vik was observant, despite how much I wished he wouldn't be. For some reason, I didn't love the idea of Vik knowing about Rohit and me.

I didn't have time to question exactly how much Vik knew. We turned the corner into the kitchen and Ratna squeed. "Vik!"

She rushed over and skittered to a stop in front of him, reaching out her hand. To my utter surprise, Vik stepped forward and together they did a special handshake. "Nice work, Ratty," he said. "You got it down."

"Been practicing," Ratna said with a smile. "How's it going?"

"Good. Been breaking any more hearts?" he asked.

"Possibly. Want seven-layer dip?"

They left me behind as they walked to the kitchen. I stood there in mild shock.

Ratty? Breaking hearts? What exactly was going on here?

I stomped into the kitchen, only to see my sister and Vik hunched over the dip, laughing. All my ire dissipated. It was hard to be angry when it was clear that Vik knew exactly how to get Ratna to laugh—and she him.

A part of me was a little jealous. Vik never acted like that with me. I couldn't remember the last time I had made him laugh, and laughing *at* me didn't count.

He looked up when I came over to the table and made a little space for me next to him. "Ratna, why exactly is it that Vik seems to know about the boys in your life before me?"

"I needed to talk to a boy. You're not a boy," Ratna said, her mouth full of chips.

"And Ratty?"

"That's a joke," Vik said. "Apparently some girls keep mispronouncing her name—"

"Which is super annoying. Like they can't say Rath-na, instead of Rat-na. Like, who would even name their kid that?" Ratna's words came out in a stream of annoyance.

She had a point.

Ratna looked down at her watch and squeaked. "Oops, I forgot my phone upstairs. Molly said she was going to call about our plans tomorrow."

She grabbed a few more chips before running upstairs, waving bye to Vik and ignoring me completely.

"Ratna—" She was already gone.

I groaned into my chips.

"I get it," Vik said, watching me as he took another bite of his chip. "Siblings."

"She seems to like you," I said accusingly.

He held up his hands. "I like your sisters. And she did come over asking me for boy advice, and we ended up playing *Mario Kart*. She's a cool kid."

"I know that," I said defensively. I sighed. "Thanks, by the way."

"Of course," Vik said, waving me away like it was no big deal. "Anyway, she beat me horribly at *Mario Kart* and I'm pretty sure she put it on YouTube, so that's cool."

I laughed, a full belly one. Vik paused mid-crunch, his eyes widening at me. His hair curled a little around his ears and it was clear he had not tried to tame the unruliness of it. Still, it looked good.

"Wow, I got a real laugh out of Deepa," he said. "Will wonders never cease?"

"Oh, shut up," I said, rolling my eyes.

The corners of his eyes crinkled, like he enjoyed me telling him to shut up. "Hey, Deepa—"

The doorbell rang, and I jogged over to get it just as Ratna came down the stairs, chattering away at the top of her lungs on the phone. Lily and Rohit were on the doorstep together. Lily's blue hair was in a tight French braid and Rohit was dressed casually in a wool sweater, which somehow still managed to look amazing on him despite it being a mustard color.

Lily held up a freshly popped bag of popcorn and a tray of cupcakes as she entered.

"I brought sustenance," she said.

"You may be allowed in," I said. I pointed at Rohit. "And you, sir? What is your offering?"

"Oh, I'm—I have gum?" Rohit said, looking mildly alarmed.

Oops. I had forgotten that Rohit hadn't known me for

years. The weirdness would have to be reduced. "That works," I said, ushering him inside.

Vik had brought the seven-layer dip over to the living room coffee table, along with the paper plates Ratna was supposed to bring. Her dulcet tones could be heard from the kitchen table. I mouthed "Thanks" at Vik and he nodded in return.

Once we had all gotten settled, I took a spot in front of our fireplace. "Welcome to the first prank war summit of the year—"

Vik made a noise in his throat.

"The first prank war summit of the year with everyone." I sent a look at Vik. "Since some of us are new, we thought we'd do a proper summit this time. First, we've got some rules and bylaws to go over. Lily, take it away."

I bowed out and took a seat next to Rohit on the couch.

Lily nodded. "We had to instate these after a little incident in seventh grade where someone, who shall not be named, prompted us to reconsider."

"What'd you do, Vikram?" Rohit said in a wheedling tone. "Come on, tell us."

Vikram scooped a big bite of dip. "It wasn't me."

"Deepa?"

I glanced over at Vik and noticed he was looking at me. His gaze always felt a bit like a focused laser, but today it seemed almost . . . appreciative. I flushed a little, from the memory and from Vik's approval.

"I'll cop to it," I said. "I've never said I wasn't competitive. Not one of my finer moments."

Vik moved as if he were going to tell the story, or maybe disagree, but I cut in first. "But that's a story for another time. Now, the rules."

"The rules," Lily said. She pulled out a sleeve of papers and handed them out. "Number one, nothing unsafe, aka your prank should not cause anyone bodily injury. Or put anyone in danger of going to jail. Number two." She held up two fingers. "You must take the target by surprise. If they catch you or see the prank coming, it doesn't count, but you can try again. This rule has come into contention before, so in case there is a disagreement, it will be arbitrated by the prank war council."

"And who's that?" Rohit leaned forward, clearly into all of this. He noticed me looking at him and nudged me with his knee. I hid a smile, and then noticed Vik staring. I looked away.

"Usually consists of one or two family members from every household involved in the prank war. And to be fair, we usually have those family members be a parent and a sibling. We've noticed that it tends to be the most fair mix. We usually draw names to determine the council."

"Rohit doesn't have a sibling, so maybe we can make it so that good friends are allowed in the mix?" I said.

"Thanks, Deepa. That's sweet of you to think of me," Rohit said. We exchanged a smile. A frown flitted across

Vik's face, but it was probably because we were changing things.

Despite his carefree nature, Vik had always been adamant about keeping the prank war the same. It was why I had even agreed to this thing in the first place, for the chance at annoying him.

"The council is only called in at the end anyway, for judging, if there's multiple successful pranks. They have a whole rubric and everything—creativity, execution, and stealth," I added. Then with a pout, "And they can be brutal."

Lily patted me on the shoulder. We both remembered that time I had missed a stealth point just because Nikhil had happened to look out the window at the wrong time.

"Number three. The prank has to occur in the cul-de-sac. This goes with one and two, because it makes sure that the pranks stay contained and safe. Obvious to say, Edison is out of territory, so we can all go to school knowing we're not going to be expelled. And finally, number four. Once the first successful prank has been pulled off, all other prank members have four weeks to pull theirs off as well to be considered in the final judging." Lily stepped back and threw her hands wide. "That's it! Go forth and prank!"

"Are you not pranking too?" Rohit said, looking confused.

"Let us go forth and prank!" Lily swiveled her head around. "Is that better?"

Rohit nodded.

"Next step is to draw names," I said, rising to get the fedora we always used.

It was an old joke, a prop that Lily and I had "borrowed" after our elementary school production of *Oliver!*, the musical. Funnily enough, Vik had been part of it too. To no one's surprise, he had played the role of the Artful Dodger with glee.

The fedora was old and worn, but I picked it up reverentially and carried it to the center of the room. Lily tore up a piece of paper and quickly scribbled names down, folding each scrap of paper into clean-edged squares. She tossed them into the hat and I swirled them around, doing a little twirl and making it clear that I wasn't looking, before I placed it on the living room table. I liked to win, but I liked to do it fair and square.

"Okay, time to get up!" I waved the hat around. To Rohit, I explained, "We like to pick all at once. More fair that way."

"What if you get your own name?" Rohit asked.

We all paused. That was a good question.

"It's never happened before, but I guess we'd just go again," I said. The others shrugged in agreement.

Vik came next to me, his hand hovering over the fedora. Lily was on my other side, and Rohit tentatively reached out in front of me.

"Ready, set, go—"

Vik and I dove into the fedora, clearly both reaching for

the same scrap. Lily got to it first. "Yes!" she said, pumping her fist in the air.

I elbowed Vik, trying to reach for my second choice. Yes, all the squares looked the same, but you had to go with your gut on these things. Vik reached for it too, and our arms collided as we tussled over the hat.

"Vikram!"

He had a look of intense concentration on his face, one that mirrored my own. I tried to reach underhand with my other arm, and Vik blocked me, grabbing my wrist. I rammed into his forearm and almost winced. When had he gotten so strong?

In between us, Rohit slid in and grabbed one of the other squares.

Vik took my split second of appreciation and swooped in, snatching the square from my fingertips.

"Ugh" was all I could say. He winked at me, and I stuck out my tongue.

I darted over to a corner of the living room, looking over my shoulder as I opened my scrap of paper. To my horror, I picked the worst name of the bunch, the one I definitely, definitely did not want to have as my target for this semester.

Vikram Mehta.

I swallowed my groan, knowing any audible noise would be an obvious giveaway as to who I had picked. We took this secrecy seriously.

Vik was the hardest to pull a prank on and it didn't hurt my pride to admit it. He was on guard and lived the prank lifestyle all year round. The boy was good. And while I would never say those words to his face, it was the unvarnished truth.

Why couldn't I have gotten Lily? I knew her schedule forward and backward. My shoulders threatened to slump and I could feel my worry like a ball of tangled yarn lodged in my chest.

The others looked unaffected.

"Who'd you get, Deepa?" Vik asked.

"You know I can't answer that," I said. I put on my best smile. "But I'm feeling good."

Vik smirked at me, as if he knew exactly how frantic my mind was at the moment. Like he could see right through me. But he didn't say anything more.

"And you, Lily?" Rohit asked, frowning down at his scrap.

"Oh, this is the year I beat you all," Lily said, her hands on her hips. And she looked like she meant it.

"That's what I like to hear," Vik said. He laughed and threw his hand up for Lily to high-five. It was Oceania Court Drive lore that Vik and Lily could never make a high five work, no matter what technique they tried. They couldn't even blame it on a height difference because I was almost a foot shorter than Vik, and Vik and I had never had a problem.

But this time, their high five landed.

Which I took as a good sign. A positive omen, really. Because there was something else that I had realized a few minutes back, something that now surged through me with a fierce burn.

I wanted to win. Badly.

Good thing I told Ratna she could be part of my planning team, because I would need every scrap of help I could get if I wanted to take Vik down.

Lily raised an eyebrow at my expression before leaning over and whispering something in Rohit's ear that made him laugh. Probably something about how intense I got in these situations, which was fair.

"Ready, Dee?" Vik said, wandering over, his hands in his pockets. His expression was focused, though, intent, the complete opposite of his laid-back posture.

Ah, this was the competitive Vik I knew and expected.

I drew myself up to my full height.

"Bring it on," I said.

13

Oceania Court Drive had a sports problem. None of us could agree on what teams were best or who to support. Sure, we all lived in Virginia, but somehow, every single family and every single person within the family had somehow developed vastly different preferences. It made for lively Super Bowls and championship games.

One thing we could all agree on? The Stuart Littles were the best soccer team on this side of the Atlantic Ocean. Rose's soccer team had won our hearts during the first soccer game Lily had forced us to come to years ago. It wasn't just that they were definite underdogs, or that we loved Rose, which were both true, but there was another huge deciding factor.

"THAT WAS A HORRIBLE CALL," Lily yelled from her seat, her face turning an interesting shade of purple. She shook her head, her blue hair streaming around her. "What idiots."

It was Lily.

We had a running bet for most games on when Lily would step in and start back-seat coaching. And when Mr. Gilbert, the current coach, would start to get annoyed.

"And we're at fifteen minutes," Mani said, looking down at her watch. She stuck her hand out. "Pay up, suckers."

I groaned. "I thought she'd last a little longer." I slapped a five-dollar bill onto Mani's palm, and to my surprise, so did Vik. He shrugged.

"I did too," he said. "I've been working with her on this new breathing technique. I really thought it would work."

"You? Breathing technique?" I snorted. "Oh, I see, is that like an add-on special for all the people you annoy?" I held my hands up, framing a fake plaque in the air. "I'll make you lose your cool and then teach you how to find it again."

Rohit snickered and quickly tried to hide it.

"Come on, man," Vik said.

Somehow, I had ended up sitting in between Vik and Rohit, each of them plopping themselves down next to me at the beginning of the game. I had thought that Rohit would sit next to Vik, given their bromance thing, so when he sat next to me, it gave me the boost of confidence I needed. It had been approximately twenty days since our last date and still nothing, even though I had turned on the charm all week.

If I was being honest, I was sweating a little. I kept going over the first date, wondering if I had done something wrong that I hadn't realized. Lily had even helped me make a chart on my handy dry-erase board, but we were both stumped. Then she had suggested that maybe he was making sure to check out the field before committing to a player, and that had caused me to panic in another way.

"You can't keep yourself open like that, Vik," Rohit said, shrugging, mirth in his eyes.

I nodded in approval. "Too true, Rohit."

We smiled at each other.

Vik jostled into me as he reached over into my bag of popcorn. "Hey!" I said, knocking his hand away. He still managed to get a fistful of popcorn. Today's batch was half-stale, probably because they had pulled from the bag from last week's game, so the joke was on him.

"What? You can't keep yourself open like that, Dee."

I made a face at him. He made a face back.

And then there was a moment of truce as Rose made another drive down the soccer field, which unified us in our screaming and cheering. We settled back down when her pass to her teammate went wide, mostly because they were looking down at their smartwatch.

Disappointing.

Vik made another grab for my popcorn and I tried to swat his hand away. Lily jogged to where we sat, a storm cloud over her head.

"And that call! Rose was a BEAST and that ridiculous teammate of hers—"

It took us about five minutes to calm her down. Once Vik offered her his soda, she seemed to chill a little, though she kept turning around to glare daggers at Rose's teammate.

"Speaking of little sisters, I heard you pulled my little sister into our war," I said casually to Vik, after I had finally managed to wrench my popcorn away.

He had the audacity to look innocent as he shoved my popcorn into his mouth.

"That's how it's going to be, huh? We're using our siblings now?" I said.

"We have been," Vik said, like it was an obvious thing. "Does anyone here think Deepa hasn't already had a planning summit with her sisters?"

Lily shook her head, but stopped when she caught me staring at her. Rohit had the presence of mind to remain silent, observing us all like zoo animals.

"Lily agrees with me."

"Lily is focusing on the game," Lily said. "Yes, Deepa probably has. But to be fair, Rose wanted in as well."

Vik sat back, looking satisfied. I opened my mouth to ask Lily when exactly she had decided to become my Benedict Arnold, but she was already gone, running down the pitch behind the team coach.

"Rohit?"

"Rohit's too sweet to pick sides."

"He's smart enough to know which is the winning team," Vik said.

Rohit looked away and then at me, giving me a heart-squeezing smile. "I'm not getting involved," he said cheerily. "I've learned that much. Plus, no sibling here. Just me."

I turned my attention back to Vik.

"Mani is one thing, but going for the baby? For Ratna?" I poked Vik's arm. "How could you?"

"Um, hello," Mani said. "Stop talking about us like we're not here."

Vik and I leaned over to see Mani, Nikhil, Pooja, and Ratna looking at us from down the bleacher seat.

Mani looked at the others, and they all nodded at each other before she turned back. "We've agreed that our interests are not being best served by our siblings in this prank war. We've unionized."

"What?" Vik and I said at the same time.

"Or whatever," Mani said. "We're using collective power to be recognized."

"Who's your union leader? Who represents you?" Rohit said, tilting his head. He was such a nice guy that it came out sounding like genuine curiosity. Which it probably was.

Mani puffed up just as Nikhil said, "Me."

"I am," Mani said.

They looked at each other. "Well, we have some things to work out."

"Does this mean that you will only work with prank war factions if you all agree on it?" Rohit said, with that same genuine tone. "Like a union would?"

Vik and I exchanged a look without meaning to, one of total agreement. Adding Rohit to the war had been a great idea, if only to see the looks on our siblings' faces at that moment.

Pooja leaned forward. "Like Mani said, we have some

things to work out. But you'll hear from us." She tossed her hair over her shoulder, tugging on her yellow cardigan.

"Though we're all technically still free agents," Nikhil said from behind Mani. "Meaning I'm free for planning work and only charge a small fee. Mostly food. Or whatever."

"Nikhil!" Mani groaned. She looked at us and then back at her group. "Give us a second."

They all huddled toward the end of the bleacher, now ignoring us.

For a second, I blinked at them, wondering if all that had really just happened.

"Well, that was interesting," I said, frowning.

"They're really smart," Rohit said. He laughed and then shook his head.

"Too smart," I said, a little darkly.

"For once, I agree with you," Vik said.

Lily bounded back into view, her cap askew and her cheeks flushed. I wasn't entirely sure it was just the game. It hadn't escaped my notice that Alex Pastor was near the dugout as well. This was proving to be an eventful game.

"What did I miss?" Lily asked, trying and failing to hide the grin on her face. It was even more obvious because the Stuart Littles were losing. Pretty badly.

"The question is, what did we miss?" Vik said, waggling his eyebrows. I nudged him hard. Not the time. Lily needed a soft touch when it came to romance.

"The younger siblings unionized," I said. "Though it's

unclear exactly how their leadership or collective bargaining is going to be organized, as identified by Oceania Court Drive's newest and hottest journalist."

I hadn't meant physically, but Rohit's eyebrow rose in a very Vik way. He looked almost . . . triumphant.

"Hottest as in on fire because of his . . . journalistic skills," I said.

Okay. Not my best save.

"Oh-kay," Lily said, sounding even more confused than before.

Thankfully, the Stuart Littles finally scored a goal, all thanks to our cul-de-sac darling, Rose. The entirety of the bleachers stood up, either in cheers or mild boos. I jumped to my feet, cheering, along with the others.

"Let's go, ROSE!" we shouted together.

Rohit and I high-fived each other. It was fun seeing him getting so into our little traditions. He had mentioned moving a lot, and I wanted him to feel like he could fit in with us.

We were all falling for him in some ways. He and Vik were always hanging out, and he had quickly won over Lily when he had offered to help with Rose's soccer team. Even at school he had become one of the standouts in fall crew training. Apparently, those muscles were actually for something.

"It's like that last practice," Rohit said to Vik. "When Crocker passed the ball to—"

And I tuned out. I had forgotten that Rohit had also

joined soccer, which meant he was on the same team as Vik.

Playing soccer or being on crew was a big deal at Edison, especially since our traditional high school teams (like football) were pretty bad. I still had no idea why he was friends with Vik, but everyone was allowed a few bad decisions.

Instead, I tuned into the little drama at the foot of the bleachers. Lily was standing and yelling about some foul—and so was Alex, the two of them in unison.

I started plotting, scheming, even. There was some clear chemistry there, obvious by the way they both looked at each other when the other was turned away.

When Lily made her way back to where we sat, I gave her a pointed look, accompanied by a lot of blinking.

"What's wrong with your eye?" Vik said.

I let out a frustrated groan. "Vikram, why do you ruin everything?"

"It's not my fault you can't blink properly."

Lily sat on the bleacher below us. Vikram offered her food, including my popcorn.

"Twizzler popcorn?" Lily said. "You're speaking my language, Vikster. Though I have a hankering for those soft pretzels they always sell. They're delicious with mayo."

Rohit gave me a look and mouthed, "Vikster?" I looked skyward and bit back a laugh. "I know," I whispered to him. "Though I guess if it's a combination of Vikram and monster, it makes sense."

142

"I heard that," Vik said over his shoulder, not bothering to look behind himself. He wrapped a friendly arm around Lily's shoulder. "Let's go get you that pretzel, Lily. These people don't understand fine dining."

"Yeah!" Lily said. She made the mistake of looking back and Vik tugged her around.

Rohit and I burst into hunched-over laughter once they had gone.

"I didn't realize Vik and Lily had a shared love of weird food combos," Rohit said, mirth still shaking his shoulders like aftershocks.

"They are weird, aren't they? I always got so much crap from them for not being 'adventurous,' but some things just don't make sense," I said.

"Totally."

We found ourselves grinning at each other, and something sparked between us then. It was a small thing, a realization that we were kindred spirits in food taste, but also . . . maybe something else?

"You know what does make sense?" Rohit said. He reached out and tucked a piece of my hair behind my ear in one smooth move.

Swoon, swoon, swoon. I'd been dying for a boy to do that to me since I'd first seen it in a movie. Verdict? Pretty darn great. It was somehow sweet and sexy and charming at the same time.

"What?" I was like a deer in headlights, frozen to the spot.

"Us," he said, increasing his charm offensive and the beating of my heart. "I've been thinking, I had such a great time on our first date. Would you want to go on another one?"

I inhaled sharply. Rohit watched me, a flicker of expectation on his face. Did Mr. Perfect really think I would say no to him? Impossible. Must be the sunlight or something.

"I'd love to," I said. My brain yelled at me about my plan. "The county fair is coming up, and it would be lots of fun. Think fried food, games, you know the deal."

I held my breath, thinking rapidly how I would handle it if Rohit didn't want to go to the county fair. That hadn't been part of the plan, but I could figure it out. Lily and I would have to have another planning session because I had totally been depending on it. Why had I been depending on it? Ugh.

Wait, Rohit had just asked me out on a second date! I tried to bask in the moment instead of worrying about the next.

"Fantastic idea," Rohit said. I heaved a sigh of relief. "I've always wanted to go to one."

He stretched and leaned back on the bleacher behind us, his arms extended out so that I could feel his presence behind me. His arm brushed my back and I let myself lean into it a little bit.

My jaw dropped. "You lived in Texas and you didn't go

to any of their famous county or state fairs? What is this travesty?"

"I know, I know," Rohit said. He took a slurp of his drink. He seemed to hesitate, and then a look of resolve settled on his face. "Moving, you know? But I've gotten to see so many cities, like my parents say. So, I guess I can't complain."

That didn't seem fair, but I understood what he meant.

"Well, you won't miss out on events here, that's for sure," I said. "And my dad has a booth at the fair, which means as many doughnuts as your—"

"Your dad has a stall again?" Vik slid onto the bleacher next to me, bumping our knees together. I frowned at him.

Vik glanced between me and Rohit, and something shifted in his face.

"Duh," I said. "He's pairing up with Smiley again. I'm sure he'll invite you over for another jam tasting, don't worry."

Vik smirked. "I'm not. I'm invaluable to your dad. Some of us have taste buds."

I rolled my eyes. "Pass me the Twizzlers," I said to Lily, who sat on Vik's other side.

Not even Vikram could ruin this moment.

The second date was on, and I couldn't be more ready.

14

Happy Tea was the best bubble tea shop in all of northern Virginia, hands down. And when I got ready that Saturday morning, that's where I thought we'd be going. That had been the plan for our next lock-in strategy session. Emphasis on *had*.

Instead, I found myself waiting outside Vik's house, trying not to angrily respond to his text from a few minutes earlier.

My house. New idea. Talk soon.

Why couldn't he text in full sentences? And how dare he change plans after we had agreed on everything? He must enjoy driving me crazy, that had to be it. I really couldn't think of any other reason.

The front door swung open and His Highness finally emerged. I was this close to telling him off for being late when I noticed that he was holding two binders in his arms. He wore dark jeans and a forest-green Henley, which I didn't understand why I was noticing. Maybe it was because he looked fairly put together for being, well, him. The binders were worrisome enough, but then I noticed Vik had a full-fledged smile on. He looked good.

The thought immediately made me flush. Vik did not look cute, nope, I was just tired and my hormonal teenage brain was latching on to the nearest human.

I eyed him uncertainly. "What's with the binders?"

"You like them?" he said, grinning, hefting them so that I could see that they were three-ring, 1.5 inch binders. My favorite kind.

I cleared my throat. I did like them. A lot. "Explain, please."

"I took a page from your book. Got a brilliant idea," he said. He jogged down the driveway, coming to a stop next to where I stood.

"Brilliance is definitely something you got from me," I said. "I'm glad you've finally recognized it."

Vik half snorted. "Are you always this cocky, or just around me?"

"Just around you," I said, not even trying to deny it. He brought out this whole other side of me, which I didn't always know if I appreciated.

"Well, Ms. Brilliant, how about a day of research planning? I know you wanted to go to Happy's, but since you have the whole day free—"

I was kind of regretting telling him that.

"—let's do something fun. A whirlwind tour. Let's hit up a bunch of spots for catering. Bubble tea, funnel cakes, taco trucks, you name it. There are a lot of new places your dad has been telling me about too, so we might as well give them a chance."

"Okay," I said slowly. "But we only have the day. And we each only have one stomach."

"And that's why it's fun. How about you forget your rules for one day?"

I frowned. I didn't have any rules about this, simply general *life* rules. I didn't love the way he made me sound.

"You like to be efficient, don't you?" he said in a wheedling tone. "We try something, give everything on the list three bites." He tapped his binders. "And if one of us dislikes it, we leave. Simple, effective, fast."

Vik smiled comically wide, his expression expectant. Maybe it was because it wasn't a half-bad idea or because he was giving me that goofy expression, but I nodded.

"Okay, I'm game. Let's do it." I stepped closer and wagged my finger at him. "But three bites only, and we both get veto power."

Vik nodded. "I'll drive."

Our first stop was Happy's, because I demanded it. I had been expecting bubble tea, I had prepared for bubble tea, and I would be drinking bubble tea. Preferably as soon as possible.

"When did you become such a tea fiend?" Vik asked, pushing open the door to Happy's. A bell jingled the tune to a song I knew but whose name I couldn't remember. Vik waved me into the café and I bowed my head graciously before walking inside.

The interior of Happy's was my favorite because it was, well, happy. Bright walls mixed with neon-colored bean-bags and upholstered pastel poufs and ottomans. The back was stuffed with vintage pinball machines, and in the corner was an eye-catching tapestry of Polaroids worthy of modern art—and one that would make any selfie aficionado very happy. But the best part was the wall full of books and board games, ranging from classic to brand-new, and all open to public use.

"Tea fiend? I kind of like that title. And to answer your question, ever since last year, when my aunt introduced me to green tea with honey and lemon," I said.

"Hmm. Fancy. Honey and lemon." Vik waggled his eyebrows.

"She was worried I wouldn't like green tea by itself, and she was right. It's definitely an acquired taste, at least to start. It's the only sort of caffeine my mom would let me have then. But she's recently allowed an upgrade to chai," I said, doing mini jazz hands. "I'm moving up in the world."

I waved Vik over to the counter, where next to the county's most comprehensive bubble tea menu lay a whole assortment of animal-shaped mochi, Technicolor cream puffs, and delicious éclairs.

"Your mom's the doctor, so she probably knows best," Vik said. He was clearly eyeing the panda-shaped mochi, but trying to make it look like he wasn't. "My mom let me start joining afternoon chai a few years ago."

"It is the gateway tea."

"So when did you get all . . . Happy's?"

I rolled my eyes. "I discovered this place last semester, when I was dropping Lily off at her sister's soccer practice," I said.

"It's pretty awesome," Vik said, looking around with clear appreciation. It was, and I was proud of my find, so Vik's words warmed me up. A group of middle schoolers scuttled past us, giggling. I waved Vik over, realizing his large frame took up more room in the small café than I would have thought. Of course, I had seen Vik grow into a tree over the years, but I hadn't noticed how broad his shoulders were until . . . now.

"Should we order?"

Vik nodded. I stepped up to the counter and then backed away. "Anything you want?" I asked Vik, not wanting to be called an absolute monarch again.

He raised an eyebrow. "I trust you, Ms. Brilliant. Make sure we get a variety to sample, though, for research purposes."

I rolled my eyes at his nickname, but turned back to the counter. The cashier was a short girl with cool purple glasses I hadn't seen before. "One Thai tea with taro boba, one milk tea with honey boba, the chocolate raspberry éclair, the vanilla lavender cream puff," I said, rattling off my favorites. "And the panda mochi."

"White and ninety-five percent dark chocolate," Vik

murmured into my ear. He was so close I nearly jumped at the sound. Why was he standing so close to me? I looked back and noticed the line forming behind us. Oh, that must be why.

"Sounds interesting," I said. "Total opposite on the spectrum. Supersweet fake chocolate and bitter, real-deal chocolate."

"Opposites are often the best combo," Vik said.

I paid for everything, and Vik took the boxes with our baked treasures. I grabbed the bubble teas and we headed to the outdoor area, where we were able to find a table with a view of the small garden nearby.

"Don't eat yet—you have to start with the tea," I said, slapping his hand. "The milk tea in particular."

"Oh?" Vik put down the éclair.

"Plus, you have to share," I said. I moved my chair closer so I could grab anything I needed to before he gobbled it up.

"What, you didn't buy all of this for me?" Vik grinned mischievously, waving the éclair in my face. "Okay, fine. Explain your reasoning. You get ten seconds."

"Ten *seconds*?"

Vik tapped a fake watch on his wrist. "We're on a time-line because of you, Ms. Brilliant."

"The éclair is a totally different flavor profile!" I said in a rush. "You start with the milk tea because the flavor will be colored by anything supersweet, like the Thai tea or the pastries. Then you try something sweet, followed by the panda. The dark chocolate will hopefully be bitter enough to cut through the other flavors. And then you end with the Thai tea, which will be like a sugar explosion in your mouth."

I took a deep breath.

"You should write them a Yelp review," he said, eyeing me. "Better yet, ask to be their ambassador."

"I've tried," I muttered. "I'm too young. Have to be eighteen or some ridiculous rule."

Vik laughed, a full, clear laugh. It coaxed a smile onto my face. I liked making Vik laugh. It felt like a victory of sorts—when we were laughing together.

"All right, Deepa, I'll go with your rules—"

"Suggestions."

"—on this, if you concede the next place to me. Deal?"

I considered it, and the hand that Vik had stuck out. "Okay. But nothing that will make my stomach hurt," I said.

"I know. You hate papayas. I think we'll be okay."

"You remembered?" I said, cheers-ing Vik's tea with my own. I took a sip. Heaven in a plastic takeaway cup.

"Of course I remember," he said, like it was nothing. "You nearly puked on me that one time."

I flushed. "Ew, no I didn't. Stop lying."

Vik snickered and I stuck my tongue out at him.

We tried the éclairs next, which garnered a thumbs-up

and a happy sigh from Vik. He mentioned that it reminded him of my dad's creations, which I agreed with. By then I could feel a bit of a sugar rush coming on, but we had barely made a dent in our pile of goods from Happy's.

I carefully split the panda cookie in half, ignoring Vik's fake cries of distress in a panda voice, and handed one piece to him.

He tapped his panda half against mine and some of the white icing on the panda's ears stuck to my side. I took a bite and made a happy noise. Maybe that was why the bakery was called Happy's, for the contented sigh that followed eating their food.

"I knew I liked pandas," Vik said happily as he nibbled off the edge of the panda's icing nose.

I gobbled up the rest in two bites. Opposites did work well together.

"Wait, come here," Vik said, gesturing at me. I turned to him and he reached over, gently brushing off the icing on my cheek. His fingers grazed my skin, warm and gentle. He had touched me for barely more than a few seconds, but I could feel my entire body flush. Vik stared down at me. Even with half a panda cream puff in his hands, he looked good.

I glanced away. I did not want to think about Vik that way.

"Um, thanks," I said, gesturing at my face.

Vik nodded, his expression a little tighter. "Ready to go to the next place?"

"Yes," I said, clearing my throat. "But you may have to roll me over."

"Already?" Vik said, tsking. "I didn't think you were going to go all amateur hour on me."

"Amateur?" I scoffed, feeling my competitive side rear its head. "How dare you? Fine. What's next? Please tell me nothing sweet."

Vik's eyes twinkled. "It's taco time."

We stopped for another bubble tea on the way to Nina's Cantina, this time from Vicky's Bubble Tea. Vik insisted we should try it because even though it was a chain, it was a chain he had discovered in New York City, which apparently changed everything. I'd been to NYC a few times before, but I didn't think it had anything on DC, a fact that Vik vehemently disagreed with.

"How could you say that?" Vik said, sounding both offended and exasperated. He threw his hands up from the steering wheel and I resisted the urge to reach over and grab it.

"Keep your eyes on the road," I said. "And I'm not saying there's anything wrong with NYC. It's a great city, but you can't beat the nation's capital. It's the . . . capital."

"DC is filled with suits."

"NYC is filled with suits," I said. "But I'll concede they're probably nicer and better-tailored suits."

"That's what I'm saying," Vik said, pulling into a parking

spot. "Those finance bros know how to dress." He took a sip from his Vicky's bubble tea and looked over at me.

"We shall never agree on this matter," I said in a faux British accent.

Vik play-choked on his bubble tea. "What. Was. That?"

"It was supposed to be a finance bro accent!"

He blinked at me. "And when did they become British?"

I shrugged. "I can't help it when the muse comes, Vikram. I must follow it."

He blinked at me again. I snickered, realizing I was enjoying the look on his face. Normally, I would have died of embarrassment. If it had been Rohit, or someone else I wanted to impress, I would've melted on the spot.

"You are . . . ," he said.

"Amazing? Unless that was your answer, you might want to stop there." Vik shook his head, like he was seriously considering it, but he kept silent.

"Tacos and truce?" I said.

Vik tilted his head in agreement. We shut the car doors behind us and turned to the orange-and-green-tiled building that greeted us. Nina's Cantina was new in town, that's all I knew. I was partial to Taqueria Fresca, but I would never pass up tacos.

I let Vik take the lead on ordering this time. He treated Nina's like his Happy's and was clearly familiar with the menu, so I left to get us a seat in the back.

Vik arrived with our food five minutes later. Two

platters of delicious-looking tacos and chips, with a tray of different salsas. Somehow my stomach still grumbled, despite all the bubble tea currently occupying it.

"Ten points for speed," Vik said, placing the platter on the table and taking the seat next to me. "Roasted cauliflower, black bean and sweet potato, pollo asado for me"—he pointed out the tacos with chicken, since I was vegetarian—"and a variety of salsas."

"And hot sauce?"

"Valentina or Cholula?"

"Both, please." Vik grabbed both from an empty table nearby.

We dove into our tacos without saying a word. I came up for air five minutes later. My stomach had made room for the tacos, as Vik had predicted, and it was demanding more of that delicious salsa verde.

"Better than Fresca?" Vik asked with that eyebrow raised.

"Hmm" was my response. I stuffed another chip into my mouth. "I'll have to think about that. But good showing, Vikram."

He inclined his head at me. "Thank you. I might get a burrito to go," he said.

"How?" I said. "I know you're all tall and broad now—"

Vik went still, just as I realized what I said. And how it might have sounded appreciative. He didn't say anything, but there was a hint of a smile at the edge of his mouth.

"I am a foot taller than you," he said. "I need more fuel. I'm seventeen."

I shook my head, feeling the edges of a blush come on.

"And for today, you're eating like me," he said. "Ready?"

I groaned. "I wasn't lying about you having to roll me."

Somehow, we managed to go to a new pizzeria and a Korean fusion food truck over the next few hours. Halfway through, I realized that I hadn't even noticed the hours flying by. It had been a while since I had lost myself in a day like that.

These days everything felt like it was so important— homework, exams, extracurriculars, driving Mani and Ratna around. A 4.0 wasn't an easy thing to acquire or keep, and I guess maybe I had forgotten how to just . . . go with the flow. I truly couldn't remember the last weekend I had done something like this.

And if I was being honest, a huge part of it was Vik.

We had decided to end the afternoon at this kitschy new ice cream place that had opened in Fairfax. Lavender's Old Shoppe was what it was called. I gave it points just for the cute vintage name. Plus, the ice cream was good.

We had taken it outside to a bench on the street, namely to get some sunshine. October was slowly stealing away summer, but today the sun was strong overhead, almost like it was refusing to leave.

"This feels like the old days, doesn't it?" I asked.

"What do you mean?" he said.

"You know, back when I first moved to the neighborhood. Back when we were children."

Vik made a noise. "Right, way back then. Not sure all of us have grown up that much since then." He gave me a pointed look.

I swatted at him. "Stop, you're ruining a perfectly good moment. Why do you have to do that?"

"What do you mean?"

I rolled my eyes and didn't respond. I licked my ice cream spoon, letting the flavors pop and burst on my tongue as I watched Vik eat his own cone. Very carefully, like he didn't even want to let a tiny drop of ice cream go to waste. It was so at odds with the rest of his carefree, live-free persona.

"Deepa? Care to explain?" Vik prompted.

"We're actually having a good time together for once—"

"Hey, I think that's unfair."

I tilted my head at him. "Like this? Anyway, we're finally having a somewhat kind of maybe nice time together."

"Thanks for the downgrade."

"And then you have to go and poke me," I said.

"I didn't touch you," he said, while nudging my sandaled foot with his own sneakered one. "There, I did."

"Okay, you know what I mean."

Vik gave me a blank-eyed stare. It was his patented obtuse look, and it normally drove me insane. This time I just sighed, and he cracked quickly. "Maybe, but I want to hear you explain," he said.

"Like—" I motioned forward with my finger. "Like poking a bear. It kind of feels like you do it on purpose."

"And you are the bear?"

"Yes."

"I'll remind you that you called yourself a bear when I use it against you later," he said. "But okay, *maybe* you have a point. And maybe it's not cool of me to do, but I can't help it with you."

"What?" I said, half mock shock and half real shock. "You admitted you were wrong? Are you going to admit I was the real winner of the sixth-grade prank war next?"

"Never," he said. "I was voted winner fair and square by a judging panel of impartial parents and neighbors. But I can admit I'm wrong. When I'm wrong."

"Which is not often—" we both said at the same time.

I chuckled. "That's my line, you know."

"I'm big enough to admit I stole it from you," he said.

"Wow, two admissions today for the price of . . . one ice cream?" I said, holding up my cup. He cheers-ed it with his own. "Though I'm definitely going to have a stomachache after all of this."

Vik took a bite out of his ice cream (because he was that type of person) and then turned to face me.

"I poke you because I think you need someone to poke you," he said. "Someone to wake you up a little. To challenge

159

you. Remind you to have fun, or that there's another way of doing something. Or to be freer."

"I'm not . . . asleep," I said, feeling mildly indignant but uncertain about what. Vik hadn't said anything mean, but I didn't like the idea that I was asleep, or boring. "I'm not boring. I enjoy myself."

I came off sounding more defensive than I wanted to.

Vik raised an eyebrow. "I never said you were boring," he said slowly. "I didn't say any of that. You're jumping to conclusions."

"So, what, you're a life coach now?"

Vik didn't say anything for long enough that a silence grew between us. It wasn't uncomfortable per se, but I wanted him to break it. The idea of being boring to Vik suddenly seemed like the worst possible thing ever.

"I never told you, or really anyone, this," Vik said. He paused, shook his head, and then spoke again. "But I had a cousin in California who was diagnosed with cancer at the end of fifth grade, right before you moved in. He was a few years older than me and he . . . got really sick. He was only eighteen and he had just entered college. He had a whole life ahead of himself and then it was . . . all gone in an instant."

"I'm so sorry," I said. I squeezed his arm, hoping it showed how much I meant it.

"Not trying to bring down the vibe, because I had my time to say my goodbyes, and my cousin was at peace at the end, but it did really make me realize that . . . life is short." He looked almost embarrassed, but then something in his expression hardened. Solidified. "I know it's cliché, but clichés exist because they have truth in them. And I just wanted to enjoy life as much as possible, while it's still mine to enjoy. The Junior Lock-In represents that to me. It's the last time all of us will get to be kids. Before college admissions and everything." He turned to look at me. "If that makes sense."

I nodded. "It does."

He looked a little surprised, but he quickly hid it.

"Is that why the prank war has always been important to you?" I asked. "Why you were so mad at me when I wanted to step out?"

"I wasn't mad—" Vik shook his head. "It's your right to say you're out, and I didn't necessarily handle all of that well." His voice was quieter, almost serious.

It took me aback, the sincerity in his voice.

"It's okay," I said, realizing I meant it. "I—"

It was on the tip of my tongue, explaining about my aunt. And it was Vik's face that pushed me over. His face was open, and warm in a way I had only seen glimpses of recently.

"My aunt had come to stay with us after her divorce," I said quietly.

Divorce wasn't a thing you really talked about in the Indian community. It happened, and it was real, but I hadn't known any other Indian families who had gone through it when my aunt came. I was wholly unprepared for how people would react.

The whispers, the gossip, all of it—it affected my aunt, and the rest of us by proxy. My aunt only recently started going back to the temple, two years later.

Vik didn't say anything. His knee pressed against mine, warm and steady.

"It was a hard time, and I didn't really feel up to all of it. It was never about you—or Lily," I quickly added. "That I didn't want to spend time with you or anything."

I had so much more to say, but even though I had been able to finally open up to Vik, something held me back from the rest. A pressure against my chest.

"I'm sorry," he said. His eyes were warm, almost too soft, despite the steadiness of his voice. "My second cousin got divorced last year and it's rough all around. People were really harsh about it, blaming her and saying all sorts of things. But sometimes, things aren't meant to be. She's happier now and that's all that matters." He nudged me again. "I . . . wish you had said something."

A beat of silence passed between us. I didn't know how to tell him that I wished I had too. Especially if it meant I had missed two years of this with Vik. But I didn't know how to quantify that feeling, or even how to approach it.

"I know" was what I ended up saying. It was hard to remember that sometimes reaching out to people was the right thing to do, even if it was scary.

I took a deep breath and put on my best smile. "Enough time down memory lane. We have a lock-in to plan, don't we?"

To Vik's credit, he didn't call out my fake cheeriness. He let me have it.

I took out my notebook. "My vote goes to the bubble tea from Happy's over the one from Vicky's."

"The bubble tea from Happy's? No way. I know you love that place, and it's real cute, but Vicky's all the way," he said. "Nothing beats that fake milk taste."

I gasped. He grinned.

And like that, we were back.

15

The smell of garlic and chili peppers lured me downstairs just as I had finished the last of my physics homework. I ran down the stairs to see my aunt attempting to open the door as she juggled three brown bags stamped with the name Taqueria Fresca. I rushed to grab the bags from her before they fell.

"Enchiladas mole and their salsa verde? Ooh, and churros?" I asked, peering at the bags. "We have been blessed tonight."

"Jeez, girl. It's like you've got a hound dog's nose for Mexican food," my aunt said, laughing.

I gave her a smug smile. My nose never led me wrong.

"Come inside," my mom yelled from the living room. "No eating before we all get to see the food."

"That rule is for Ratna, not for me," I said to no one in particular.

The chaos had already started. Ratna had scurried down the stairs and Mani was stomping down after her, hollering about how curling irons should never be borrowed by younger sisters (ha, that felt ironic coming from her). My dad had snatched the other bag of chips from my aunt's tower and my sisters were following her into the dining room.

I snuck a chip on my way in. Heaven. Their chips were always perfectly salted.

We set up the dining room for taqueria night the way we always did—burritos on one side, tacos on the other, multiple bowls of salsas drawing the line in the middle. Each one of us was firmly in one camp or another and we rarely switched sides. Ratna, Nanna, and my aunt were Team Burrito; Mani, Amma, and I were Team Taco. My grandmother just enjoyed the guacamole, and watching us argue about what was better, burritos or tacos, for the thousandth time.

We skipped the spirited discussion because tonight was game night, and that meant whoever got to the living room first got the best seats in the house. You'd think it wouldn't matter, but optimal seating was vital to success during a Josyula game night. Tonight, we'd be playing charades and Taboo, which meant maneuvering yourself so you were on the right team, especially if you were as competitive as we all were.

Mani and I dove onto the couch, grabbing opposite sides, since we counted the two teams off. We were a pretty solid team, and if we got the couch, then we knew our dad would sit in the middle and be on the second team. We all loved him dearly, but he was seriously horrible at Taboo and only my mom could decipher half the things that came from his brain.

Ratna ran into the room next, half a taco sticking out of her mouth.

"Hey!" She pouted at us.

"Snoozers losers," Mani said.

My aunt laughed and took a seat on the floor near the coffee table. "I see nothing has changed when it comes to game night."

All three of us shook our heads.

"Does this mean I'm stuck with those two?" she said with a sigh. "Great."

My mom sashayed into the living room with boxes of games piled in her arms.

"Let the games begin!"

Right on cue, my dad sank into the couch cushion between me and Mani.

Two hours later, and after an exceptionally painful round of charades where my dad tried to act out *The Empire Strikes Back*, Mani and I had been declared the winners. Obviously.

Now Ratna was snoring on the other couch, and everyone else had gone up to bed.

It usually ended up like this when Urmila Pinni visited these days—me and her on the couch, everyone else asleep. After putting in another order of nachos, this time for delivery, we had settled in to watch an old movie where two best friends fought over their mutual wedding weekend. It wasn't very good, but it made for quality gossip time since we didn't really need to pay attention to the movie. Urmila Pinni was telling me another story about her best friend's nightmare wedding planning.

"And so she had to wear the lime-green shoes because he had already said yes," she said, laughing. "It's a good thing they had been dating for so long by then, otherwise the wedding may have been called off, she was so annoyed."

The words tumbled out before I could stop them. "Do you ever regret your marriage? You know, because of the divorce?"

Urmila Pinni put down her plate carefully. I didn't miss how her body tensed up, how her eyes screwed shut for a brief second, like she was looking for strength still. But the moment passed.

She let out a deep sigh and looked at me carefully, taking my hand into her own. "Is this what you've been thinking?"

I looked away and then back.

"You were so sad," I said quietly. "And those first few weeks, I could . . . hear you. Crying. A lot. The walls are not that thick."

Urmila Pinni's lips thinned, her expression growing heavy.

"And it was my idea to make those brownies that finally brought you out of the room," I said.

"Turtle, my favorite," she said.

"So . . . yes. I have been thinking that?" I said, more of a question than a statement. I didn't know how to explain how often the thought had wormed into my head, and I wasn't proud of it. But for the first time, I wanted to know the answer. Really badly.

"No, I don't regret it," Urmila Pinni said before I could say anything else. "Despite the pain at the end—and divorce is very, very painful—despite that, I don't regret it. It wasn't a mistake, per se. Or rather, everything about life is a mistake if you look at it in a certain way."

I wasn't sure I understood what she meant by that. Sure, making a mistake on a test was a learning opportunity— you saw what you did wrong and you tried not to do it again. That was life too.

"I don't think Amma would agree," I said. "Both she and Nanna never make mistakes. They have the perfect relationship and the perfect life. I mean, partially thanks to their three amazing girls, but also otherwise. Amma has never failed at anything. She aced college, got into a top med school, and she's somehow even vision boarded her way into a book deal. And Nanna? He gave up his finance career on purpose to follow his passion."

Urmila Pinni laughed. "I wouldn't call Asha's and Suraj's lives, or their relationship, perfect. You've got to look a little closer, Deepa. Nothing is perfect . . . ever. And life isn't about that anyway."

I pursed my lips, considering her words.

"If there were a right way to do this whole life thing, someone would have figured it out by now," Urmila Pinni said. "And they would have sold it. Trust me."

I laughed. "That's true."

Still, I couldn't completely shake the idea that there was a right way, a right path, and that I just had to find it. Like my parents.

My aunt squeezed my hand, and then before I could say anything, she pulled me into a tight squeeze of a hug. She let go just as quickly.

"Don't be eager to grow up too fast, Deepa," my aunt said. "You'll have your whole life to be an adult and worry about your life and its direction. Try to just . . . be a little more carefree."

I gave my aunt a look. When had that advice ever really worked? I went to one of the top, most competitive public high schools in the country. People started studying for their SATs two weeks into freshman year.

"Okay, okay, I don't mean like stop doing your home-work or whatever. Do what you're supposed to do, and listen to your parents"—she said that with a stern shake of her finger—"but you just seem brittle, Deeps. Don't put so much pressure on yourself to get the best grades ever and be like your mom. Just be yourself."

This time, I went for the hug. My aunt gave the best hugs because she put all of herself into them. It was like the warmest teddy-bear-meets-octopus hug ever. Also, I didn't know what to say to her at that moment, and a hug was worth a thousand words.

My aunt let go just as the doorbell rang and our second

round of food arrived. The next half hour went to debating guacamole toppings and me getting the details on my aunt's latest slew of dates (and getting all the info she wouldn't say in front of my sisters). We even tossed on our favorite classic rom-com, *10 Things I Hate About You*. My aunt had gotten me hooked on it years ago, and it had become our thing, even if it was kind of old.

And right on schedule, the minute we scooted back to watch our favorite part of the movie (the bleachers scene, of course), my aunt fell asleep. It gave me a moment to think about what she had said earlier.

Sure, I was stressed about college and grades and all of that. Who wasn't? But that brittleness that my aunt had mentioned . . . it wasn't because of academics. It had started the moment my aunt had walked through our door, tears streaming down her face.

We had grieved with her for that entire year, and even after. I had lost an uncle too then. I had liked Anil Babai, but now none of us talked to him anymore. Plus, I wasn't sure I could ever put into words how much I had wanted to save my aunt from all of that, how much it had hurt me to watch her in pain.

But here she was, years later, stronger than ever, enjoying life again in a way I hadn't been sure I would ever see. My aunt was right. Okay, not about everything. My parents were an abomination of perfection and no one would convince me otherwise.

This, though? The brittleness?

I didn't know if she was right, but I hated the idea that she might be. I grabbed my phone before I could chicken out, and sent off a quick text.

Deepa: Fine. Let's go with your new lock-in idea.

Let's try it out, see if it's worthwhile. I'm willing to give it a shot.

Vik responded almost immediately. Well, at least I wasn't the only one near my phone on a Friday night.

Vik: Really?

Deepa: Why not?

He didn't respond immediately this time. I saw the three dots pop up and then go away, and then again, like he wasn't sure how to respond. Honestly, I wouldn't know how to respond if I were him either. This was a bit out of character for me. But it felt right.

And after what Urmila Pinni had said, well, I was ready to try something new.

Deepa: Seriously. I'm saying let's try your idea.

Vik: Okay.

Are you on something?

Either way, I have it in writing. Can't take it back now.

A laugh burst out of me, surprising me and making my aunt's eyes flutter open. She sat up and rubbed her eyes, staring blearily at the flickering TV screen and our forgotten movie.

"What'd I miss?" she asked.

"Nothing," I said. "Nothing at all."

16

The county fair was one of those things that everyone liked to either complain about or pretend to hate but secretly loved. Not me, though.

I loved it completely and totally, ever since my dad had taken me when I was six and I had eaten my first funnel cake. To be fair, the complaints were somewhat legitimate, especially when it came to the local roads that had to be closed off to make room for all the rides and the tractors that carried them in. Definitely a traffic jam in the making.

But the funnel cakes were worth it.

Smokey Grill Farm was the usual host of the county fair, a mere five minutes away from our neighborhood. We made the trek out every year as a family, but recently, with my mom's workload increasing and the fact that my dad was a local food celebrity, we had split up.

My dad would go earliest, getting there just as the stalls were setting up and helping out at the food corner within the fair. His stall was always the one that smelled the best, especially once he decided to pair up with Smiley's Doughnuts and they created a jam custard doughnut together.

That's right, jam custard. Not jelly. The distinction was important to my dad.

The doughnut itself was surprisingly delicious, and as a result, my dad's stall became the one stall that always sold out. Ratna used to go with my dad to help every year, but apparently she was too old this year. Had friends she wanted to go with.

I'd have to keep an eye out for any friend named Toby.

The thought made me frown into the vat of raspberry jelly I was currently stirring. My mom had a massive deadline for her upcoming book and Mani had something or other. She'd become really secretive recently, but that was part of being fourteen, so I had come early to help my dad, and to sneak in a couple of fresh doughnuts before the hordes descended.

"Aren't you happy I'm here instead of Ratna? She'd have eaten half of the raspberries and the chocolate for the chocolate drizzle," I said. I nudged my dad with my elbow, a teasing grin at the edges of my mouth. He wore a backward baseball cap and an apron that said "Always Stirring the Pot."

"Deepa, you know I would never play favorites with my daughters," my dad said. He looked up from his steaming tray of freshly fried doughnuts and winked at me. "Though you're not wrong. I brought Ratna to the spring fair and I had to make an emergency trip to the grocery store halfway through."

"Chocolate?"

"Chocolate."

"It's surprising how she can, and will, eat any form of it," I said, carefully spooning out raspberry jam from the cooled batch into a tall mason jar. Smiley Chen, from Smiley's Doughnuts, would come over soon with his famous custard, and that's where the magic happened. A jammy, custardy doughnut. My mouth watered just thinking about it. "Even white chocolate."

"That used to be your mom's favorite, you know," my dad said. "Back when I first met her. She had the taste buds of a fifth grader until the age of twenty-five."

"Ahh, it all makes sense now."

My dad put down his spoon and wiped his hands on the cloth napkin at his waist, tied into his apron. "I'm the jam maker, but I like to think I have an elevated palate. I've never had that much of a sweet tooth." He took out a new spoon and tasted the jam. His face relaxed into a pleased-as-punch expression.

"Is that a new flavor?" I asked.

"Want to try?"

I hesitated, and then nodded. "Nothing weird, right?"

My dad laughed and waved the spoon at me. "Come and find out."

I furrowed my brow, but went in for a taste. Tart, sweet, and something earthy. I thought about it for a few seconds. "Is that basil?"

"Good job, Deepu," he said. "Strawberry, lemon, and basil."

"Just interesting enough, but also a classic," I said. "I approve." I nodded at my dad and leaned in for another taste. He handed me the spoon and I licked it clean.

"One of Vikram's suggestions, actually. Though I was waiting for my favorite taste tester to approve it before I served it." He nudged me and waggled his eyebrows.

"Me?" I said, catching his look, pretending to be shocked. "What happened to Vikram? Your partner in crime?"

My dad rolled his eyes. "Jealousy doesn't look good on you."

"I'm not . . . jealous."

Not really, anyway. I liked that Vik was such a huge supporter of my dad's business. It had been hard on my dad when he had first switched careers, from finance to making jam and other treats, and having an overly excited teen boy encouraging his every attempt had been good for him. I was naturally a bit more critical, more focused on how to make every single one of my dad's sweets a success. But Vik had been the first non-family-member to show up consistently for my dad, asking him about his business, going out and giving flyers to people, helping him with his website. It was sweet, actually.

Which was what made me wonder why Vik was so spicy to me. Though after last weekend's research trip, I wasn't even sure that was true anymore. Maybe I had organized away my friendship with Vik too quickly. Maybe there was still a spot for it, under "kinda complicated."

"So what's going on later that you're abandoning me for?" my dad asked.

"I'm not abandoning you," I said. "I made sure you'd have a troop of minions to order around. Pooja and Nikhil. Rose is coming too."

"All the younger siblings of the cul-de-sac," my dad said. "I'm glad your grandmother is coming, then. I'll need help rounding everyone up."

"Oh, she'll probably join right in." I examined the mason jar, wondering how much of it I could eat without compromising the integrity of the custard jam Smiley would be making.

"Mani and Ratna will be stopping by later to help too," my dad said.

"How'd you manage that?"

My dad lifted the last batch of doughnuts from the deep fryer with his spider spatula, carefully placing them on top of the drying rack. Those would need to cool down, but they had prepped enough doughnuts that they'd be able to assemble them quickly later, whenever the crush of people started.

"They volunteered, actually. I think they enjoy hanging out with their old man," my dad said. He nudged me with his elbow, his eyes crinkling.

"Huh. I'm not abandoning you, you know. Or if I am, it's for a good reason," I said.

"Prank war?" he said.

I sighed. "No, Nanna. I do have a life outside of that. And outside of the cul-de-sac."

Okay, so I was meeting Rohit, who technically lived in the cul-de-sac, but it didn't really count. He was new to town, and new to the neighborhood.

"How's Rohit doing so far, by the way?"

I froze. But my dad was focused on prepping, and didn't seem to notice my reaction. When had my dad become a mind reader? Usually, it was my mom who I needed to avoid.

"In the prank thing. Your mom told me he joined your prank summit, right? It's always difficult joining a group like yours late," Nanna said. "I hope you guys have been welcoming. It can be tough to be a kid who has to move around a lot, hard to make real friends."

My muscles relaxed as I realized that my dad had no idea I was going on a date with Rohit. I picked up the tray nearby and started to line up doughnuts. I wasn't trying to lie to my parents or hide anything—they were okay with me and my sisters dating.

Or so they said. So far, none of us had really tested it. Going to homecoming or formals was one thing, but I had no idea how my dad would react to me going on real, official dates.

And I didn't really want to find out. Not at that moment.

"We've been welcoming, of course," I said. "He's our neighbor."

My dad's look was sly, his voice light. "Right, because he's our neighbor. Not because he seems to have captured the attention of every girl in the neighborhood? Not because he's a hunk?" He stretched out the last word.

"That took a turn," I said. I took off my apron. "I think that's my cue to leave."

"Aw, come on, Deepa," my dad said, grinning. "We can talk about cute boys."

"Nope. No, nope."

My dad laughed, which I didn't appreciate, because it was definitely at my expense. Good thing I saw a small figure with a tight bun elbowing her way through a group of eighth graders. My grandmother always knew how to make an entrance. My phone said it was half past four—Rohit would be on his way here soon. I grabbed my bag with a change of clothes and makeup.

"Amamma's here," I said. "So that covers me."

He put his tray down and gave me a kiss on my head, which meant there was probably a ring of powdered sugar in my hair now. "I'll see you back at home. Be safe, okay?"

"Nanna, I'm not going anywhere else."

"County fairs can be dangerous places, kiddo." He tried to keep his face straight and failed. "Have fun, all right? And later, please explain to me when all my daughters grew up and started to have mysterious plans. And when I became the doughnut man." He looked down at his apron and made a face.

"That's Smiley," I said. "You're the jam man."

"Is that better?"

"Totally," I lied. I pecked my dad on the cheek and ran to the bathroom, leaving my dad's mutterings about jam behind.

Twenty minutes later, I was jam and powdered sugar free, clad in a warm but cute outfit that was quality second-date material. Short cardigan set, jeans, and this time, my signature red lip. Lily had been right. Though my date had gone well, the red lip was definitely more me.

I made my way over to the middle of the fair, bobbing past groups of teens I didn't recognize and young families. That was another thing I loved about these fairs. They meant something different, yet special, to everyone who came. A moment to gather and celebrate the season shifting and how time never really stood still.

That was what I was pondering when Rohit found me.

"Deepa, hey," Rohit said, his warm voice breaking through my thoughts.

"Hey!"

Rohit was in a dusty blue cable-knit sweater and rolled-up jeans, looking like he had walked out of a J.Crew catalog. To no one's surprise, the look did it for me. I was glad I had gone a little more prep classic for my outfit as well. I loved the idea that we would match on our date. Something about it felt so picture perfect.

"So what's the plan?" Rohit asked.

I smiled broadly, loving the fact that he had already realized I would have a plan. And seemed okay with following it.

"Okay, quick intro to the county fair. Food stalls are over there," I said, pointing to the left. "And games and rides are over there. I'm thinking we start with the rides and then make our way over to food?"

"To avoid any stomach mishaps?" Rohit said. "Wise."

"Thank you," I said.

Lily and I had once done the opposite and I had ruined one of my favorite sweaters in the process. Never again. Rohit would not want to hear that story, and honestly, I didn't want him to think about me with my head in a trash can.

We chatted on the way to the Ferris wheel, me telling him more about the history of the fair and him telling me about his obsession with a Texas classic, deep-fried Oreos, as a kid. I kept trying to ask more about Texas, but he would move the conversation back.

Expertly, but still.

"The Ferris wheel," I announced as we arrived in front of it. "I actually haven't been on it since I was twelve." And the aforementioned trash can incident.

Still, it had stuck in my mind as the pinnacle of romance. Maybe it was because every movie had a Ferris wheel scene. You know what I mean. When the couple gets stuck and has to kiss or snuggle, or when someone makes a big sweeping gesture hanging off one—you could always rely on a Ferris wheel to ramp up the romance.

"Sure," Rohit said. "Let's do it."

The Ferris wheel looked different than it had the years before, its shine a little dull, its metal a little rusted, but it was still the Ferris wheel. The one I had set most of my first-kiss dreams in when I was thirteen and the one that I imagined would sweep Rohit off his feet tonight.

I focused on getting us to the front of the line with minimal line cutting, which was a feat in and of itself at a county fair like ours. There was always some group or another of kids who chose one of the rides and clogged the line. This year the target was the Ferris wheel, clearly.

But I wasn't about to let anyone ruin our date. One of the many things you learn as a petite girl is how to use your elbows in precise ways, namely to get your way through crowds who would normally push you around.

I let my elbows lead the way and pulled Rohit along behind me. Thankfully, he didn't mind following. We got to the front of the line, and after ten minutes of waiting, we were in.

I turned to Rohit with a gleeful expression on my face. I had been dreaming of this Ferris wheel moment for so long and I couldn't believe it was actually happening. Rohit smiled back, giving me major swoon vibes. A part of me did wonder if I was forcing him to do something he didn't want to do. But I figured he would just tell me, even though I couldn't remember the last time Rohit had actually disagreed with me . . . or anyone. He was the epitome of chill.

We got into the wooden seats after the attendant waved us in. My knee knocked against Rohit's as I got myself situated. The Ferris wheel seat was smaller than I had thought.

"Oh, sorry," he said, making room for me by scooting over.

"No, no worries," I said. There was an awkward beat of silence where I didn't know exactly what to do or where to put my limbs, but eventually we figured it out. Rohit slid his arm around my shoulders and I nudged my body into him. He was tense, like a petrified tree. Was he nervous as well? Did he want to kiss me already? I slowed my roll on that thought, especially because a wave of worry washed over me at it.

"I've never been on a Ferris wheel before," he said. The ride lurched to a start and in seconds we were moving. We passed by the tops of the trees and my heart started to beat faster.

"I have," I said. "But not like this."

"It's something else," Rohit said, his eyes cast out on the landscape and horizon beyond. The sun was setting, filling the sky with purple and orange as far as the horizon. Up here, I could almost see all the way to the Blue Ridge Mountains. "We didn't have scenery like this in Texas.

It's a lot of beige flatlands and lots and lots of four-lane highways."

I could feel the muscles of Rohit's arm tightening as he shifted, almost like he was trying very hard to keep himself still. He glanced down at the ground and bit his lip, so quickly I might not have noticed it if I wasn't paying attention. Huh.

"Did you grow up in Texas?" I asked, searching for some sort of conversation topic we hadn't already gone over. The silence between us still felt a smidge uncomfortable. I knew everyone said that being able to be silent was the mark of a good relationship or something, but we were only on our second date and I wanted this to feel special.

The ride lurched, this time hard enough that I could feel it in my stomach. I ignored it, trying to focus on the boy next to me.

"No, I was actually born in Miami," Rohit said.

"Miami?" Well, that explained the innate hotness. "That's . . ."

"Very different?" Rohit laughed. "I know. We've moved around a lot because of my dad's job. I've also lived in San Diego, St. Louis, Kansas City, and a suburb right outside of Chicago for six months." He ticked them off on his fingers.

"Wow," I said, thinking about what my dad had said. "I moved from one county to the other and thought it was the end of the world. Multiple different states? Must have been hard."

He looked away, his gaze dragging over the horizon. His body tensed again, or maybe it was just that up here the wind was a bit more sharp. A tendril of hair swept across his forehead, making him look like one of those old-timey movie stars. I wondered what it would be like to have our kiss up here, in the cool wind, on the top of the Ferris wheel. I wondered if Rohit would be as good at kissing as he seemed to be at everything else.

"It was a bit hard," Rohit said slowly after a slight pause. "But it's okay. It all worked out."

Something felt off about his reply. It occurred to me that Rohit never really talked about his other schools, only mentioning two best friends from childhood.

"Worked out? How?"

"I met you," Rohit said. He was avoiding my question, I could tell that pretty obviously, but he was doing it so well that I had to applaud him.

I looked up at him at that moment, he looked down at me, and there was half a second when I saw that soft look in his eyes, the one that boys have when they want to kiss you, like it's the only thing they've ever wanted.

The Ferris wheel lurched again.

This time, I almost went over. The only thing that stopped me from vaulting forward was the safety belt. Rohit grabbed on to my arm and pulled me back into his chest. His heart was beating rapidly and he kept looking at the ground and back up. I could've sworn I saw a flash of terror.

Was he . . . scared? Of heights? And if he was, why hadn't he said anything before we got on the ride? I didn't have time to think about that more. Seconds later, the Ferris wheel jerked to a total stop.

Over the loudspeaker, a voice yelled, "Just having some technical difficulties. Please keep all of your limbs inside the ride . . . to be safe."

"Keep your limbs inside," I said. "That's a joke, right?" I gulped, worry rising in my throat like a wave. Our moment from before had disappeared into thin air. The wind was stronger up here, and the metal frame around us rattled every time the breeze hit. When the ride had been moving, I hadn't noticed how thin the railing was or how high we were.

"Yeah, yeah," Rohit said quickly. "Definitely. I think."

Rohit's expression was nervous, tinged with worry at the edges. I gave him a weak smile, trying my best to make it seem like I was okay, but even I noticed that my knuckles were white as they grasped the metal railing.

Logically, I knew everything would be okay, but it wasn't like brains were entirely logical all the time. Mine kept thinking of every single possible horrible outcome, and somehow every one of them resulted in me falling off the Ferris wheel. None of the movies had ever mentioned this. I had thought a rickety Ferris wheel would be romantic, and it almost had been, but this was more like horror-movie stomach churning.

"Tell me we're not going to die," I said.

Rohit looked at me with a panicked expression. "What?"

Wrong thing to say. I forgot about the cool Deepa role I had been trying to play. And for a second, it seemed like Rohit had as well.

"I'm kidding! Not like actually die, but like . . . we're going to be okay?"

"Oh, yeah, yeah, I totally got that you were joking," Rohit said with a nervous laugh. "It'll be fine! Don't worry."

I hated when people said that. If you're ever in a situation where you might tell someone "don't worry," they are probably already worrying. I could tell Rohit was racking his brain, trying to find the right words to turn me back into the chill, calm girl from before.

"It's okay," I said. "I'm okay." I was trying to convince Rohit as much as myself. I wanted that concerned look, all pinched lips and eyes, to disappear. This was not how I wanted the date to go. "I'm sure this happens often."

Rohit looked at me, and then gave a short nod. "Uh-huh. You're right. I'm sure it happens all the time." His voice was trying to be soothing, but somehow it put me even more on edge. I realized, no matter how ridiculous it sounded, what I needed right then was not this. But I didn't know what I needed and I didn't want to be *that* girl.

The difficult one. The not-chill one who had too many neuroses.

I swallowed and tried to smile, minus any frenzy eyes. Lily always said I got a frenzied look on my face when I was worried. I was not worried. I was cool as a cucumber sunning in the south of France.

Would a cucumber be cool if it were sunning in the south of— Stop. I needed to stop. A distraction.

I scooted closer to Rohit. The wind played with the edges of his collar, tossing little swoops of hair onto his forehead. His hands clutched the railings like they were a life vest.

"Getting stuck up here is probably not what you were hoping for," I said. My inkling from before was stronger now, that maybe Rohit *was* scared of heights and this had been a disaster from the start. Part of me wished he would say it. Admit it.

"I wasn't really hoping for anything," Rohit said, his cheek dimple creasing. "Just a good time. With you."

"Oh."

That was sweet, and it melted a little of my worry away.

Still, I felt this desperate need to perform in that moment. I wondered if Rohit had felt the same way, if that was why he hadn't mentioned he was scared of heights. We were silent for a few moments.

"Look at the stars," he said.

My first instinct was to tell him that they were airplanes. But actually, from up here, a smattering of stars was apparent across the sky. Northern Virginia wasn't exactly the city, but there was enough smog and pollution that you couldn't see much more than the North Star or a few airplanes.

Tonight, however, the stars were bright and twinkling like jewels in the sky.

"They're beautiful, aren't they?"

I tilted my head up, scanning the sky. "They are."

The thought calmed me down, enough that I could turn some of my charm back on. Be the Deepa I was supposed to be. But the moment was definitely gone.

The ride jolted, starting up again. I clutched the railing tightly until the motion of the Ferris wheel evened out again. Rohit and I exchanged faint smiles, and we chatted about something or other until we hit the ground, vague words that I wouldn't have remembered if you had paid me to—I was just glad to be distracted.

I could tell that we both breathed a sigh of relief once our box hit the ground and the attendant came. Clearly, we had both been trying to keep our cool up there. Rohit excused himself for a minute and threw away something in the trash can.

I really didn't know Rohit that well, I realized.

I'd loved how easily our conversation had gone during our first date. But part of that easiness seemed to be because he always said the right thing. Exactly what I wanted him to say, whatever I had already said.

Problem was, Rohit agreeing with me all the time was getting a little . . . boring. Tiring, in a way. I wanted to know his opinions, but maybe he just didn't want to bombard me with them. Mani would probably say it was because he didn't have any opinions. I glanced at Rohit from the corner of my eye, taking in his strong profile. He turned and caught my glance, giving me a tentative smile, like the sun peeking through clouds.

Maybe I shouldn't be so harsh. It was only our second date and he probably was just nervous.

I tried to keep that in mind as we walked toward the food stalls. We were talking about the weather, and then Smiley's, when a mop of hair came into view.

"Vik?" Rohit said. "Hey!"

Rohit greeted the other boys in the group, giving Vik one of those bro hugs reserved for close friends. When had that happened?

I faintly heard someone mention joining groups and Rohit agreeing. Vik and his friends were crashing our date. Classic. I probably should have been offended that Rohit waved over Vik and the group he was with, but I wasn't. Still, I didn't know why there was a loosening sense of relief in my chest when I saw Vik.

The groups mixed together and soon we were all laughing about something Kyle had said as we walked over to get pizza at the Sliced stall.

Vik made a beeline for me. "Been enjoying yourself so far?" he said.

"Up until this point, yes."

Vik raised that eyebrow of his, a smirk curling up the sides of his lips.

Rohit glanced over and smiled, the warmth of it melting my doubt. Getting stuck on a Ferris wheel would probably strain any second date, and I was feeling restless from being stuck. Obviously. That was the only reason I felt relieved.

That had to be it.

17

You would think that convincing my sisters to help me with the prank war would be an easy task, but I was realizing it was going to take more than the typical mound of chocolate to win them over.

At the moment, Mani was driving a hard bargain.

"I'll take that pink sweater as payment," Mani said, lounging against the couch arm as if she were a princess in a palanquin.

"Payment?" I shook my head. "Nuh-uh. You said you wanted to help."

"But you're cutting into my choreography learning time," Mani said in an utterly calm and annoying voice. "I have to learn this K-pop routine for the dance showcase next week, otherwise I won't have any friends going into high school, and you wouldn't want that, right?"

No, I did not want to be blamed for that. Mani would hold that over my head for eternity. Ratna sat in a corner, watching us like we were a particularly interesting tennis match.

"And you," I said, whipping around. "What do you have to say?"

Ratna threw up her hands. "I'm sitting here, aren't I? You two are the ones wasting time." Her eyes were bright and she did look excited. "I'm just waiting for the moment when I can reveal my diabolical ideas."

I scrunched my face.

"And yes, I did learn that word recently," Ratna said proudly. "And no, it wasn't from a video game."

"Did you actually pick up a book this time?" Mani said.

"Sorry I'm not a nerd like you," Ratna said, sticking her tongue out at Mani.

"Nerds are cool! And you like video games! Plus, I'm not even—" Mani heaved a big sigh. "Why did Amma and Nanna put *her* in school a year earlier?"

"January birthday," Ratna and I said at the same time.

"I could be in high school already," Mani groaned.

It was one of Mani's biggest annoyances that Ratna, by some flick of fate, was in middle school at the same time as her. I commiserated, because it was easy to sympathize with Mani when I had a tidy little moat around my school years.

Still, Mani would be in high school next year with me anyway, which I didn't point out. Ratna always got a little sad when it was mentioned, like she was going to be left out. I don't think Mani realized, but Ratna really looked up to her, even if they were very different.

"Fine, you can borrow my pink sweater—"

"Borrow?"

"—for long stretches of time. Not permanently." I waggled my finger at her. "You're renting it from me. Free of charge. But I will add interest if you spill anything like you did that one time on my little black dress."

Mani rolled her eyes. "It was black, no one could tell."

"I could tell!" I said. "Do we have a deal or not?"

"Fine."

Well, that was as good as I was going to get. "Good." I plopped myself on the couch in between her and Ratna and poked Mani. "Now help me." I didn't mean for it to come out whiny, but I was feeling a little in over my head when it came to prank planning.

I had tried that morning to get ideas down in my favorite notebook, but it was like the blank page was laughing at me. Somehow, I had forgotten how to think, let alone prank.

"I said I had ideas," Ratna said.

Mani shook her head. "We can't superglue everything, Ratna. Have some originality."

Ratna frowned. "I only did it once. What's wrong with doing it again? Superglue Vik's laces together. Ooh, or put a fake spider in his bed. Or what about switching out his milk for something super gross, like sour cream."

"I like sour cream," I said. "And that might be a little obvious, since they're different textures." Ratna's lips quirked downward. "But all good ideas! Keep them coming. Let's think a little bigger, though. Vik is"—I gave a deep sigh—"very good at pranking. We have to do something he won't see coming."

"You could Saran Wrap his car," Mani said, and then snickered.

I leveled her with my worst stare. "Unhelpful. But . . ." I paused. "Let's think along those lines. I need something that can provide a photo op as well."

"Now we're talking," Mani said. She brushed her bangs out of her eyes and squinted at me. "Prank plus prank humiliation. I dig it. What about changing all his shirts with his brother's so he wonders why nothing is fitting?"

"Solid," I said, nodding in approval. "It's been done, though. I did that after Vik went through that growth spurt in middle school."

"I forgot about that," Mani said, grinning.

It was a good reminder that even though Vik was the winner of the prank war, I had gotten in a number of good hits. I could do this.

Soon, we had wheeled my dry-erase board down to the living room. Every idea, even if it was as simple as "tooth-paste," went on the board, and an hour later, we were laughing as much as we were scheming. Ratna's stomach started to grumble, so we took a break for snacks, reheating some of the vadas and samosas my grandmother had fried earlier in the week.

Mani was complaining about learning that new K-pop dance and I listened, taking a bite of a samosa. It was hot, and I burned my tongue instantly, but it was worth it.

Amamma always made her samosas with extra cumin seeds, which was my favorite.

"—and Emily Thorne always looks so good doing it, and I just want to show her up. But I need help. It's hard choreography—"

"Why don't you ask Rohit?" I said. "He dances and sings. Or used to."

Mani pondered that for a moment. "Maybe. Do you think he would say yes?"

I pursed my lips, thinking about it for a second longer that I should have needed to. "He's super nice."

"Sure, but would he say yes? There's nice but not kind, and kind but not nice," Mani said. "I was watching this video about New Yorkers and how they'll yell at you, but they'll help you dig your car out of the snow. I think it makes sense."

Huh. I hadn't ever thought about it that way. She had a point. A lot of people said the polite or right thing but never showed up when you needed them most. "I think he'll say yes if you ask nicely," I finally said. "He likes to be helpful."

I realized that was true, but that I didn't have an answer to whether Rohit was nice or kind or both. The thought niggled at me, but I shoved it down.

Only two dates, right? And he was a solid friend. He was a good guy, it was just that sometimes it was hard to know what he really thought.

We settled into that easy silence of ours, listening to

Ratna make a mess in the kitchen. Pots and pans and lots of dishes clanging about. Too many for the nachos she was trying to make herself. The samosas "weren't enough."

"You think this can work? That I can do this?" I said, tilting my head at the board.

"Yes," Mani said, sincerity in her voice for once. We stared at the board together, reveling in the good work we had done.

"If you don't mess it up," she added a beat later. The smirk she gave me as she bit into her samosa could rival Vik's.

I threw a pillow at her. "You're the worst."

Mani was right, though. I had a chance here. If I played my cards well, I could finally win this year.

I laid my trap on a Saturday.

The Mehtas' house was quiet that evening, compared with the hustle and bustle of the day. I had been monitoring them all afternoon with my binoculars. Ratna had promised to help with reconnaissance but had gotten distracted by the new version of some video game that had been released, which was all she had been talking about for the past week.

Vik had pulled out of the driveway only moments ago, and I was waiting for all traces of his car to be gone before I let myself in with the key Pooja had given me.

I'd orchestrated it all. Vik had been sent an email that

there was an urgent emergency student council meeting about the lock-in at school, something I knew Vik would care deeply about and would rush to attend. Pooja had helped me do it—given me updates on her brother in the hour since he had received the email. All it had required was some light bartering and bribing.

It paid to know what the younger siblings wanted, because they held the keys to this prank war. And they knew how to negotiate. Most of the time, the siblings kept to their family battle lines, but some of them were chaos monsters—or easily bribed. It was hard to know who would switch sides when, and this year, I was unsure about my own sisters. Especially after Ratna had gone and developed a secret handshake with one of my direct enemies in this war.

Finally, all traces of Vik were gone. The cul-de-sac was silent.

The coast was clear.

I tiptoed over to the Mehtas' house, making my way from our backyard to their backyard with my backpack full of supplies in tow. There was a small fence around their yard, but I knew the way to jiggle that little gate open. It really wasn't much of a lock—more of a deterrent for the neighborhood cats that always seemed to get lost and end up using people's flower beds as their nap-time pillows.

The lock opened easily and I slid into their backyard. The brick path was simple to follow, curving around Reshma auntie's vegetable garden and a number of half-deflated soccer balls, courtesy of her two sons. I remembered spending afternoons here with Vik and Lily, way back when. We'd bring sleeping bags out here and lay them out for cloud watching and for figuring out ways to play pranks on Nikhil, who was a bit of a menace back then. He'd chilled out now, but he still definitely fell into the possible chaos monster territory.

The back door was locked, as Pooja had warned, but the key she gave me fit perfectly, and seconds later, I was in. The best way to describe the Mehtas' house was like a giant hug from an old comforter. Reshma auntie and Pratik uncle had inherited the house from their parents and there were touches of them all around, from the woven tapestries from India hanging on the walls to the faded yellow walls of a bygone decade.

I crept through the living room and up the stairs to Vik's room. It had been years since I had taken this path. Since Lily moved in, really. The third step creaked as I walked up, just the way I remembered.

And Vik's room? It was . . . very different.

Gone were the soccer and band posters; gone were the trophies that I remembered. Instead, it was almost sparse, which surprised me.

I guess I had kept an image of Vik in my head that hadn't grown up the way he had. His room was all blue and white now, with a monochrome navy bedspread and sleek black furniture. His walls were dotted with photos that looked familiar—I squinted at them, trying to make them out in the low light. To my surprise, among the photos of his old soccer team and bandmates was a photo of the three of us—me, Lily, and him—from middle school.

Huh. I was surprised, which wasn't hard to admit, especially since I had the same photo on my corkboard in my room. Sure, it was half-covered by a few other things, but I had kept it up. And so had he. For some reason it warmed me, seeing that photo there.

And it reminded me why I was there.

I took out all my supplies with care—two hundred plastic cups, three cartons of soda, and a tarp. Vik was going to come home to his floor covered in soda-filled plastic cups, which was my take on the classic prank of wrapping a room in aluminum foil or gift paper. This way, one wrong step from Vik would result in catastrophe, and a lot of complaining and frustration.

I couldn't wait.

And because I adored Reshma auntie and would never want to ruin her beautiful home's wood floors, the tarp went down first. I was halfway through laying out and filling up the plastic cups when I heard a noise from downstairs.

It sounded suspiciously like a door opening.

Crap. I hurried through putting down as many of the rest of the cups as I could, trying to leave myself a path out.

A door slammed.

"Hello?" a voice called out.

Crap, crap. Vik was home. Good thing I had kept the light off and only used my flashlight. Ugh, I was so close to being done.

So, so close that it was eating at me to have to stop. His bedroom floor beckoned at me to continue, but I wouldn't get any credit if Vik found me here. It wouldn't count as a finished prank if I was caught in the act.

I had to get out.

Okay, new plan. I put down the cup I was working on and snatched my bag of supplies. This would have to do. There was a slight possibility I could hide in Pooja's room until the coast was clear enough for me to sprint downstairs.

I rushed to the door and swung it open—only to run into Vik on the other side. We tumbled back and hit the staircase railing.

Vik caught me. Thankfully, his grip was strong enough to keep both him and me upright. I tried to hide my face, but I knew it was too late.

"I knew it," he said, sounding annoyingly supercilious. "Caught in the act."

"How? When?" I sputtered. "Pooja said you'd be out."

"Can't reveal my secrets," he said. "Call it a feeling."

I turned to angry-glare at him when I realized he was still holding on to me. He seemed to realize it at the same time, and let go. Slowly.

"Someone betrayed me. Was it Pooja?" I demanded. Then, with a groan, "No, it can't be Pooja. She literally texted me ten minutes ago to check in—"

"Always a pleasure to discover that my sister has abandoned me for the enemy camp," Vik said. "Good to know I can rely on my family."

"—and I made sure everyone would be out. Tell me how you knew. I demand to know," I said. My fists curled into balls, my frustration rising. I wanted to breathe out a huge stream of "uggghhhhh," but it would probably only give Vik more satisfaction.

Even now he looked way too smug and happy.

"Tell me," I said, poking him in the arm. He raised an eyebrow at me and I mock raised one back. "Come on, you know you want to. Lord it over me."

Vik chuckled. "You do know me. Okay, fine, if you have to know, it was your email."

"What email?" I said automatically. I tried to look innocent, but inside my stomach fell. I thought it had worked! I had even spent two hours perfecting the wording to make it seem like it came from a teacher.

"Deepa." Vik leaned against the railing, which made me worried for the railing. "I'll admit it took me longer than it should have, but I put the pieces together. It was good—you covered most of your bases, but . . ."

I leaned closer.

". . . you didn't cover all of them. An emergency student

council meeting? That got me into my car almost immediately, but then I texted you. And you didn't respond." He paused. "*You* didn't respond. To a summons from a teacher. Normally, you'd be banging down my door and dragging me to school yourself."

He was right. Kind of annoying that he was so right, and that he knew me so well. It all felt so obvious now. I had planned for everything—except Vik's reaction.

I bit back a groan, thinking through all the ways I could've solved for this problem. "I was so close."

Vik crossed his arms, looking down at me. He was so tall that it was like he was literally looking down his nose at me. "Dee, you're such an overthinker I can literally hear your mind whirring from miles away," he said.

"That is clearly hyperbolic," I said, frowning. "And anyway, a good prank requires good planning."

"True, but if you want to be able to pull a prank on me, you're going to have to stop overthinking."

I made a choking noise. "That is so condescending. You're not the god of pranks, Vikram."

"No, but I am the three-time winner of our war." He leaned closer. "Know what that means? I beat you. Three times. Four times, if you count how this war is shaping up. And I know a thing or two about you."

Heat rose up my core, like an oven turned on too quickly. Vik did that to me. Apparently. These days. What was my body doing? I tried to ignore it.

It was very unfair that Vik—Vikram, of all people!—was able to make me feel this way, even when he was lecturing me. I couldn't help but notice the way his forearm muscles flexed and how his lips moved. I was annoyed at him and at myself for getting distracted. And by the wrong boy.

And then he had the audacity to wink at me.

"You're right, you need a good plan," Vik continued, oblivious to my internal screaming. "And you had a . . . decent one."

"Thanks."

"But you forgot that it's not just about a good prank. It's about the crafting the right prank for the right person."

"Sure," I scoffed. "Pranks should work for anyone. That's the whole point. It's a prank."

"You're wrong on that," Vik said.

"Your face is wrong," I muttered.

Vik laughed, that stupid full-throated one that meant he was definitely laughing *at* me. But that felt more normal, in a way.

"Very mature," Vik said. "But I'm still right. At least, that's my opinion."

I was about to let him know where he could shove his opinion when the front doorbell rang.

"And that's Lily and Rohit, to witness your failure," Vik said in a singsong voice, his eyes dancing. Vik darted out of the way and down the stairs before I could smack his arm. I frowned at his back.

Maybe he was right. Maybe I hadn't planned well enough for Vik specifically. Whatever that meant.

But there was one thing Vik didn't realize.

I wouldn't make the same mistake twice.

And he had made his first: underestimating me.

The rest of the weekend was a drag, with me trying and failing to think of another prank that I could successfully pull over Vik. I kept thinking about what he'd said—and getting more and more annoyed about it.

It followed me to Monday morning as I made my way to our lockers before first period. Lily was chattering about something to my right, but for the life of me, I couldn't focus. It wasn't like I wanted to be a bad friend. But Vik's words kept eating at me. And I couldn't stop thinking of a way to beat him for good.

Glue in shoes? Done that already.

The toothpaste trick? Small potatoes.

Change his car horn to a clown car noise? Ooh. That could work. But it'd require a lot of careful—

"Deepa!"

I snapped to attention and gave my best friend a sheepish look. "Yes?"

She sighed, crossing her arms over her chest. "Seriously, dude? It's so obvious you're not listening to a word I'm saying."

"I'm sorry," I said, squeezing her arm. "I just can't stop—"

"Thinking about Vik?" Lily said.

"What?" My cheeks burned. "No. Ew." It surprised me how not gross her comment made me feel. More embarrassed. Which was somehow worse. "No, I was thinking about how I can prank him better. Because I was so close. So, so close . . ." I caught the look on her face. "And it doesn't matter. What were you saying?"

I smiled bright and wide at my best friend, hoping she would forgive me. Lily rolled her eyes, which meant all was good.

"I was saying that the Winterfest dance committee apparently has some surprises up their sleeves," Lily said. Today's beanie was a dark eggplant with tiny silver stars sewn in, and a piece of Lily's blue hair kept sticking out of it no matter how many times she tried to tuck it behind her ear.

I stopped in my tracks at that, also because we were at my locker. "Intriguing. I wonder what it could be."

"Right?" Lily jumped onto her toes. "I've been putting together a list of potential surprises. It's better than fretting about how I did on that last physics exam."

I nodded in agreement. That one had been a doozy.

"It could be a surprise performance?" I said, twisting my locker open to grab my textbooks. "Maybe they got—"

"Taylor Swift?" Lily said.

I laughed, and it came out as a cross between a snort and a cough. "I was not going to say that."

Lily deflated. "Okay, yeah, unlikely. But a girl can dream."

"She certainly can. A surprise performance could be it, but I'm thinking it would probably be a local band? Or maybe a cool new DJ?" I frowned. "Whatever it is, I really hope it isn't something Vik and I have already thought of for the lock-in."

"Have you guys decided on your plans?" Lily asked.

I shook my head. "Not completely, but we're close. We have our last research and planning session next week. Though Vik said he wanted to take me somewhere new before that . . . and I'm a little scared."

"More intrigue," Lily said, giving me a look I couldn't quite decipher. There was a little too much glee on her face.

"Or he's trying to get rid of the competition in some sneaky way. Keep me occupied on a Saturday," I said darkly. "Not that I have any idea what I'm going to try next—"

"Deepa?"

I smiled, recognizing that musical voice. I turned to see Rohit standing across from my locker, a bouquet of roses in his hands. He was wearing an ivory fisherman's sweater and a smile. It took my brain a few seconds to register everything, and then it hit me.

It was the first day of Winterfest asking week. Asking weeks were a tradition for the two big dances at Edison and I had completely and totally forgotten in my post-prank-fail haze. I clutched my textbooks a little tighter.

"Hi," I said, because my brain had stopped working. "How are you?"

I winced. Good thing Rohit laughed. "I'm good. Didn't mean to catch you off guard, but I wanted to ask you something."

I tried not to squeak as he handed me the flowers. A crowd was gathering near the far end of the lockers. Well, duh. It was asking week and Rohit was one of the top bachelors in the junior class at the moment.

Then he got down on one knee. The entire hall went pin-drop silent, even the two drama kids rehearsing for the upcoming musical in the far corner. Good thing I was holding my textbooks, because otherwise, I'd have no idea what to do with my hands.

"Deepa, will you go to Winterfest with me?" he said.

The answer was obvious, but for some reason, my brain was still thinking about Vik—the prank, of course. It took me just a half second longer to respond than totally necessary, and a flicker of uncertainty flashed across Rohit's face.

"Yes, of course. I'd love to!" I said.

Rohit smiled wide enough that it made me smile too. What a picture-perfect Winterfest proposal. Rohit got to his feet and swept me up into a hug. I tried not to giggle.

I couldn't believe it. I thought about pinching myself, to make sure it was real. But the evidence was right in front of my face.

It had happened. The third date was a go. My plan was

still on. I had lost sight of it for a second there. Somewhere in the far reaches of my brain, I noticed that Lily had disappeared from view. Had she known?

My question was answered.

A squealing Lily came rushing into my peripheral vision, latching on to me the minute Rohit let go of my hand. I pulled her to the side. "You had no idea. Tell me you had no idea," she said.

"I had no idea," I admitted.

"You were right," Rohit said to Lily. "Best partner ever."

Lily saluted. "I reported for duty and I delivered. That's what I do."

I laughed and noticed a tall figure at the end of the hall. Was that Vik? Had he seen this whole thing?

The crowd moved to surround us, with high fives being given to Rohit.

"That was so romantic," Jenny Porter said, sidling up to me, her voice dreamy. "You guys kicked off Winterfest asking week with a bang. Everyone's going to be talking about it."

Jenny Boateng showed up to her right at that moment.

"Rohit asked you? I can't believe I missed it," Jenny said, her eyes skimming over me and then Rohit, who stood a few feet away. There wasn't any judgment in her eyes, only a faint sense of appreciation. "Damn, girl, you got a solid one. You guys look so good together. Honestly, you're like the *perfect* couple."

"Thanks," I said, allowing myself a small smile.

We would look good together. But when Jenny turned around, my smile fell. My aunt's words came back to me.

Nothing is perfect . . . ever. And life isn't about that anyway.

I wasn't unhappy. I was honestly thrilled, and yet . . .

Something felt off, like a teetering porcelain plate, but I didn't know what. This was exactly what I had wanted, what I had hoped for, what I had planned. My third date would happen and with it, the seal-the-deal kiss.

It was all coming along perfectly, and I should be ecstatic, jumping-from-the-roof ecstatic. Instead, all I could hear was what my aunt had said.

Perfect was a lie.

But this didn't feel like a lie. Rohit turned and waved at me, and I waved back.

Right?

18

Vik insisted that our outing today was secret, meaning I had no idea where we were going, something I truly hated. That's probably why he had insisted on it. Pushing me out of my comfort zone or something super irritating like that.

When I showed up at Vik's front door, he was holding a thick scarf in his hand.

"Trying out a new look?" I asked.

Vik's lips quirked. "This is for you."

"Not quite my style," I said, eyeing the yellow paisley floral scarf. "But thanks for the thought?"

Now Vik rolled his eyes. He stopped leaning against the door frame, which the door was probably thankful for, and walked up to me. "Turn around. I want today to be a surprise. And I couldn't find anything else that would work as a blindfold."

Vik moved toward me and I stepped back.

"Is this really necessary?" I said.

"No," he said. "But I think it'll be fun. Remember fun, Dee?"

I didn't have a chance to snap back because Vik came

up close to me. Very close. And with a very wry smile on his face.

He didn't think I would say yes. That made me want to prove him wrong.

"Fine," I said.

I did a semi-turn so my back was to Vik. He stepped closer, his arms going around me. I could feel the heat from his skin, he was so close. I teetered, feeling suddenly self-conscious in the outfit I had chosen.

Vik steadied me as I fell back. Which was the wrong thing, because now I knew exactly what Vik's chest felt like, and it was solid. Very, very solid. A flush threatened at the edges of my cheeks. It was a good thing that I was facing away from Vik.

"Ready?"

I nodded.

Very gently, Vik reached around and tied the scarf around my eyes, engulfing my vision in murky darkness. I could still see peeks of light, and I could see my own feet.

He chuckled. "Already looking for loopholes? I tied it so you won't trip."

"Oh. Thanks, I guess."

"You're very welcome, Dee. Sometimes I can be nice."

I snorted at that, and almost tumbled over the front doorstep. Vik grabbed my arm and steadied me.

"Though maybe I should stay near you. Just in case," he said.

"Yeah," I said quickly. "That might be a good idea."

Was I totally confident that I would not trip down the stairs? No. This whole blindfold thing was harder than it looked. That was the only reason I wanted him to stay close.

Not because he smelled like a mixture of old leather and pine. Or that I liked the way his cool fingers brushed against my warm skin.

Vik helped me into the car and I tugged the seat belt across my body. I tried to get comfortable, but the anticipation was getting to me. Maybe that's why I was so bad with surprises. I so desperately wanted to know everything, all the time, that I hated having to wait for it.

But it was also nice to know someone had taken the time to plan something for me. Even though my brain kept thinking of the worst-case scenarios, especially because it was Vik. But maybe this would be good for me. A change of pace.

My newly Zen mindset didn't last long.

"What are we doing?" I asked, unable to help myself. It had only been five minutes since we had pulled out of the cul-de-sac.

"Not telling."

"Is it more food? I may not be able to survive another day of eating like the last one we did, to tell you the truth."

"What a lie. You're a total foodie."

He had me there. I had secretly loved that all-day food bonanza. My stomach complained the next day, but it had been worth it. I loved discovering new places, and I had to credit Vik for pushing me to do that. Since then, I'd convinced my family to get Nina's for our taco night and even gone to a new coffee shop that had opened in Sterling with my dad.

"Am I appropriately dressed? Do we need to stop by my house and get anything?" I asked.

"Stop fishing for clues," Vik said. "And you look great."

Even though I knew there was no way I should, I could feel the heat of his gaze on me.

"Are we there yet?" I said.

I could almost imagine Vik rolling his eyes to my left. My blindfold was itchy and I reached up to fix it. Vik slapped my hand lightly.

"Rules are rules," he said. "You're the rule lover here."

I grumbled to myself. "I wasn't taking it off."

Vik chuckled, as if he knew that I was hoping to inch off the blindfold. Damn, he knew me well. Usually, that thought annoyed me, but not today. Today, it felt kind of nice. A warm blanket on a frigid night.

The car came to a stop and I tried to unbuckle myself and get out.

"Wait," Vik said. I heard the car door shut, and then footsteps. My door swung open and a fresh breeze buffeted the car, reminding me again that it was November. Vik reached down to unbuckle me. His warm hands wrapped around my upper arm, and he pulled me up.

"Watch your step," he said, just as I stumbled on a rock. He caught me around the waist and there it was again. The full-body flush. He was warm, and solid, and I really wasn't used to thinking about Vik that way.

So I wouldn't.

"Can I take this thing off yet?" I said, trying to pull on the endless reserves of annoyance I usually had for Vikram Mehta.

"Nope," he said.

"Worried I'm going to run off or something? Are you sure you didn't bring me to some abandoned cornfield to hide my body so you can win the prank war?"

"I don't need to," Vik said, scoffing. "I have no concerns about my ability to beat you. Also, if that were actually my plan, should you really be poking the bear? Shouldn't you be begging for your life?"

I could hear the chuckle in his voice. The taunt.

"Never," I said dramatically. "I have dignity."

Vik laughed, a full-throated one. I hid a smile. I had grown to like that laugh. It was funny, the fact that I had known Vik for so long and only now understood his real laughs.

"Take my arm," Vik said. I reached out and looped my arm through his, trying to ignore the fact that this was the most touching we had done in a long time, and it felt very different than it had in middle school. His muscles were taut under his flannel shirt, holding me steady as we walked over the unpaved ground.

"This is definitely a cornfield," I said. "Not a road, because it's too bumpy. I stand by my theory."

"You're half right," Vik said. "I did bring you somewhere a little off the beaten path."

Huh. I tried to think where he could've brought me. I ran through the list of places we had left on the research list, and I couldn't think of anything.

"Okay, okay," I said. "Show me. I can't stand it anymore."

I reached up to yank off my blindfold. Large hands covered mine, pulling my hands away. "Patience is a virtue, Deepa." His voice was close enough that I startled, his breath tickling against my cheek.

I cleared my throat. "Not a virtue to me. I like results."

"You are impossible sometimes, you know? I'm *trying* to surprise you."

"I know," I said, smiling. "But no one does that for me. I do that for people." The words were out before I thought about it too much. I was always the planner, the thinker, the strategizer.

"I noticed," he said.

I was about to open my mouth, another smart comment on my tongue, when Vik pulled off my blindfold.

I blinked a few times, resisting the urge to rub my eyes. The midday sun was covered by clouds, but it was still bright and my eyes took a second to adjust.

Then my mouth dropped open.

My gaze swept across the large field in front of us, covered in rusted metal barrels and fake camouflage. Bright

215

red inflatables peppered the field in a zigzag, some short, some tall, and all very noticeable. People of all ages walked around in helmets with color-splotched shirts.

"Paintball?" I said incredulously. "That wasn't on our initial list."

The memory came back to me: Vik scratching something in at the bottom of our list after a heated discussion on fun, competitive activities for the lock-in.

"You said you'd never been," Vik said. "And we still have research to do, Dee. We talked about a showstopper. What's more showstopping than outdoor paintball on the lacrosse field? I talked to Principal Goldberg and she's on board if we're able to get water-soluble paint. Think about it. No one else has ever done something this cool. We'd go down in Edison High history. For life."

Vik's excitement was palpable, his energy cresting over me like a wave.

"Hmm," I said. "I have to say . . ."

Vik raised an eyebrow.

"This is pretty cool," I admitted.

He laughed. "You don't have to sound so unhappy."

I fake hit his shoulder. "I'm supposed to be the planner. You're taking my job."

"You need a break," he said. Vik grabbed my hand and pulled me forward toward the office in the back. "And once you mentioned you and your aunt love *10 Things I Hate About You*, I knew we had to do it."

He remembered that? I did love that scene in the movie.

"Isn't this considered mismanagement of funds?" I said.

"I cleared it with Principal Goldberg," Vik said over his shoulder. I let him lead me, buoyed along by his excitement. "She told me to find a place that could do what we needed, and that's what we're doing."

Vik threw a helmet at me. "Suit up."

After an hour of chasing and being chased by other teams, I was wiped. To no one's surprise, the group that came in with all sixth graders was the most vicious. I held my hip as I limped over to Vik.

He handed me a water bottle and I gulped it down in one go.

"You thirsty?"

I threw my empty water bottle at him, and he caught it. "This is hard work," I said. "And those kids?"

"Terrifying," Vik said. He grabbed another water bottle from the ice cooler near the rest station and took a swig. His helmet was off, and despite the heavy helmet hair, he looked good. I couldn't help looking.

Vik caught my gaze, and I immediately glanced away, but not before a slow grin crept up his face. Okay, fine. Vik was cute. I found him . . . attractive.

But that was normal. He was a good-looking boy and I was attracted to many good-looking boys. That was it.

"You know, this wasn't as bad as I thought it would be,"

I said, gazing out at the two teams battling it out on the field.

"Meaning?"

"I mean, paintball looks like chaos incarnate."

"Which is half the fun."

"Of course you'd think that," I said. "It sounded fun, but I thought it would be too much. Which is probably exactly why you brought me here."

"I wasn't sure you were going to come, to be honest," Vik said. "I thought you might refuse, especially since it was my surprise. You're not good at letting go of control."

I was mildly offended by that, but I knew it rang true. "Surprised you, didn't I? See? I contain multitudes."

Vik released a half-snort that sounded suspiciously like something I would do. Maybe he wasn't just rubbing off on me, but I was on him as well.

"And I didn't mind getting messy," I added as an after-thought. I was concerned it might take me two hot showers and a quart of shampoo to get the paint out of my hair, but even that sounded okay.

I glanced over at Vik since he was silent. Vik was looking at me with a curious expression, his mouth curving into what I could only describe as a dangerous smile.

Oh no. That was Vik's trademark prank grin. What had I said? Something about not minding getting messy—

I started to back away just as he stepped toward me.

"No," I said.

"But you said you were okay getting a little messy," Vik said, his voice low. Teasing.

"Uhh, I meant like, I'm okay with a little paint here or there, but the look on your face is promising—"

"What? The look on my face is promising what, exactly?"

"Mischief!"

That stopped him in his tracks. "Mischief?"

"Yup. Very, very devious . . . mischief."

Vik gave me that look, the one like I had lost my mind. But this time, his face was softer, thoughtful.

"Your radar is very good, Ms. Brilliant." Before I could even defend myself, or move away, or anything, really, Vik sprinted over. He grabbed a half-exploded paintball nearby and swiped hot-pink paint down my cheek.

I turned around slowly to face Vik.

And then grabbed some of the paint myself.

Vik dashed away.

"Come back here, Vikram!"

"Catch me!"

I ran after him, laughter bubbling up to my lips.

19

The next weekend I had promised to go with Lily to her sister's soccer practice and help with the snacks and drinks. Her parents couldn't make it, and I didn't have any exams coming up, so I said yes.

To no one's surprise, catering for young kids was a bit of an ordeal, not just because there was a shortage of the Melon Medley juice flavor but because the parents were there. The kids themselves were easygoing, mainly focused on practicing their plays before their game with their neighbors, the Fighting Wasps, but the parents were all demands and complaints.

We drove back home after, Lily and me both singing along to the song on the radio at the top of our lungs. My voice cracked on the high note and we both shattered into peals of laughter.

"Apparently, I'm not going to win any musical contests," I said.

"Hey, if you could, that would be unfair," Lily said. "Too much good in one package. I might have to come over at night and cut your hair in a weird bob, just to even it out."

"You're too good to me. Seriously, who needs romantic love when you have best friend love?" I giggled. "Anyway, I would never be able to pull off a bob, not like you."

Lily fluttered her eyelashes and coiffed her pretend bob. "I do have good hair luck."

"Hey, how did the soccer practice go?" I asked. "I spent most of my time in the bleachers trying to control the parents and I totally missed it."

Lily's face fell. "Horrible. Rose's coach is incompetent. Utterly incompetent. Just last game he made a horrible call in the crucial last five minutes." I could sense a tirade coming.

"Hey," I said quickly, trying to fend off her bad mood. "Their soccer coach is a volunteer, right?"

Lily nodded. "Yeah, we're still in regional leagues, so it's all volunteers. But when Rose gets into the travel clubs . . ."

"The game changes."

It was sweet how invested Lily was in her sister's soccer career, and I knew how much Rose appreciated it. Both their parents worked a lot—they were civil rights attorneys. During one of their big high-profile cases, Lily had stepped in to help with her little sister, and she had never stepped back. She enjoyed being a "soccer sister" and it was obvious to me that Lily would be an amazing coach.

"Have you considered coaching yourself?" I said tentatively. We pulled into my driveway and I put the car in park.

I did a double check of everything before closing the car door. Ever since my car had been Saran Wrapped, I was a little on edge.

"Coaching?" Lily paused while getting out of the car. "Me?"

"Yeah. You."

"But I'm not . . ."

"You're not?" I said. I tugged Lily out of the car and shut the door behind her. "A soccer expert? Coach material? And Mr. Gilbert is? He's an accountant."

"But he's an adult," Lily whispered.

"So?" I said, walking to the front door, bag in tow. "You're almost an adult. And I'm sure they'd make an exception. There's no harm asking at least, checking to see if there is an age restriction." I stopped and faced Lily. "Now that I think about it, I've definitely heard about a teenager coaching a local league before."

I turned back to the house.

That's when I noticed it.

"Really?" Lily squeaked from behind me. "You think I could do it?"

"Stop!"

"Oh, sorry," Lily said, running into me.

"No, I mean, stop moving. Yes to your question on if you can do it. We'll talk about it later, I promise, but right now we have a problem." I squinted at the front door.

Lily came up to my shoulder and stared at the front door too. "Why exactly did we stop?"

"Something's off," I said. "I can smell it."

Literally.

I could smell it.

Our front door was nothing special. A white door with blue trim and long glass windows inserted on the sides. There was a *Welcome, Travelers!* doormat in front of it, and along both sides were my dad's rosebushes. My grandmother had taken the dying things from my dad's care when she had come to America to stay with us, and now they were a blooming hedge that drifted a sweet scent, even in fall.

But right now, I was smelling more than roses.

I was smelling . . .

"Pie?"

"Pie?" Lily repeated. She sniffed the air and then her eyes bulged. "Wait, I do smell pie. Apple pie, to be exact."

I nodded, sniffing as well. "Tons of cinnamon. A hint of . . ."

"Cloves?" we both said.

No one was supposed to be home right now—even Amamma had her weekly neighborhood carrom board game that afternoon. At first, I considered that maybe my dad was trying a new jam flavor, but then I remembered he was supposed to be at Smiley's for a meeting until dinnertime. And I didn't see his, or my mom's, car in the driveway.

A sneaking suspicion slithered into my mind.

I put my finger to my lips and motioned for Lily to move forward with me.

223

"Ooh, smells like apple pie!" I said loudly. "My dad must have gotten home early, must be that new flavor he said he was going to test."

Lily blinked at me, and then caught on. "I remember him mentioning it, can't wait to try." She paused. "Yum!"

I stifled a laugh. She shrugged helplessly. Subterfuge was not Lily's strongest suit.

I closed the distance to the front door slowly, keeping an eye on the sides of the house, even as I stomped loudly. We didn't have a fence, so anyone could be lurking around. And we were in a war.

I stomped again, like I was going up the few steps to our door.

A shadow, and then a rustle of leaves.

Rohit lunged out of the bushes on the side of the house just as I ducked to the side. An apple pie with a mound of whipped cream went flying across our lawn, and Rohit followed. He tried to right himself, only to tumble over into the grass, narrowly missing the strewn bits of apple pie.

I burst into laughter.

"Bad luck, my friend," Lily said, shaking her head.

"I was so close!" he said. Rohit looked genuinely disappointed. He got to his feet and wiped the grass off his pants.

I felt a little bad, but also weirdly triumphant for defending my territory. My instincts had been honed over the years, and I knew to trust them the second something felt off. But it was Rohit, so I tamped down my initial instinct to pump my fist in the air.

"You were . . . kind of close," I said. "I knew something was off. But it was a good effort!"

Lily nodded. "Really good first effort. You don't even want to hear about what an epic disaster my first attempted prank was. And no one ever wins on their first try."

"Thanks," Rohit said. He didn't sound convinced. "But you guys don't have to take it easy on me."

"Well, if that's the case . . ." I exchanged a look with Lily. She nodded. "I was drawing you out with that fake voice. I had a hunch once I got to the door."

"I really thought I was close—how did you know?" Now Rohit looked a little intrigued.

"The smell," I said. "And the fact that we've honed super senses when it's prank war time."

"But how?" Rohit said, looking at me expectantly.

That stumped me. I thought back to exactly what had tripped me up. I wasn't lying about the super senses, but I tried my best to really think about it.

"I planned everything. I knew your family would be out and I even had a backup pie," Rohit said with a groan.

That lit up the bulb in my brain.

"You're overthinking it," I said. "But not the part you need to overthink."

"Huh?"

I waved my hands around, trying to find a way to explain.

"A prank doesn't work just because you've checked off a few things. Unfortunately, I'm highly attuned to smells because of all my dad's jam experiments. If you had considered that with the prank execution, it would have been perfect," I said, landing on words that someone else had once told me. "It's about crafting the prank to the right person."

Huh. I guess Vik had a point.

Rohit's prank had failed because he hadn't taken me into account in the planning. We were all on our guard, sure, but if he knew me, he should've known what would trigger suspicion—it was the same mistake I had made with Vik. And there had to be some instinct, if I was being honest. A plan could only take you so far.

Vik hadn't known that my car would be outside on the driveway that morning, but he knew me, and he knew how to adjust accordingly. I was sure that he had planned everything to a T, but it was that added little bit that had made the pranks so good. It also helped that he had picked the one thing that would drive me, and specifically me, up a wall.

"Huh," Rohit said. "I think that kind of makes sense?" He squinted his eyes like he was in thought. "I guess I was trying to plan the best prank and not necessarily a prank for you. Though I do think a pie in the face is a pretty good prank for anyone."

I had to agree, it was classic. But I was thankful I wouldn't be picking bits of apple out of my hair in the shower.

Lily made a face at the now-ruined pie. "Shame we didn't get to eat it, though." She jumped. "Crap, I forgot I need to get home and finish my chores otherwise I'm never going to hear the end of it."

"Shoo," I said. "We'll clean up the pie."

"And I might have an extra one," Rohit said. "Remember the backup?"

I was pretty sure I made googly eyes at him right then and there. "I do think backup pie is a good 'I'm sorry for nearly pieing you' apology."

Rohit's cheeks turned red. "It was the first prank that came to mind."

"And a good one!" I rushed to say. I forgot Rohit didn't really know me or my humor. Though it had been a few weeks. "I have to say, I love that you had a backup. A good plan A always requires a plan B."

I tried to keep my voice light and teasing. Flirty, not harsh.

Rohit's body language relaxed, his shoulders dropping a bit. He brushed his hair aside and smiled that megawatt smile. The one that always managed to distract me.

"You're so smart," he said. "And so together. I planned extra hard knowing you were my target, because otherwise, how would I pull one over on you?"

Sweeter words had never been spoken. I stepped closer to him, looking up at him through my lashes. "You really think that? Even though the first time you saw me I was in my pajamas?"

Rohit laughed. "That was cute. It made you seem approachable. Plus, you had great taste in music."

He reached out and twirled my hair around his finger.

A scream crashed through the gentle afternoon wind. Rohit and I whipped our heads around.

"What was that?" he said.

The scream had come from the right, and it sounded strangely familiar. . . .

I connected the dots. And gasped. "Lily!"

I motioned for Rohit to follow me and ran straight across the cul-de-sac to Lily's house. Immediately, I berated myself. I knew it was war time and I hadn't walked her to her house. We hadn't officially entered an alliance, and alliances were hard during the prank war, but if the two of us were here, then that only meant one thing. . . .

Vikram.

Lily stood in the middle of her driveway, soaked down to her very shoes in bright blue liquid. "You were supposed to be at a friend's house! Nikhil told me you would be!"

I looked over to see Vikram leaning against my mailbox, his arms crossed as he watched the chaos in front of him. "Never trust a younger brother," Vik said, shaking his head. "They will turn on you for a ride to the movie theater."

I came to a stop in front of him, gaping at the rows of broken balloons that hung at the top edge of Lily's garage door. He had hung them under the garage lights and strung a loop of balloons up and over onto the roof so when Lily had put in the code to enter, they had exploded.

How, I had no idea.

"Lily, I'm sorry! I should've come with you, but I was with Rohit and I was—"

"Distracted?" Vik grinned, looking smug and triumphant at the same time. "I may have suggested that today would be a good day to attempt a prank."

Rohit's eyes widened. "Sneaky. So sneaky." I didn't appreciate how admiring Rohit sounded. He rubbed his temples. "I may have gotten in over my head with this whole prank war. You guys are intense."

I should've taken offense at that, but instead I found myself looking over at Vik, who happened to be looking at me. "We know," he said.

Lily blinked rapidly. Some of the blue liquid had dripped down her face. She stuck her tongue out. "Is that . . . Gatorade?"

Her frown bloomed into a grin. "Okay, that's pretty fun. It's like what they do to winning coaches in the Super Bowl. I dig it." She looked down at her ruined jersey. "Though I definitely need to change now."

Vik threw a towel at her, which she accepted gratefully. "For our favorite soccer sideline coach."

"Don't give up," I said, turning back to Rohit. "Even though I will be on total guard around you now."

"I'm not giving up," Rohit said, sounding determined. "I just need to work a little harder. I'll catch up."

"Good attitude, Rohit," Lily said, wiping her hair down. "Trust me, you're going to need it with these two."

I frowned. Lily sounded like she admired Vik's prank, even though *she* was the one who had been pranked. Granted, this was a solid effort from Vik. He had literally played us all off each other to time it, and he had managed to pull a prank that made Lily grin.

"So you knew I'd be out?" I said to Vik. He stood near me, hands in pockets, looking pleased as punch. "You following me, Mehta?"

"I know what's going on in my cul-de-sac."

But it was bugging me—Lily had only asked me to help her with her sister's soccer practice a few days ago. How did he know? Was he watching me? All of us?

Or did he have an informant? I thought of his and Ratna's secret handshake and my gaze narrowed. I'd have to keep a close eye on her. Give that girl chocolate, and she would do anything. I made a note to check my phone and room for anything suspicious in it.

"You have a scheming look on your face," Vik said. "You're going to need it if you're going to catch up."

He was right. Vik had pulled off his prank, and the countdown had started for the rest of us.

Which meant that now, he was in the lead for winning the prank war.

20

Soon the first event of the neighborhood calendar—the Mid-Autumn Festival block party—arrived. And just like that, the official party circuit had started in our neighborhood. The pre–High Holidays brunch at the Steins' led to the Navratri garba dance at the Patels' to the Diwali fireworks that we had in the neighborhood gazebo.

To no one's surprise, Rohit was swarmed by other girls at all the events. Granted, we hadn't become official-official, but it was rather annoying given that we had been on a couple dates and he had asked me out to Winterfest. Apparently, that didn't mean the prank war was off, which I oddly appreciated.

I had narrowly avoided another prank attempt from Rohit right before the Navratri garba, when he had tried to tie all my strappy heels together. Mani had caught him, but it was a better attempt than the apple pie. I did like my heels, despite how much they hated me.

We finally had a Saturday off from festivities and I had planned to spend the entire day relaxing. Or I had hoped.

It was the afternoon when I smelled betrayal in the air.

The morning started out pretty normal, with me waking up later than I had hoped and missing my mom's early-morning yoga workout. I tried to join sometimes, if only to make me feel like I was doing something good for my body before eating my weight in pancakes.

After pancakes and dosas had been consumed, we all went our separate ways and I ended up falling asleep on my bed while reading the latest cozy mystery that Lily had recommended to me, one about a young widow in the Victorian era. That, plus the cool air from my cracked-open window and my big fluffy blanket, sent me off, even though Lady Lindensnood was actually a firecracker character. I fell asleep imagining myself in the Victorian era. The crimes I would solve, the handsome earl I might meet, the fabulous dresses and hats I would wear.

The afternoon sun woke me up, as did the sounds of something highly suspicious: Ratna laughing. It's not that Ratna didn't laugh; it was that it was hard to get a full, real laugh out of her. She was more judicious with them than my mom was with advanced reader copies of her new medical book. And trust me, I had tried to get my mom to give me one, but she said she was only giving them to her patients.

I tiptoed outside my bedroom and waited for the sound again. There it was. A loud, woodpecker-like, rhythmic sound, like joy come to life. I couldn't for the life of me figure out what might be causing such a noise. Ratna wasn't supposed to have anyone over, at least not according to the calendar.

A low voice filtered through the door. A boy's voice.

Curiouser and curiouser. I thought she had said no to that boy who had asked her out. Toby. I couldn't help the way I frowned at that name. I inched closer to the door, trying to figure out the best way to confront my sister—and the fact that she had a boy in her room with the door closed—when it hit me.

I recognized that voice. The boy's voice erupted into laughter and—yes.

That was Vikram, all right.

What was he doing here? And how had he snuck past my bedroom?

I gasped. My suspicions had been correct. Ratna was working with the enemy. Maybe I should've let her do her superglue plan.

Before I could help myself, I ran to the door and threw it open.

"I knew it! You recruited my sister to help you. And now I have proof!" I yelled.

Vik sat on the floor, a game controller in his hand. He blinked at me in surprise, his eyes widening. Ratna was above him, lying on her stomach, sprawled across her bed. She completely ignored me, her eyes glued onto the large monitor in the front of the room.

I turned to see a video game of some sort on the screen.

And a small little purple character crossing the finish line.

"Yes!" Ratna pumped her fist in the air, dropping her controller. Half her hair was in a braid and the other half was falling out, like she had forgotten halfway through. Knowing her, it was very possible.

"Aww, no, that doesn't count. Sabotage!" Vik said, throwing down his controller.

"Not my fault you got distracted," Ratna said, grinning like a maniac.

Vik sputtered. "She's your sister, Ratty. Control her."

"Hello," I said, tapping my foot, my arms crossed. My stomach was sinking as I realized this was not the ultimate planning session I had been picturing in my mind, but I still felt a bubble of annoyance in my gut. "What exactly is going on here?"

"We're playing video games," Vik said.

I tried not to roll my eyes. "Obviously, but why?"

Vik and Ratna looked at each other, some unspoken dialogue passing between them. Finally, Ratna spoke up. "Vik convinced me to try out for this e-sports tournament, and I got past qualifiers. So, he's helping me practice. Aka, I'm beating his butt into the ground."

Vik laughed at that. "She actually is."

I did a double take. Vik admitting that he was beaten? Would wonders never cease?

"Oh," I said. I didn't know why, but it made me feel a

little sad and a little proud that Ratna was doing this. Sad because she couldn't come to me, and proud because she had been talking about these types of tournaments for a while. "That's . . . really cool of you, Vik."

"Thanks, Dee," he said. "And just so you know, I don't need to recruit your little sister to defeat you." He said it so simply, like it was a fact of life. "Plus, I already have one prank under my belt for judging. And you? Zero." I stuck my tongue out at him.

Shooing Ratna aside, I took a seat next to her on the bed. The bedspread was a Nintendo one, and I still remembered running around the mall on Black Friday trying to find it for her. It was well loved and covered in crumbs.

"Ratna," I said, putting myself in Ratna's path so she couldn't ignore me. "When's the tournament?"

"Three weeks from now, right after Winterfest," Ratna said.

I nodded. "I'll help you practice."

Ratna opened her mouth. She always complained that I was so horrible at video games that it made her worse.

"Or I'll drive you," I said quickly.

Ratna shut her mouth. "Fine, but I'm not forcing you or anything."

"I want to be there, you silly goose," I said, ruffling her hair. She knocked my hand aside, like always. I turned to Vik. "And you, you better make sure she wins. If you're going to be her coach and all."

Ratna seemed really pleased by the idea that Vik might be her coach. I squashed that little feeling of jealousy in my chest. Vik looked nonplussed, like he had expected it. He saluted at me. "Aye, aye, captain."

I narrowed my eyes at him, looking for any sarcasm. He seemed sincere. That was one thing about Vik—he had always been sincere when it came to my family. You could count on Vik to be unflinchingly real and authentic. He didn't care what anyone thought of him, except for the people who mattered.

"Are we going to talk about how you barged in here thinking your sister had betrayed you and accusing me of—" Vik started.

"No," I said, cutting him off. "And I have to go meet Lily to go Winterfest dress shopping, so I better not hear a single word of this when I get back."

Mainly because if the rest of my family heard about this, I'd never heard the end of it. It would fuel Mani for weeks, if not months.

"Pinky promise," Ratna said. She looked shifty-eyed for a moment. "If you promise not to tell Amma that I ate the last chocolate from La Jolie. Again."

"Promise," I said.

Honestly, not a bad trade. Ratna looked satisfied and turned back to the screen, setting up a new game.

"Your Winterfest dress?" Vik said, sounding mildly interested. He wrapped his arms around his knees and looked up at me. "You and Lily? What are you thinking of wearing?"

"Why?" I said. "You want to come dress shopping with us?"

"Maybe I'm just curious." Vik tilted his head at me.

I raised an eyebrow at that. "Curious? Hmm. Who are you going with anyway?" It flew out of my mouth before I could even realize what I was saying.

"Who said I was going with anyone?" He shrugged, his eyes still intent on me.

The Jennys, that's who. I had overheard them discussing it yesterday. Why wasn't he just telling me? I couldn't mention any of that, though. It would seem like I cared.

My lips pursed, holding back questions. Vik stared back at me.

I left the room quickly after that, and didn't think about why I was suddenly feeling so very warm.

Lily and I met at the outdoor mall in Reston, where a cute new boutique had opened up just a few months ago. I had been afraid that it would be thronged with high school girls shopping for their dresses, so we decided to come late to avoid the crowds. Selection might be lower, but neither of us wanted to fight for dressing rooms, and one simply did not order a dress online for Winterfest.

The boutique itself was sectioned off into different areas, and Lily and I made a beeline for the classic gowns in the back. I already had my look in mind. Think old-timey Hollywood starlet—satin, loose curls, dark red lips. This would be my first kiss with Rohit and I wanted it to feel like the silver screen.

That energy carried me through the first hour of shopping, where I debated between a few dresses. My silver screen vision had led me to a row of old-Hollywood-inspired dresses, but there was a bright red corseted dress that I kept being drawn to, though I didn't know why. It wasn't very on theme, or very Rohit, so I tucked it away.

This was Winterfest, after all.

Lily tried on about thirty dresses, going back and forth on whether she wanted to match her hair or dye it a new color.

I had finally decided on my dress, a royal-blue tea-length satin one with a small side slit, and went to the front section to see if I could uncover any new options for Lily. She kept gravitating to yellows, which weren't doing much for her complexion, so I was looking for a dark green gown for her. Something that would set off the blue in her hair nicely, but also bring out the olive in her skin tone.

A tall blond suddenly stepped in front of the mirror and I started, until I realized it was Alex Pastor from school. She had on a dark pink gown with an interesting beaded halter neckline, and it looked killer on her. I nudged Lily.

"Look who else is here," I whispered.

Lily spun around, a new dress in her hands, an excited expression on her face. Her smile dropped immediately when she spotted Alex and melted into a horrified grimace. I could almost feel her entire body freeze up next to me.

"Lily?" I waved a hand in front of her face. And then pinched her arm. That brought her back to life.

"Why is she here?" Lily whispered, dragging me to the side so we were hidden.

"Uh, because she's also shopping for dresses. Like us," I said. "What's wrong?"

"She's not supposed to be here. She's soccer Alex. She's not supposed to be standing there, looking great and stuff." Lily smoothed down her hair nervously, glancing at her clothes and frowning.

"And she's not supposed to be here when you haven't had the chance to look cute?" I ventured.

"Exactly!" Lily said. "This is why we're best friends. You get me."

"It's true. I do consider understanding your insecurities to be one of my jobs," I said sagely.

Lily grabbed on to my arm. "What do I do?"

I grabbed her arm back and looked her in the eye. "You talk to her."

"What? I can't do that."

"You talk to her every weekend, don't you? At soccer games?" I said. I wouldn't call Lily super confident on a regular day, but she wasn't usually this . . . terrified. Lily must really like her if she was this nervous.

"Not every weekend, she's not always . . ." Lily saw my expression. "But yes, fine, I do."

"Go! She's right there," I whispered, tugging Lily forward.

Lily shook her head so fast and quick she could've given a bobblehead a run for its money. "I can't."

"You definitely can. She's right here, shopping in the same place as us, for the same event. It's like the universe is putting her in your path and yelling."

"Well, maybe the universe is wrong," Lily hissed back.

I gasped. "Why would you say that?"

Lily looked down at her shoes. "She kind of gave me the brush-off last week after physics. I went up to her locker and she basically ran away."

I pursed my lips, thinking. "Don't you have physics fourth period? And doesn't she have debate on Thursdays?"

Lily nodded slowly.

"Don't you see? It wasn't you! She was in a rush. The debate club meets on the other side of the school." I bounced on my toes. Lily didn't look convinced, so I decided to bring out the big guns. "I'm invoking The List, Lily. I didn't want it to come to this."

Lily groaned. "Fine, fine. I just . . . don't know how to be like you. How do I be all confident and grab life by the horns?"

I burst into laughter. Was that really what Lily thought?

"Me? I'm so confident I wished for a high school boyfriend. You had to pump me up to ask Rohit on the first date. And now I'm trying to do the same. If you let me."

Lily wriggled around a little, playing with the hanger in her hands. Then, in the smallest of voices, she said, "What if it's Martin all over again?"

Martin had ghosted her after six months of actual full-on dating. A surprisingly hard thing to do when you went to the same high school, but he had done it. Lily had tried to fit the pieces together for weeks. Weeks where I had come up with a very good murder plan that I would never follow through on. Maybe.

I grabbed her hands and squeezed. "Martin was an asshole. You can't mummify yourself because he did you majorly wrong. That'd be letting him, and all the trolls of the world, win."

Lily nodded slowly. "Like your aunt, right? She's been such a badass since the divorce, which must have been so hard. Six years gone, and then all those people who were so rude to her? If she could get through all of that, I can do this. Right?"

Huh. Lily's words hit me. I supposed all those people who had opinions about my aunt's divorce were kind of like trolls. Observing and criticizing from the outside, as if appearances mattered more than anything. More than the human beings involved.

I hadn't ever thought about it like that before.

"You can definitely do this. Just go say hi," I said. I took the hanger from her and put it away. "It would be awkward if you didn't at this point, you know?"

"That's true," Lily said. "We can't leave without passing her."

"Go say hi," I said, wheedling. I fixed Lily's hair, fluffing it at the top and looping the ends around to make sure the blue strands shone just so in the light.

"Okay," Lily said, with a deep breath.

I watched her approach Alex from behind one of the dress racks. It felt good to see her flying again after being grounded. I took my phone out, feeling a sudden urge to text Vik.

Deepa: She did it. She talked to Alex.

Vik: You sure?

Deepa: Yes, I am, you weirdo. I was there.

Vik: Nice.

And then a beat later:

Vik: She deserves it. Are we on for Thursday? Home stretch.

I texted back a quick yes, and was about to put my phone away when a text came from Rohit. It was a photo of him in a gray suit, and then another in navy. Looking really hot in both, to be honest. No baggy knees or blown-out shoulders. Rohit knew how to make himself look good, and I was happy to appreciate it.

Rohit: I'm kinda into the navy, because it is called the "Winterfest." And gray is too summery.

According to my dad. But what do you think?

I thought for a second.

Deepa: Navy. It'll match my dress. ☺

A little frisson of excitement for Winterfest shot through me. We were going to look so good together.

And if I happened to double-check my phone for any other texts before I tucked it away and walked over to Lily and Alex, I chalked it up to having a phone addiction.

Nothing more.

21

Thursday after school, and our last planning session, came quicker than I'd anticipated. Before I knew it, I found myself across from Vik in the chemistry classroom again. This time our long research checklists were crossed off, our binders were stuffed, and the large rolling whiteboard in the center of the room was filled with our scribblings.

Our initial proposal was due right before winter break started, but we wanted to get it in a little earlier. We'd made a lot of progress, but there was still something missing.

I tapped my pen across my lips as I stared at the whiteboard.

"Are you trying to glare the whiteboard into revealing its secrets?" Vik said. I didn't bother to look at him.

"Something like that."

He moved into my peripheral vision, looming over me so I couldn't ignore him. I turned to face him, an exaggerated expression of annoyance on my face. "Yes? Can I help you?"

"What exactly are you trying to get the whiteboard to reveal?" he said. He perched on the table next to me, his arms crossed, his thigh close to mine. Very close to mine. Of course my brain noticed that detail.

"Its deepest, darkest desire, obviously." Vik tilted his head, giving me a look. My shoulders dropped and I sighed. "Something's off."

"Like . . . ?" he prompted.

"I don't know," I said. "That's why I'm here."

"Right. Okay." Vik rubbed his temples. "Can you please elaborate?"

"We've done all the research. We've made a list of caterers and vendors. We even have the special element you so wanted."

"Yes, Vik, paintball was a brilliant idea and I really enjoyed it," Vik said, mimicking me in a high-pitched voice.

"I don't sound like that," I said, smacking his upper arm lightly. "Or I hope I don't. Anyway, I mean that there's a missing component to our proposal. Something to make it an absolute 'must immediately fund' lock-in proposal."

"That's the special element," he said. "We discussed this."

I shook my head. "That's set. But we're presenting to a bunch of teachers and school admin. How do we make this an easy yes? How do we make it so they allocate more funds to our lock-in than to anyone else?"

Vik turned to me slowly, his eyebrow rising, an expression of approval on his face. He gave me an intrigued once-over.

"Diabolical, Dee."

"It's not diabolical," I protested. "It's practical. It's planning."

"Well, I like that your practicality and planning are finally working on my side." He saw my face. "On our side."

I nodded. That was much better. And it was our side.

Somehow, slowly, the lock-in had become as important to me as it was to Vik. It would be our stamp on our class's junior year, before all the stress and college chaos started. I had grown to really love the idea that we'd be a part of building this memory for everyone.

And I'd had fun planning with Vik.

"Well, let's think. What do adults love?" Vik said. We both went silent, considering the question.

"Thoroughness," I said.

"Thoughtfulness," he added.

We exchanged a look.

"You know, those aren't that far off from each other." I knocked my knee into his. He knocked his back into mine. "And now I have an idea."

It took me a little bit to convince Vik that traipsing around the school with a measuring tape was a good idea. Or even a fun one. But I had an epiphany.

What was more thoughtful and thorough than putting together a layout for the entire lock-in? A floor plan, so to speak. With precise and exact measurements. We had the budget planning under lock, but I knew that it wouldn't be easy to see our vision without something concrete to look at—even if it did mean a tedious amount of work.

"We're almost done," I said, tugging at Vik's arm. "We just need to go to the second floor."

Vik shuddered. "Freshman hall? No, thank you."

"Stop being such a snob. You were a little freshman two years ago."

Vik sniffed. "That was two years ago."

I rolled my eyes and tugged him along. We had been doing that more often—touching lightly, sitting closer together. It was like there was some sort of magnet that was pulling us toward each other, ever since paintball.

We climbed up the stairs to the freshman hallway, lined with lockers and classrooms till the end, where two long windows stood. The second floor was shaped like an H, with the freshman and sophomore hallways connected in the middle by a short row of classrooms and labs. Most of the classrooms were for underclassmen, but some of the math and history classes were still up here.

"Is it just me, or does the hallway seem smaller?" Vik said. "And the lockers. The lockers definitely seem shorter."

"Nope, you just grew a foot," I said. I frowned. "But wasn't there a locker bay right there?" I vaguely remembered trying to flirt with an upperclassman against those lockers and failing miserably.

Like I said, there was a reason I had made the wish.

Vik looked in the direction I pointed, where there was a series of new doors. "No, I don't think so. I think that was a classroom?"

"Huh."

I stood there, arms akimbo, staring at the new door. I could've sworn—well, apparently, I was two years older and very bad at holding on to facts.

"This hallway would be perfect for Dessert Row," Vik said, pacing the hallway juncture. "It'd be nice to keep some of the food vendors away, mainly to make space for all the activities downstairs."

"We'll need access to the parking lot and the tennis courts outside for the water balloon wheel. The lacrosse field is all paintball. So, what if it's Dessert Row and the makeshift movie theater? I remember that Ms. Sharp's projector is really good. And that classroom is wide enough to set up about forty or fifty chairs."

"Really?" Vik pursed his lips. "That seems like a lot. Which classroom is hers?"

"That one," I said, pointing to the classroom near the imaginary locker bays. "I think."

Most of the classrooms stayed open for a few hours after school, so a lot of clubs and teams held their meetings right after the last period ended. But we only had about thirty minutes now to investigate, until the janitors came to lock the rooms.

"Come on," I said. "Let's check it out."

I waved to Vik to follow me. "Are you sure? It's kind of dark."

I jiggled the handle of the door, pushing it open. It was

dark inside, but I walked in. There was enough light from the hallway that the room was illuminated. Vik came in behind me, easing the door so it was slightly ajar.

And the big reveal? A classroom supply closet.

"Okay, so this is on me and my faulty memory," I said. "But I could've sworn—"

I turned to face Vik when I realized that this supply closet was not that big.

I could feel the outline of Vik behind me, making the hairs on my arm stand on end. There was that scent again, worn leather and crisp pine. Why was it that he always smelled so good? Was it that men's cologne got better scents?

"Hey, I don't think you were so off," he said, pointing at the far wall.

There was another door there, and a small, vertical window slat that peeked into a darkened classroom. I stuck my face against the window. Old-fashioned globes and huge tomes lined the window shelves. Yup, that was Ms. Sharp's classroom.

"Weird," I said. "This must have been covered by the locker bays before."

Vik stepped forward. I immediately stepped back and collided into the metal shelves lining the far wall. They shook, and before we could stop it, the door slammed shut.

"That didn't sound good," I said.

That sounded very bad.

All the light had disappeared except for a faint haze from the window slat on the classroom door. Vik jiggled the door to the closet.

"It's shut tight," Vik said, sounding a little frustrated. "I think we're locked in."

Panic rose in my chest. I did not want to die in a supply closet, least of all here with Vik. Then logic set in. I had seen Bernard, the janitor, downstairs before we had left, which meant he would be coming up here and would eventually see us. That was followed by another wave of panic.

Bernard would find us here, stuck in a tiny supply closet, after hours. That would be highly, highly embarrassing, to say the least.

And now Vik would never let me live this down.

"Don't say anything," I said.

I knew he was smirking in the dark.

"Was this what you had been envisioning when you said planning? Because it's going really well, Dee."

I ignored him. These rooms always had keys or a lock mechanism built in. This couldn't have been the first time some kid had gotten themselves stuck inside. Ms. Sharp was a super meticulous teacher, so there had to be keys somewhere. Or a buzzer of some kind.

My eyes adjusted to the dim light and I felt around the wall in front of me and ran my fingers down the lines between the stones.

"What exactly are you looking for over there?" Vik asked, his voice close.

"There has to be something, some way to get out of here," I muttered to myself. "I refuse to be stuck in here with you."

I whipped around to check the other wall for keys.

What I hadn't anticipated was Vik still standing there.

I fell against Vik, my palms on his chest. I made the mistake of glancing up and immediately felt like I was drowning. His eyes were so dark brown they looked almost black and they were focused on me, like I was the only person in the room. Which I was, but this was different. I could feel it.

He bent his head down to whisper in my ear.

"This all seems very convenient. You sure you didn't bring me in here for another reason?"

"What? You're so full of yourself," I said. "You know I didn't."

But my hands were still on his chest and my head was still bent upward toward his at the perfect angle for a kiss.

He hadn't let go of me yet, and part of me wanted him to keep pulling me closer. I got my wish quickly. Vik wrapped one of his arms around my waist, tugging me so that the top of my head grazed his chin. I looked up at him and my breath hitched.

Vik pulled me closer, and one of his hands curled around my head and then . . . pulled a cobweb from my hair.

I groaned internally. Of course. Exactly what every girl wanted during a moment like this.

Vik showed it to me and started laughing, turning me

251

to the side. I grumbled as he reached around and ran his hands through the ends of my hair, making my skin tingle. I tried to hide my reaction.

"Only you, Deepa," he said. "Only you."

I didn't know if that was a good thing, but I couldn't help but laugh, especially as I had come to one life-altering, unconscionably stupid realization.

I had wanted Vik to kiss me. So badly.

It was hard to deny it anymore. I was attracted to Vik.

"The door," I said, clearing my throat, trying to pull away. Vik held on to my shoulders, turning me around.

"Not so fast. I have to do a complete cobweb check."

He really didn't.

His fingers brushed against my temple, featherlight and gentle.

"No cobwebs here," he said. Vik moved his hands down my hair, his fingers cool as they skimmed the side of my face, and then my neck. "And here."

"You know," I said, my voice coming out a little more breathless than normal, "if Bernard finds us here, we'll never live it down."

"Then he won't find us," Vik said calmly. His hands were at my collarbones now. He stopped there. "I think you're cobweb free."

I didn't miss that his voice sounded deeper, huskier than before. We were still standing very close together. So close that I could see the way his eyelashes fluttered. The way his lips quirked to the right as he spoke.

I tried to shake myself out of it. I shouldn't be noticing anything about Vikram, of all people. But something drew me to him. And him to me, from the way he didn't move away either.

And the way he was looking at me.

A loud creak sounded through the doors and we both jumped. It was followed by the sound of wheels.

"Bernard," we both whispered at the same time.

That snapped us out of whatever weird chokehold the supply closet had put us in. Yes, that must be it. The supply closet was the problem. The moment we got outside, this . . . tension between us would disappear and we'd just be Vikram and Deepa, neighbor enemies, again.

"What were you trying to do before? Look for a key?"

"Ms. Sharp would have one, I think. Especially for after hours."

"Most people are probably not entering through the supply closet door," Vik said.

"Do you have a better idea?" I asked.

Silence met me for a moment. All I could hear was a rustle from Vik. I squinted into the dark to see him rummaging through the shelves. "Okay, no. I don't."

Apparently, there was a first time for everything. I didn't lord my small victory over him; instead I turned to the task. "There are also buzzers on some of these supply closets that are attached to classrooms, especially if they used to be used for lab supplies."

"Smart," Vik said. "I remember someone got stuck in

a biology room freshman year during our carbon lab and then he buzzed into the intercom."

"That's actually what I remembered too."

Together, we searched the walls for hanging keys or a buzzer.

The squeak of wheels against tile sounded from outside. Marvin was close.

"I got something," Vik said. He held up a set of keys in an envelope. It had been tucked between the metal shelf and the wall, almost as if Ms. Sharp had planned for two kids to get stuck in the supply closet after hours.

"Quick," I said. From the sounds outside, Bernard was at the classroom across the hall.

Vik unlocked the door to the classroom, and we snuck inside. He dropped the keys on Ms. Sharp's desk just as a door shut across the hallway.

We looked at each other, eyes wide, as we rushed out of the classroom. Half of Bernard peeked out of a door. If he turned, he would see us. Vik grabbed my hand and tugged me the opposite way just as I turned to try to head down the stairs. He shook his head at me.

"He'll see us. We can enter on the other side of the school," Vik said. "Get back to the chemistry classroom."

I nodded and we ran down the opposite hallway together. I didn't let go of his hand. He didn't let go either.

We pushed through the doors to the parking lot and collapsed against the brick wall of the school. I started laughing, in that sort of delirious way that only happened once in a while, when you realized that life is kind of a beautiful mess.

"Are you okay?" Vik asked, breathing heavily. I kept laughing, waving around my hands at him as if that would explain what I was thinking.

Another mess. I had wanted Vik to kiss me. The most annoying boy in all of Edison. In all of northern Virginia, where I was concerned.

Where had Rohit been in my mind? Shouldn't I have thought of my Winterfest date? My perfect match?

The laughter kept coming up, bubbling out of me. I must have lost my mind. Vik was looking at me as if I had. Still, his mouth was curving up into a smile as he watched me.

We said our goodbyes and made our way to our separate cars. Vik was staying later for a soccer team practice, and I had a date with an AP US History essay. My phone pinged as I got into my car, a text from Rohit.

Corsage or no? He sent a photo of two flower corsages. **Also, can't wait to hang tomorrow.**

I was about to text Rohit back when another ping came in. It was from Vik.

You look good in cobwebs.

It shot through me, shoving me back into that moment. I was hit with a strong realization.

He hadn't pulled away.

Vik had wanted to kiss me as well.

22

It became pretty clear the week after the supply closet incident that something had changed between me and Vik.

Nothing obvious at first. Nothing that someone else could point at and acknowledge. It was in the little things. The way his hand lingered near mine when we met after school. The way we stood closer together as we talked before first period. The way we sought each other out more often, lounging near our lockers and staying even after everyone else had left.

It wasn't anything, and at the same time, it was something.

And I couldn't stop thinking about it.

Even though I hadn't told Lily—Lily, of all people!— anything about the supply closet incident. About our almost kiss. I couldn't figure out exactly what it was that was holding me back, especially when I told her literally everything, even if it was the most embarrassing thing ever. And this wasn't embarrassing. Not necessarily.

But still, something held me back.

I kept telling myself the almost kiss didn't really matter,

especially because Winterfest was in two weeks. I was going to Winterfest with Rohit, something I had been wanting and working toward for months now.

Plus, Winterfest was my favorite dance, even though it was an awkward middle school kind of a dance. It wasn't homecoming, which had all the pomp and circumstance of being the kickoff dance of the season. Add in the home-coming football game and you had a classic.

It wasn't upperclassmen prom, which was so firmly embedded in the American high school experience that *promposal* was probably a word in the dictionary. Definitely Urban Dictionary.

But Winterfest was uniquely an Edison High thing. It had been started by a particularly stressed-out senior class who had desperately needed something fun to look forward to before first-semester finals. And through the years it had taken on a new life—it was consistently one of the most attended dances by underclassmen and upperclassmen alike.

Plus, the decorations were always over the top. Last year there had even been fake snow brought in by some-one's dad.

All to say, Winterfest was a big deal. Especially to me.

I had written a kiss at Winterfest on the whiteboard months ago with Lily because Winterfest was the ultimate moment for a romantic kiss. Lily had been playing detective after our conversation on the potential surprise the committee was planning, and she had found out that the surprise was a local band. And she had confirmed that there would be fake snow again.

It would be the right event for my first kiss with Rohit. To seal a magical wish for the perfect boyfriend, something I desperately wanted. And it was right there in front of me if I was willing to take it. I had to put any doubts aside.

Not that I was having any doubts. Not with Rohit around.

I did my best to spend time with Rohit that week, which was how I found myself eating lunch with him and some of his crew team friends. They were talking about some collegiate rowing regatta coming up in DC and I was having trouble paying attention.

To start with, the crew team had a tendency of only talking about crew, even when they were off season, and I only knew a few things about it—like that they woke up at dawn for training and that somehow the coxswain was always a tiny spitfire who was very good at yelling.

I hated to admit it, but I was preoccupied. I kept reliving that moment in the supply closet with Vik. When his arms had gone around me and . . .

"Deepa? Hey, Deepa."

A hand waved in front of my face. I glanced up at Rohit. He wore a mildly concerned expression. "You okay? Something wrong?" His brow scrunched at the thought, which I found adorable.

Yes! More of that, brain. Rohit was the one I should be thinking about.

"Nope, nope, I'm all good."

My smile was so wide they'd see it from Mars. Rohit and the others seemed to buy it.

What was wrong with me? I had the cutest guy in all of Edison High at my side and there I was, thinking about someone else. Someone totally, utterly wrong for me.

I just had to keep telling myself that.

No one knew how it had started, but Thanksgiving, or Friendsgiving, dinner in our cul-de-sac was an absolute must. Every year, my dad would bring a new version of cranberry sauce that only Vik liked, Reshma auntie would bring the Tofurkey, which was a surprising hit, and Lily's mom, Mrs. Liu-Garcia, would bring her famous egg roll taquitos. You could always count on my dad to badger Lily's mom all night for the recipe, and so far, she still hadn't given in.

That conversation was loud enough that us kids could hear it from our station in the living room. We were playing an intense game of Monopoly. Still, there was only one topic on the table for everyone in the room: Winterfest.

Whispers of who was going to be performing, who would accidentally be wearing the same dress like those two senior girls last year—anything and everything Winterfest was on the docket. Asking week was over, but Thanksgiving marked the start of the two week Winterfest gossip season. It was better than worrying about finals, anyway.

"Did you hear Sharon DaSilva is going with Arnold? Arnold!" Lily said, reaching for the dice.

Rose smacked her hand. "It's not your turn, it's mine. And Arnold has really filled out."

Lily waved her hand. "I don't have a problem with how he looks, I have a problem with the fact that he tried to cheat off my biology exam freshman year."

"Yeah, that's no good," Rohit said. He squinted at the Monopoly board, trying to covertly look between Park Place and Atlantic Avenue, clearly deciding which to go for on his next turn.

He was cute, but not very sneaky. Though he had done really well at fending off Lily's latest attempt at a prank, which had been a crate full of fake crickets released into his garden when he was weeding.

Unfortunately, Rohit, a Texas boy at heart, was all too familiar with real crickets and had seen right through it. Lily was currently plotting another attempt, though she wouldn't share it with me yet. Something about the idea needing time to "steep."

"I heard that the football team is renting a huge limo."

"Of course," Mani said, rolling her eyes. We all looked at her. "Cordelia's older brother is on the football team and they're so full of themselves this season. They won two games."

Lily nodded. "It's true." She paused and looked at me. "Should we get a limo?"

Vik and I both said "No" at the same time. We exchanged a quick glance, but it was a slightly heavy one. We hadn't talked about Winterfest, or that I was going with Rohit. Or anything about the closet incident. Vik knocked his knee into me and pointed at the dice, tilting his head. His expression was unreadable, his eyes intent on me.

I grabbed them and rolled, hoping that no one could tell that my face was burning. I rolled a five and Rohit helped me move my little metal car, for which he earned a smile. He smiled back, and that face-burning feeling returned.

"Who do you think is going to win Most Winter this year?" Mani said, her face going a little dreamy. "That's like the ultimate."

"No idea," I said. "But I can safely guess Best Dressed will go to Jenny Boateng. I heard she's designing her own dress again this year, and that girl is talented."

"Definitely going to FIT for college," Lily agreed. "We'll see her on the cover of *Vogue* in five years."

"Kids! Food is ready!" My mom stuck her head around the corner, her freshly curled hair bouncing. "Ratna's already in line."

We all jumped to our feet and ran into the kitchen, our game forgotten. The food smelled delicious, like walking into an all-you-can-eat buffet of all your favorite things. I got into line, leaning over to see what new delicacies our neighborhood had dreamed of. Rohit had gotten waylaid by Lily's dad and was loudly being asked about Winterfest.

Rohit turned and looked at me, and I immediately looked away.

"So are you two a thing?" Vik said from behind me. I nearly jumped out of my skin. "Official?" His voice was surprisingly casual, but it sounded off.

That look was there again, the one I couldn't quite decipher.

And I hadn't been expecting that question. First, it was weird coming from Vik. Second . . . well, it was weird. All of it.

"I thought you guys were besties," I said. "Shouldn't you know?"

"I wanted to hear from you."

I turned my face away from him, biting my lip.

"Um, no. We're not official. But it's been going well. Why, what has Rohit said?" I said, trying to sound casual.

Vik rolled his eyes and smirked, though there was something tight about it. "Bro code. I'm not telling you anything."

"You're so annoying," I said, miming like I was about to throw the dinner roll I picked up at him.

"You love it" was his reply. He reached around me to give himself two huge scoops of kimchi mashed potatoes.

I instantly wanted to deny it, but if I was being totally honest with myself, sometimes I didn't mind it. It was almost . . . fun.

"I heard you asked Violet to Winterfest," I said casually, before I could help myself. I didn't know why I was bringing it up. Except that I wanted to know more. Suddenly, I understood Vik's earlier question better. It was curiosity.

"I did," he said slowly.

We both noticed that I stabbed the mashed potatoes a little bit harder than I needed to. I didn't know why the idea of Vik asking someone else was getting under my skin. Maybe it was just because now I had to go warn her about him. Or something.

"And you're going with Rohit, right?" Vik said, even though we both knew the answer to that.

He was right. I was going with the most eligible bachelor in the junior class. I tried to be a little kinder to the green beans.

"Yup," I said. "I think we're going in a group with some of the crew kids."

"Then I guess I'll see you there?"

I nodded quickly. "Of course. I'll save a dance for you."

Vik froze for a second, his hand stuck midair while spooning curry sweet potatoes onto his plate. A blink later, he was moving as normal.

"Sure, I'll find you for the 'Cupid Shuffle,'" he said, grinning. "If you think you can stay upright this time."

And like that, we were back. "Hey!" I smacked his arm. "It was my first time in heels ever. I didn't know I was going to—"

"Take out a whole line of the soccer team before the

middle school regional finals?" Vik snickered, I frowned. It was the first time our neighborhood had gone to a middle school dance with dates. The dance was right after a particularly brutal prank, and I had been furious at Vik. When I found out Vik had asked out Lucy Mathers, I told her that Vik still wet the bed, and he had retaliated during the slow dance, making me trip so I fell into my date, Scotty Kim.

Taking down the soccer team, though? That had been all me, and those dratted strappy stilettos I had begged my mom to let me wear. I had to move lunch tables for a whole month until the story had died down.

"Thanks, Vikram. I really needed to be reminded of that particularly traumatic memory," I said.

"All of middle school is one traumatic memory," Vik said.

"That I agree on—"

"—for you."

I threw my dinner roll at him this time. Vik caught it and took a bite out of it.

"Nice catch," Rohit said, coming up next to him. He took a huge bite out of his pumpkin pie slice. He noticed our looks and colored a little. "Oh, I like dessert first."

"Love it," I said. "I'm a pecan pie kind of girl, though."

Vik looked at me like I had grown horns. "Pecan pie?"

"Sorry I have taste," I said.

I turned to Rohit. "Pumpkin or pecan?"

He looked up mid-bite, his eyes wide. "Both?"

I giggled at his expression before realizing that Rohit was actually a little flustered. That was something I had finally picked up on. Rohit was the ultimate nice guy and he always agreed with me, The List had been right about that, but I wondered if it was because he really did agree or because he was too nervous to say otherwise.

"No need to pick between us, Rohit." I leaned closer and whispered loudly. "Though it's clear who's right."

Rohit visibly relaxed. "My best frie—my friends in Texas always had the same battle. Glad I don't have to pick here."

"You should send them a text now," I said. "We could take a photo—"

"No, no," Rohit said quickly. "That's okay." He looked away and then back at us. "We kind of lost touch."

"All the more—" I started.

"It happens," Vik said, giving me a look. "But anyway, pumpkin for life."

"What about pumpkin and pecan pie in one?" Ratna said, popping up next to me. She had smashed together two slices of pie, one pumpkin and one pecan.

Rohit started laughing. "Now, that's the right answer."

I couldn't help but laugh too, especially when Ratna took a bite and mimed fainting from how good it was.

We took our food back to the living room, and Rohit stayed behind with me.

"So, do you think we could get Most Winter?" he said.

"Unlikely," I said, shaking my head. "That campaign starts the first day of school. Plus, Most Winter is another level of school spirit. Not sure that's me, or you."

"What about Best Dressed?" he said. Rohit leaned a little closer than necessary. "We could be, if you're really going to be wearing that dress you sent."

My heart fluttered a little. "Possible," I said. "If you're wearing that suit."

We took our seats opposite each other. Rohit sent me a small smile, and I couldn't help the one that crept up my face, or the way my skin warmed from head to toe. That boy could flirt. Winterfest was going to be magical for sure.

Vik sat down heavily next to me, the scent of pumpkin pie wafting over. In his other hand, he had a plate of pecan pie, which he handed to me.

"Me? What did I do to deserve this?" I narrowed my eyes at him. "Did you steal some of my Monopoly bills when I wasn't looking?"

Vik rolled his eyes. "Just eat it."

I did, and it was delicious, which I proceeded to tell Vik. Rohit looked over, his eyes lingering on the plate of pie and flickering over to Vik, but he didn't say anything.

My face flushed, but I wasn't sure why.

23

Before I knew it, Winterfest arrived at our doorstep, accompa-
nied by a snap of frigid winter weather. Frost covered the
grass, making our lawn look almost otherworldly from the
foggy window of my bedroom. A frisson of anticipation
had followed me since the morning, when I realized that
this was the day. The Day.

I would finally be able to cross off The List as soon as I
made my wish real.

Music thumped from my portable speaker, some playlist
that Lily had put on claiming that it was the *ultimate* pre-
dance playlist. I hummed along to the mix of electro-pop,
Top 40, Latin hits, and rap.

"Lily, where's the Christmas music on this playlist?"
I yelled over her music.

"I'm going to pretend I didn't hear that blasphemy," Lily
said, sticking her half-curled head out of the bathroom.
"This is a pre-dance playlist, no Christmas music allowed."

I ventured into the bathroom and watched as Lily carefully wound her curling iron around her hair and tugged
the strands into waves. "You know I need Christmas music
for the entirety of December."

"Stop distracting me, Deeps," Lily said. "We have to meet the group in thirty minutes, and I'm running late."

"I didn't say it," I muttered.

She rolled her eyes at me in the mirror. I sighed and went back to my bed.

"Don't you dare put on any holiday music!"

"No promises!"

I'd finished putting on my midnight-blue satin tea dress and styling my hair (curling was a hopeless cause with my stick-straight hair) before Lily had arrived. I checked my makeup in the mirror and decided to start the process of getting my heels on.

"How are you feeling?" Lily asked.

"What do you mean?" I said, tugging at my strappy black heels.

"About tonight. About your wish." She said the last word in a whisper, as if she was worried that someone might hear even though we were in my room and the door was closed.

"Good," I said automatically.

"Yeah?"

A wave of heat spread over me and I ducked my head, not wanting her to see me. Somehow, even a week later, the topic of my and Vik's almost-kiss hadn't come up. I hadn't told Lily and I was worried she'd see it on my face.

"Yeah. Why? Am I emanating stressed vibes or something?" I tried to keep my voice casual.

"You've just been a little quiet this week. Wanted to

268

make sure you were okay." She ducked her head outside, only one straight blue piece of hair remaining. "Was it that surprise AP Calculus exam? I know you were pretty unhappy about that."

"Yeah, yeah, it was really hard," I said immediately, grateful for the excuse. I wasn't really lying anyway; the exam had been brutal.

Thankfully, Lily didn't push any harder. We finished getting ready and drove to meet up with the rest of the group before Winterfest.

Dinner was raucous as our group ran into other Edison Winterfest-bound students and we combined forces to create a group so huge that the waitresses began sweating as they ran back and forth with our orders.

Rohit was attentive and we spent all of dinner laughing and talking with our group. If there was one thing I could say about Rohit, it was that he was charming. It was exactly the distraction I needed from my thoughts, even if I sometimes wanted to push back on Rohit and ask him what he really thought, to maybe even be a little less perfect. Be more authentic.

But our packed tables were full of laughter and I used it to squash any uneasiness I felt in my stomach.

I let that propel me for the rest of the night, and onto the dance floor once we arrived at Edison. The dance was in the gym, as all Edison dances were, but tonight the planning committee had really outdone themselves.

Fake icicles dripped from the ceiling in unnatural patterns, cascading over the folded-up bleachers on the edges of the gym. In fact, it didn't look like the gym anymore. The lighting cast a shimmery glow over a silver-and-white dance floor that was shaped like a snowflake. There was even a faint drift of fake snow gently falling over the dancers, adding a dreamlike quality to the event.

To my and Lily's delight, the band was phenomenal, playing mixes from all across the decades and interspersing their live acts with a very enthusiastic DJ who was a little too into line dances.

Rohit and I had just finished knocking into each other during the Wobble when I felt a tap on my shoulder.

"Can I cut in?" Vik's head appeared behind Rohit, and my stomach did a flip.

"Sure, man," Rohit said. "I was just about to go get some water."

"Wait—"

Rohit let go and waved at someone near the door. I turned to face Vik, who was looking at me with a curious expression.

I nodded at him. "Vikram."

My heart stuttered, standing across from Vik. He looked good in a suit and tie, even with his hands stuffed in his pockets. His normally unruly hair was slicked back, showing off the angles of his face.

The music shifted and the band started the notes of a

slower song. Vik held his hand out to me, and I couldn't really say no. I took it and let him lead me onto the dance floor.

"So . . . ," he said.

"How's your night been?" I said quickly.

"Good."

"Glad to hear that. I know you were coming with some of the kids from student council. Were the Jennys in your group? I heard they almost wore the same dress—" I was rambling. I knew it. From Vik's face, he knew it too.

"Deepa . . ." His voice was low, and I made the mistake of glancing up. Vik's eyes were warm, too warm, and intent on me. I wanted to look away but something prevented me, like two magnets you couldn't tear apart.

"Our proposal! Any news on our proposal? After our early submit?" I said, hoping that might distract me and him from whatever was happening between us. I didn't see Violet around either, which didn't help. She would have been the perfect reason to flee.

"Not really," Vik said, tilting his head. "Are you nervous, Dee?" Mischief crept up his face.

"What? No. Not at all."

I was. Half of me wanted to run away from the way Vik was looking at me and the other half wanted to lean in. We were on the precipice of something, something that terrified me.

"Am *I* making you nervous?" Vik seemed to be amused

by the idea, like he hadn't thought it possible. "I know you're a good dancer, so it can't be that."

"No," I said, a little too forcefully. "I just haven't—we haven't—"

Vik pulled me closer, as if he knew exactly what I meant, his fingers light on my back. "Ever danced together? Yeah. Unless that square dance in middle school counts. To answer your question, Mr. Costa hasn't said anything. I'm feeling confident, though."

He leaned in. The light amusement on Vik's face shifted into something serious, intent.

"I really enjoyed planning with you, Deepa."

It was sincere enough to catch me off guard.

"Me too," I said softly.

The song was coming to an end, but our eyes were on each other. Locked together.

"Sorry about that!" Rohit said, startling the both of us. The song ended and the entire gym burst into applause. I took the opportunity to step back and clap, composing myself in the process. I gave Rohit a shaky smile and took the glass he offered me.

And Vik? I didn't look at him. Couldn't look at him.

If the song had lasted a little longer, if Rohit hadn't turned up . . .

If, if, if.

Everything would've changed. I would've kissed the wrong boy at Winterfest.

Rohit held out a hand to me to join the group. He waved

Vik in as well, but Vik shook his head, motioning that he was getting a drink.

I looked back at Vik as Rohit pulled me into the dance circle.

The wrong boy.

Right?

An hour later, my feet were aching and my head was still a confused mess. Lily and I stumbled outside the gym as the band shifted to another slow song, determined to get some more punch and a brownie or two from the PTA snacks table. And maybe find a seat where I could take off my heels for a moment. Mani had warned me that strappy heels always made my soles hurt, but I had ignored her and now I was paying for it.

I had done my best to dance away all my thoughts, but in the bright lights of the auditorium lobby, surrounded by other students I knew and parent chaperones, they all came rushing back to me.

We got the last two turtle brownies and snagged a seat in the corner, close enough to the snacks table for a quick refill, but out of the hubbub.

"—and the band is *so* good," Lily said, continuing on with her assessment of Winterfest. She had a lot of thoughts about the decor and surprise elements. "And that 360 photo booth is surprisingly fun, though at an unflattering angle for, like, everyone. I did get one doing the whole dance from—"

"I don't think I can go through with it, Lily," I said, grabbing her hands. She almost dropped her brownie. "Rohit's been great, but something feels off."

Lily rolled with the change in topic. "Go through with . . ."

"The kiss," I said. "I know my grandmother said it's the only way, but something feels wrong."

Lily pursed her lips in thought, searching my face for something. Finally, she sighed. "Does that something wrong have something to do with Vik?"

My hands dropped into my lap. I considered denying it.

"How'd you know?" I said finally.

"Well, you've been acting weird ever since that last planning meeting you guys had. Usually, I come back home to multiple long text messages from you giving me the details." Lily took a sip from her cup, looking at me thoughtfully. "This time? Nothing. And given what happened at paintball, I put two and two together that something must have happened."

I flushed, thinking of the moment between me and Vik. Something had happened.

"Lily, don't hate me, but you're right."

"Of course I'm right." She sniffed in the air. "But tell me exactly how I'm right, please. With details."

"Paintball was really fun. But you're right, the 'thing' happened at our last meeting. There was a . . . moment," I said, my voice dropping to a whisper at the end.

"A moment?" Lily leaned in, intrigue across her face.

"What kind of a moment? Like a 'we've been crushing on each other forever and are now finally getting our crap together' moment?"

I blinked. "What? No. Like a 'there might be something here, almost-kiss' moment."

Lily gasped. I shook my head.

"You think we've been crushing on each other forever?" I asked.

Lily shrugged, pulling at the edge of her bag strap as she looked anywhere but my face. "It might have crossed my mind. Many times. The bickering is a lot!"

"We bicker because we truly annoy each other!" I said, exasperated.

"Maybe," she said. "Looks like I'm not totally off base, because you guys almost *kissed*." She gave me a very, very pointed look. I winced.

"Key word, *almost*."

And everything had been different since then.

"So that's why you guys have been extra weird recently," Lily said, her lips pursed in thought. "What are you going to do about it?"

I wrung my hands, glad that I had put down my punch cup.

"Nothing?"

"Nothing?" Lily sounded aghast.

"Because Rohit," I said, as if it were obvious.

"But Vikram," Lily said.

"But the wish. Don't you think it's the universe?" I said,

my anxiety rising. The universe literally plopped a perfect boy down across the cul-de-sac after my wish. How could I ignore that?

"Deepa, you need to think about what you want," Lily said. "What *you* want."

"I don't know what I want! That's why I made a wish for the perfect boyfriend. That's why Rohit showed up."

I rubbed my temples, feeling an epic tension headache coming along. Lily said I had to think about what I wanted, but I had everything I had asked for in a boy, right there. He was perfect on paper and off. Wasn't that what I should want?

And why was it so hard for me to want it? What was wrong with me?

I gritted my teeth.

"That's why I have to kiss Rohit to seal the deal, Lily," I said. "That's why this whole night had to happen. That's the only thing that matters tonight."

"Deepa, I don't think—" Lily started.

A loud noise jolted us out of our conversation. Somebody had spilled a row of cups filled with punch, and a group of girls had narrowly missed getting drenched. Suffice it to say, they were not happy.

I turned back to Lily, shaking my head. "I have to do it tonight. Don't I?"

Lily's eyes widened. She blinked rapidly, trying to tell me something. I didn't know what.

"I have to kiss Rohit. Otherwise all of this was pointless." Lily didn't seem to move and I waved a hand in front of her face. "Hello? Please, send help, my best friend's body's been snatched."

I whipped around to figure out why the spilled punch was more interesting.

Everything that followed happened in slow motion.

Vik stood in the corner, a few feet away from us. From the pinched, tense look on his face, he had heard what I had said. My heart dropped into my heels.

Had he heard everything?

His expression turned tight as we locked eyes.

"Vik—" I started forward.

He sidled away from my touch. "Have a great time with Rohit, Deepa."

It was worse. He hadn't heard what I'd said about him, only about Rohit, which meant . . . he must think I wanted to kiss Rohit.

He wasn't wrong, was he? Despite the way my stomach clenched, he wasn't wrong. I had wanted to kiss Rohit; I had planned for this.

But things had changed. How could I explain?

Vik stepped away and I followed.

"Wait, you've got it wrong. We're just—"

But Vik didn't hear me.

24

The December air crashed into me as I rushed outside after Vik, covering my bare arms with goose bumps. He was striding toward the parking lot and his car like he had somewhere to be. But I couldn't let him go. Even if I hadn't technically done anything wrong, I knew I couldn't leave it like this.

"Vik. Vikram. Wait," I said.

I caught up to him, ignoring the way my feet ached as I ran in my heels. That seemed to be the only reason Vik slowed down, and then stopped.

"Why? Shouldn't you go back to Rohit?" Vik almost spat the words at me.

"You knew I was coming to Winterfest with Rohit," I said slowly. "And you came with your own date."

That seemed to calm him down. "Violet and I came as friends. And yes, okay, I knew you were coming with Rohit. But I heard you. I heard what you said to Lily." Vik spun around. The look on his face was one I'd never seen before, like he was lost. "Was it all fake? Did I imagine it? Were you just laughing at me the whole time?"

I almost fell back, I was so surprised. "What? Why would you think that?"

"What do you mean why would I think that? Deepa, I heard you. I heard you saying that you've been planning this kiss with Rohit, which means you're serious about it. About him. I know you and I know you don't do things halfway."

He did. And right now, I hated that he did. Then I could find some way to play off what I said, to make him think it was nothing. I knew it wouldn't work, but I couldn't help but try.

"I was just saying stuff," I said.

"Uh-huh."

I hated the way Vik was looking at me anymore. Like he could see right through me and he didn't like what he saw. That familiar feeling of irritation rose and I grasped at it. Technically, I hadn't done anything wrong. Rohit was my date. It wouldn't be weird to want to have a good night with him. To even share a kiss at the end of the date.

The argument rang false even to me, but I held on to it for dear life.

"Vikram, he's my date. *He's* the one who asked me out. You don't really get to be upset about that," I said, a little more sternly than I had intended.

Vik's lost expression turned hard. Cold. He looked at me as if I had lost my mind on the dance floor somewhere. "You still don't get it, do you?"

I shook my head, wrapping my arms around myself. "Don't get what?"

"Stop, Deepa. Just . . . stop. I know you and I know you've felt—"

My heartbeat stuttered. "Felt?"

Vik turned away and turned back. "This," he said, pointing at me and then himself. His movements were staccato, caustic. I could see an emotion cresting on his face before he pulled it back. "You and me. We almost kissed. We have something. And since then—"

I shivered. "He had already asked me, Vik. It wasn't like that."

"It's always not 'like that.' I thought for the first time that you saw what I've been seeing. That you and me, we are something. Something that could be really good." His voice was taut, laced with hope.

I laughed, hoarse and unsteady. Suddenly, it was too much. "Us? You don't even like me. You tolerate me. You didn't want me as your partner for the lock-in. You want to beat me at the prank war."

"Maybe before, but now—"

"I'm your nemesis. I thought that was all." The words tore out of my throat. I didn't believe them, not completely, and yet I wanted to. It would be so much easier.

Suddenly, I wanted to hear him say it. I needed to hear him say it. To define the amorphous thing that had bloomed between us.

"Right," Vik said. He shook his head. "Then to make it clear, Deepa, I like you. I like you very much. And yes, you've also annoyed me almost every day since you knocked on my door in fifth grade and barged into my life without asking permission, but here we are. And maybe it took being partners for me to realize it, but I have now. I like you. I want . . . you."

I inhaled sharply.

"And you can be so frustrating. In fact, you are the most frustrating, infuriating girl I've probably ever known, but I love it. And I've denied it for weeks, maybe even years, according to Pooja, but for the first time at paintball I saw that maybe you might feel the same way, and I . . ."

Vik trailed off.

"Vik, I like—I think I—" For some reason, my words kept drying up in my mouth. I could feel them at the tip of my tongue.

I liked Vik, I did, but it was all too soon. Too unfamiliar. Too unplanned.

My aunt's face flashed across my mind, unbidden, like a gust of harsh, cold wind.

A voice whispered in my head that I'd known Vik forever. But that was what held me back.

"What?" Vik said, staring me down. "Say it. I can tell you want to."

His words were harsh, but his tone was pleading.

"You don't understand. Rohit. He's—"

"Perfect?" Vik sighed, and it was like all the air went out of him. "Yeah, I've heard. And you know what's worse? I really like the guy. But this isn't about perfection. This is about how you feel."

No, it was about the wish I had made. Feelings couldn't be trusted, not really. And how could I go against what the universe had decided for me?

I couldn't say that, though.

"That doesn't make sense," I said, shaking my head. "It's more than about how I feel."

How could I explain that the universe had answered my wish?

Decisions, choices—especially the wrong ones—they could hurt you so deeply you might never see the world the same way. I had watched that story play out in front of me with my aunt.

"Oh, of course." Vik stepped away, his face shuttering. "You'd rather have something you think is perfect. News flash, Deepa. Perfect doesn't exist. It's fiction, it's fake. Of course, you'd rather go for that than take a chance on something real. You're that scared."

I staggered back.

"That's not fair."

"You know what's not fair? This. Making me think—"

"Making you think what? I haven't lied to you. In fact—" I stopped cold. I didn't know how to say it. How to tell him that nothing real had happened between us, nothing like that moment in the supply closet. But I couldn't, wasn't able to admit it. "We haven't kissed."

I had wished for Rohit, and Rohit was waiting for me inside right now.

"I'm sure Rohit is going to ask you to be his girlfriend soon. I thought all the time we've spent together—" Vik ran a hand through his hair. "I'm an idiot."

"No, you're not," I said.

Vik suddenly deflated. "I can't do this." He looked at me for a long second before turning on his heel and walking away.

This time, I let him.

I wandered back into the auditorium lobby, picking up a cup of punch before I wound my way back to the gym. I spotted our group by the bleachers, dancing their hearts out to yet another line dance. Rohit waved at me, pulling me over into the group. I plastered on a smile and tried to get into it. Mostly so no one would notice something was off.

And when the music turned slow and Rohit held out a hand, I took it. The lights twinkled above and fake snow fell as the last song of Winterfest played.

The moment presented itself to me. Rohit looked down at me with the soft lighting, a hesitant look in his eyes. All I had to do was tilt my head up and it would be done.

An ideal kiss with an ideal boy.

But it felt all wrong. Everything felt utterly, horribly, and incandescently wrong.

Instead, I made a joke, Rohit laughed, and the moment passed.

This wasn't how things were supposed to go, not by a mile. But here I was. Standing under the fake night sky at Winterfest, rejecting a perfect kiss from a perfect boy, because my heart demanded something else.

Someone else.

25

The next day came way too slowly, and yet too soon. I woke up at the crack of dawn, my worries having invaded my head at the earliest moment.

I grabbed my phone from my bedside and checked. No text from Vik, but there was a good-morning text from Rohit. Seriously, he wasn't real. What boy did that? Especially after we *didn't* kiss last night.

My dreams had been of Winterfest, my subconscious brain going through everything over and over again, like a movie that kept looping itself. So, yes, I woke up feeling about as fresh as a month-old vase of flowers. But I had a plan to fix everything from the night before.

The one thing I had realized from my looping movie of a dream was that I had never gotten the chance to explain to Vik. If I could just get him aside to talk, I'd be able to explain what I had actually been telling Lily last night. Maybe even about the wish. And maybe suss out what exactly was going on in the feelings department of my heart.

And his.

Part of me was surprised at how he had reacted—I hadn't thought he would care. Even after our almost-kiss, I had thought that maybe it was all a mistake. He would probably text me after having calmed down from the previous night. We had gotten into the groove of chatting every morning. I kept my eyes peeled for another text, even as I dragged myself through the motions of getting ready. It was going to require a lot of work today to look as if I hadn't slept in a trash can.

Fifteen minutes later and I still had no text from Vik, so I sent one myself.

I couldn't stop thinking about the night before. It hadn't looked good, but what did Vik want from me? Rohit was my date to Winterfest. And Vik didn't know it, but I had blown a major magical moment (literally and figuratively) by not kissing Rohit.

Logically, I knew I had to find the next best moment to kiss Rohit and seal my wish, but my eyes kept pinging back to my phone and my blank screen. And to the hurt on Vik's face.

I just needed Vik to respond. I decided to call him.

No response. Straight to voice mail. And even that was full.

I called his home phone and his mom picked up.

"Oh, hi, Reshma auntie!" I said, trying to sound cheerful. "Is Vikram home?"

"Sorry, Deepa, you just missed him," she said with her

soft voice. "He's staying at a friend's place for the weekend. He went there last night after the dance. You should try his cell phone."

"Thanks, auntie. I'll do that," I said, even though I had already done that.

I hung up the phone as I gnawed on my lip. Was he ignoring me?

Suddenly, the one thing I had wanted for most of freshman year seemed like the worst possible outcome.

Now I was worrying. All I wanted to do since Winterfest ended was to talk to Vik. Tell him that the kiss hadn't happened. I still didn't think I had necessarily done anything wrong, but I also knew I hadn't done anything right.

And worse, my heart was telling me the same.

Next week at school, it was as if he had disappeared. Vik's presence had become such a constant over the past few months that his absence was striking.

My hours after school suddenly seemed endless. Without lock-in planning, I almost didn't know what to do with myself, even though I had been so excited to get my time back. Now all that time, all alone, felt . . . empty.

I hated to say it, but I missed Vik and his annoying presence as much as I did planning and working toward something. Now that we had turned in our proposal, there was no reason for us to really see each other.

Vik seemed to be taking that to heart a little too well.

To make matters worse, when I did see him, he would somehow disappear. At first it had been more subtle, in that he wasn't where he normally would be. When I went to his locker, that's when it became more obvious what Vik was doing.

That morning, he saw me, stopped, and walked the opposite direction.

Message received. Loud and clear.

I didn't have to like it. I knew that if I could get a few words in with Vik, I could explain everything. But how could I when he wouldn't even let me? And without lock-in planning, I had no built-in reason for him to see me. He could keep ignoring me for all existence.

I considered walking up to his door after school and making him talk to me, but that opened up a whole can of worms with the neighborhood. I wasn't interested in getting his (and my) entire family involved.

School it would have to be. Unfortunately, Vik and I didn't have any classes with each other this semester, which left me having to piece together his schedule. I spent the better part of the week trying to do just that, with minimal success. One of the soccer boys mentioned that Vik had AP Chemistry fourth period, but I could never manage to find him.

That Friday, I got lucky. I was leaving my lunch meeting with my counselor, my nose in my career-planning binder as I walked to my locker. I didn't normally come to this side of the school during lunch, mostly because all my classes were on the other side.

I saw Vik across the hallway and dashed over before he could leave, right as he shut his locker. He looked up, startled to see me. The initial surprise turned into a frown.

"Hey," I said.

"Hey."

It was funny how one word could contain so much.

Hey, why have you been avoiding me? Hey, I'm sorry you overheard something you shouldn't have. Hey, I hate the thought that you might be mad at me. Hey, I'm so, so confused.

"I've been calling." I didn't mention my unreturned texts.

"Yeah, my mom told me." His face was an impassive mask. I stepped closer, and that mask cracked. "Proposal is submitted. We're all good."

A beat. And then a heavy look. There were so many words lingering in the air, so many things unsaid. I took a deep breath.

"I don't really care about the lock-in proposal," I said. I reached out to Vik, my hand brushing his arm. "I was calling to talk to you."

"Why?" The word came out a bit harsh, and I flinched.

"You know why."

I attempted a wobbly smile. Vik's body language relaxed a little. He stepped away from his locker to face me fully.

"No, I really don't," he said softly.

I fidgeted. "Really?"

"Or maybe I want to hear you say it." A smile played at the corners of his lips. He squashed it quickly, but it was encouraging.

"It was a misunderstanding," I said. "You didn't hear everything. You didn't hear what I said before, how I was telling Lily that I wasn't sure anymore, that Rohit and I didn't quite feel right." My shoulders dropped.

Vik considered me, his face inscrutable. "Okay. So?"

"We didn't kiss."

It was the wrong thing to say.

"Wonderful," he said, his jaw tight. He slammed his locker shut and gathered up his books. "See you later, Deepa."

I reached for him. "Vik. Vikram. I just told you—"

Vik whipped around, stopping me in my tracks.

"Are you and Rohit still dating?"

The words died in my throat. I didn't know what to say. I couldn't tell him no because I hadn't officially ended things with Rohit. Part of me was still holding back. Part of me was protesting that it had only been a few dates. But I wanted to—

That seemed to decide it for Vik.

Vik's face shuttered, and just as I thought he was going to say something, he clenched his jaw shut.

He didn't even look at me as he walked away.

26

My mom was sprawled across the couch, napping, when I came back home from school that afternoon. That in and of itself was a weird thing. I wasn't sure I had ever seen my mom look so exhausted. She wasn't the napping type.

I grabbed one of the blankets from the armchair and draped it over her. I knew she had been staying up late for her book deadlines, but I hadn't known it was this bad. I started dinner, deciding that my mom needed a break and that I desperately needed a distraction from my conversation with Vik. Nanna wasn't home, so I pulled out what I was best at making—macaroni and cheese. I went through the motions, letting the stirring and measuring fill my mind.

Still, Vik came popping back in.

Part of me was upset that Vik wouldn't hear me out. The other part understood. I never enjoyed the idea of Vik being right, but in this case, maybe he was.

Either way, I knew I had to tell Rohit something. I hadn't been spending as much time with him as I should, especially after a date like Winterfest. But I had been so confused all week.

Could my wish have been wrong? And could I turn

my back on it? How could I know I wasn't making a huge mistake?

I was stirring the pot of mac and cheese, wondering what sort of vegetable I could sneak in without Ratna noticing, when I heard my mom yawn. She stretched and sat up, rubbing her eyes.

"Deepa? Are you home already?"

"Amma, it's past six," I said.

She blinked at her watch. "Oh."

"It's okay, I started dinner. Granted, it won't be anything like Nanna's creations, but it'll be sustenance and it'll be ready by the time the others get back." I tried a bite of the mac and cheese, and then grabbed the jar of crushed red chili peppers. And some broccoli.

"You're a lifesaver," my mom said. "I didn't mean to fall asleep."

She walked over, rubbing the side of her face. I handed her a glass of water.

"I . . . have a question for you," I said. We were alone—everyone else was out and my grandmother was at her weekly carrom board game again. This was as good of a time as ever. "Last time Urmila Pinni came over, we were just . . . casually talking about relationships . . . and stuff. And I mentioned how perfect your and Nanna's relationship is. And she said that it's not as perfect as I think."

I paused. My mom took the knife from me and started to chop up the broccoli.

"But you guys met your junior year and have the best

love story. How did you guys know you'd be each other's first loves? Was it because you guys had a plan?"

"Erm," my mom said. "We didn't know, to be honest."

I frowned. "You guys are like the ultimate. The way to be," I said, prompting her. "And after Urmila Pinni's divorce, you were always saying that she had to find someone who 'fit the bill' and was a good match."

My mom sighed. "Deepa, I was angry and grieving for my sister. I never meant to give you the impression that there's only one way to do love, or to do life. And while things seem together on the surface, there are many times when my relationship with your dad is hard work. But we both *want* to make it work. We choose each other every day. That's why we're perfect for each other. That's it."

I shook my head. It all seemed so . . . uncertain.

"How do you know you won't get hurt? Like Urmila Pinni?" I said.

My mom's smile was gentle, and a little thoughtful. "There's no guarantee you won't. Or that anyone won't. But that's what trust is all about. That's the beauty of life—you only feel hurt if something matters to you."

She took my hands in her own and rubbed my knuckles. It was something she used to do when I was a little girl, and it calmed me now as it had then. "Life isn't about getting things right. It's about finding what matters to you and going after it with all your heart, because those other things? Hurt and disappointment? They're inevitable. In some form or another, they will find you."

I frowned. She didn't sound unhappy about the idea, while the very thought of being hurt, let alone disappointed, sounded wretched to me.

"And that's a good thing?" I said slowly.

"It's a great thing," my mom said, her eyes bright. "It means you're living a full life. Highs and lows. And your relationships? Love? It is something worth fighting for. Sure, it's an unknown. But tell me, Deepa, what in life is known for sure?"

I glanced down at our hands and swallowed hard. I could feel her words in the very center of my heart, like a small, hot arrow had been aimed true.

"But can't I make life known?" I said, still unwilling to let go.

"You can try," my mom said. "But don't do it at the expense of your happiness."

My happiness.

I wasn't entirely sure what was my happiness, but for the first time, the idea of figuring it out, and making a few mistakes along the way . . . well, it didn't sound as horrible as before.

Still, the idea of letting go sounded so scary.

"What if I could get it right, though? Avoid any hurt? Nanna always says that certain choices increase the probability of a good outcome, so what if I—"

"No," my mom said quickly, in a very decisive and firm tone that she only used on business calls. "Your dad is right, in his own way. Going to bed on time will increase the possibility that you'll do well on a test the next morning. But, Deepa—" She took my chin in her hands and tilted my head so that she was looking me straight in the eyes.

"Let me tell you a secret." She cleared her throat, looking a little nervous. "I was actually planning on asking another boy to homecoming at the beginning of my junior year."

"Wait, what?"

That was a major revelation. My nose scrunched as I tried to put the pieces together.

"He was my perfect boy. Your dad was . . . not." She laughed a little, as if reliving a memory. "But one fateful weekend together, at a random garba of all things, made me start to see your dad in a different light. And when he asked me, I realized I had a choice. And I'm glad I took the choice to go on the adventure of life with your dad."

"Okay, wait, this is mind-blowing. First of all, why has no one ever told us this?" I rubbed my forehead. "And also, you guys weren't some power couple from the beginning?"

My mom burst out into laughter. "Not at all. But I took a chance on the boy who made me laugh and who made me feel like me. I'm realizing we should have told you this earlier." She cupped my cheek, her eyes soft. "I never meant to make you feel as if we had it all figured out. No one does, kannamma. And you don't need to either."

I hung my head, emotion swelling in my throat.

"Thanks, Amma," I said, my voice breaking. I wrapped

my mom in a hug, taking her by surprise. I let my head rest on her chest for the first time in a while, the way I used to when I was a child. It felt comforting and reassuring. A few seconds later, I lifted my head to see my mom tearing up again.

"Amma."

Not this again.

"I'm sorry," she wailed. "You'll understand when you have teenagers!"

I rolled my eyes but patted my mom's back. When she finally stopped sobbing, she decided that what we needed now were chocolate chip cookies to go along with the mac and cheese. Which was also unusual for my mom. She went to the pantry and I continued stirring the mac and cheese, deep in thought.

I hadn't realized how much I had been trying to control things. I was a planner, and I liked being organized, but I didn't know when it had all transformed into . . . fear.

And my mom—and my aunt—were right. I didn't want to be scared. There were no guarantees. I didn't even have to look very far for examples. Like my fabulous AP US History essay about the Vanderbilts that had been so thoroughly researched and meticulously written and had still not gotten an A+ because of Mr. Stickler's dislike of robber barons. Totally unfair, but how could I have known? And I stood by my essay.

Okay, so not the perfect analogy.

But I think I understood what my mom was saying.

Some things were worth gambling on. Some things demanded it, and only paid out after.

So was I willing to accept the uncertainty? Was I willing to finally ask myself what I wanted, instead of what I should want?

The real question—was I willing to take the risk?

27

I found Rohit outside that weekend, pruning the gardenia bushes in their front lawn with his mom. I spotted him from my front window, watching and trying to gather the courage to go over there. And waiting for his mom to go inside.

"What are you doing?" Mani said, popping up next to me.

I shrieked. "Jeez, Mani. Are you trying to give me a heart attack?"

"Not my fault you're jumpy," she said, shrugging. She peered out the window. "Stalking Rohit again? Aren't you guys dating now?"

I winced. "That's kind of why I'm here," I said slowly. I looked over at my younger sister, wondering how much I should tell her. I sighed. "I need to end things, and I'm trying to muster up the courage."

"Why?" Mani said. There was no malice in the question.

"Because . . ."

"Is it because he's so perfect? It's almost too much. Like please, have a flaw. Or is it because you and Vik are finally admitting that you like each other?"

My jaw dropped open.

"Don't look so surprised. The YSU has had a bet going for a while," Mani said. I looked at her in question. "Younger Sibs Union. I let Nikhil pick the name, which may have been a mistake."

"You better not have bet against me," I muttered.

"That's not really the point. And yes, for your information, I did place a bet that you would come to your senses and see that Vik's into you. Has been into you."

I flushed, thinking of the supply closet.

"Ewww, are you blushing? I do not want to know why," Mani said, making a face.

I smacked her on the arm and she pushed me back. "You're so annoying," I grumbled.

"That's why you love me."

We stood there for a few moments, both of us watching Rohit and his mom weeding and tending to the garden.

"What if I'm making a mistake?" I whispered. "What if—"

I was bracing myself for a snarky comment or jibe that would remind me why it never paid to be vulnerable with younger siblings when Mani reached over and wrapped her arms around me.

"Sometimes you just have to try," she said.

I hugged her back, nuzzling my face into her hair. I remembered how Mani had smelled as a baby, all fresh powder and soft baby scent. "When did you become so wise?"

"Over the summer. Growth spurt." Mani wiggled out of my arms and pushed me toward the door. "Now go."

* * *

Rohit's mom had finally gone inside when I walked over. I breathed an internal sigh of relief. That wouldn't have been fun to explain.

His head popped up from the bushes and he waved. In the buttery morning sun, and in a short-sleeved Henley, Rohit looked godly. But seeing him reminded me that there was another boy across the street, one who I cared about a lot. I took a deep breath and waved back.

"Hey! Have a second?"

Rohit straightened, shielding his eyes with his gloved hands. "Sure thing. What about?"

I inhaled deeply, trying to steel myself.

"How are you, by the way?" he said. "I didn't see much of you this week after Winterfest." I flinched, noting the hint of accusation. His tone softened. "I was thinking, are you free this weekend?"

I pulled my cardigan tighter around my body. Now or never.

"I'm sorry I missed you, it was a hectic week," I said. I didn't mention how I had been in a frantic haze for most of it. "But about Winterfest . . . and this weekend . . ."

Rohit leaned into me and I realized I had to rip the Band-Aid off.

"I had a great time at Winterfest. And I'd love to hang out this weekend. But as friends," I said. "You're lovely. And I've had such a good time with you. It's just . . ."

300

"I get it," Rohit said. He quirked a half smile at me.

"I'm sorry," I said. "I really like you and I wanted to give it a chance—"

"But you like someone else more," he said.

I stepped back.

"What?" I shook my head quickly. "No. No. It wasn't anything like that."

"I don't mean it in a bad way. We'd only been on a few dates," he said, his voice gentle. And his eyes? Way too kind and understanding. Like he could see right through me.

Or maybe it had been that obvious to everyone around me.

I didn't want to admit it to Rohit, that he was right. But he wasn't completely right.

"I really did have a wonderful time with you at Winterfest," I said. "But I think I'm . . . looking for something else."

Despite Rohit being a great guy, he wasn't the right guy for me. Maybe I was looking for something a little less perfect and a little more . . . real. And honestly, both of us deserved that.

Rohit nodded. He put down the watering pot in his hand.

"For what it's worth, I think Vik's fantastic. Seeing you two together, well, you're a good pair."

I scoffed. "The first time you saw us together, we were at each other's throats." The words came easily, a story I had told hundreds of times before.

"True," Rohit said. "But I don't think that's a bad thing in this case."

"Why?" I said, curiosity getting the better of me.

"Well, he doesn't let you get away with crap. He pushes you to be better, like to think outside the box with the lock-in planning or to put together a better prank. More important, he cares enough to do that. Most people wouldn't. He's your biggest pain, yeah, but he's also your biggest fan."

"Huh? Are we talking about the same person here?" But even as I said the words, I wasn't sure I meant them. There was more truth in what Rohit said than I wanted to admit.

He was right.

Sure, I had wanted to explore this thing with Vik, but part of me still struggled with it. With making the wrong decision with the wrong person.

But it wasn't about that, was it? The perfect boyfriend didn't exist. I thought back to what Ratna had told me as she had parroted back my own words.

A boyfriend is someone who should make you feel like you could take on the world.

Vik did that. He saw me. He did push me to be better—by challenging me and making me think and arguing with me (which was annoying). But it worked. And he also knew me deeply. My humor, my weird traits, my pet peeves. So, so well.

It hit my gut, and I knew it then. Maybe I had always known it in some way.

Vik was my wish come true.

Not because he needed to be conjured up but because I had missed that my perfect match had been there all along. That's what the universe had been trying to tell me.

"Actually, now is as good of a time to tell you as any," Rohit said. "But my dad's contract has been renewed, so we're . . . staying here. On Oceania Court Drive." Rohit stuck his hands in his pockets and looked away, almost like he was scared of my reaction.

"What?" I said. "That's amazing! I thought your dad's contract would be over at the end of the year, and I know all of us have been counting down the days until we could ask you whether you were staying. This is great news!"

"Really? You're not just saying that?" Rohit glanced up at me, his expression so open that I finally saw the real boy behind the fantasy. And it clicked for me then. The times he had mentioned his old friends, the way he was always just a little careful around us all, the mask he sometimes wore. My dad had been right. Making friends was hard for everyone.

Even for someone "perfect" like Rohit.

"Really." I placed a hand on his upper arm in a way that I hoped was reassuring. "I can honestly speak for all of us here on the cul-de-sac in saying that we're thrilled. Especially Vik, I'm sure. And Mani adores you now after you helped her learn that new TikTok dance. Your fan club is pretty big on this street."

"And you?" he said softly.

We'd dated, so I guess we were exes of a sort, but I realized I still wanted him in my life. The thing was, we did get along really well, even if it wasn't romantically. And more important, I could hear the question behind his words. The worry.

"Oh, I'm the president," I said, grinning. "You're a part of the cul-de-sac crew now. Stop trying to get out of it. You're a member for life, Rohit. You'll have to leave all your other allegiances behind, especially to horrible football teams from other cities. It's possible you may come to regret moving here."

A few months ago, Rohit would have startled at my words, taken them too seriously, but he knew me—and he knew us now.

"You don't mind? Really?" The relief was clear on his face, and for a second, I hated the people who had made him feel this way in the past. I mentally pictured tracking them down and making them eat dirt.

"Why would I mind? You're like the best thing that has ever happened to Vik, by the way. I'm pretty sure he had no decent friends before you."

Rohit laughed, the questions on his face finally melting away. "He's a really good guy, you know. If I had to lose to anyone, I'm glad it's him."

Rohit really was a great guy, and a great friend.

"Well, we'll see. Vik may have moved on—he went to Winterfest with Violet and—"

"He hasn't," Rohit said, cutting me off, his tone final.

I swallowed roughly at that. Maybe, maybe not. I had messed up and I knew it.

We chatted a little more, catching up about the week, Lily's latest failed prank attempt, and Edison gossip. I helped him with the gardenias as he told me about one of the neighbors down the street and how they had a noise violation the other night, and we speculated about what kind of rager their kids had attempted to throw.

Talking with Rohit seemed easier, lighter. We were more open with each other, and Rohit cracked jokes, revealing a side of him I hadn't quite seen before. Almost as if without the pressure of dating, we were getting the chance to finally know the other person.

I caught Rohit's eye, and for a moment over the gardenias I saw what might have possibly been—if I had seen this version of Rohit earlier. There was a part of me that still thought he would make a wonderful boyfriend.

But the heart wants what it wants, and what I wanted . . . wasn't so obvious.

An hour later, I waved goodbye to Rohit. I could really see us being friends. He had mentioned needing some time, which I understood. But when he was ready, he'd be the first person I'd call if the Flaming Moths ever did that reunion tour. The way we had left things felt right.

Now I had something much bigger looming over me. How exactly did I win Vik back? Or really, win him in the first place. I hated to admit it, but Vik had clearly under-stood that there was something between us before I had. I had lagged behind. For all I knew, Vik had already moved on after I hurt him.

I hated that idea. A lot.

There was only one thought I could focus on, something I kept thinking back to—I had wished for the perfect boy-friend. And like the perfect prank, the perfect boyfriend had to be tailored to the person. So, wasn't Vik who I'd wished for, if you really thought about it?

I stumbled back, the realization literally throwing me off-balance.

The solution was clear.

The wish still needed to be earned and the deal was still waiting to be sealed.

With a kiss.

But this time, with the right boy.

I ran into the living room to find my sisters sprawled across the couch, watching the latest holiday baking show competition.

"I have a problem," I said.

"Is it the problem where you have two boys to pick from and there's an obvious choice, so it's not really that much of a problem?" Mani said.

Ratna looked at us. "Huh?"

"How'd you know?" I said, sinking into the couch across from them.

She gave me a sidelong glance and tossed her hair behind her shoulder. "I see all" was her response.

"Oh, are we talking about Rohit and Vik?" Ratna said. She had somehow managed to contort herself upside down and half off the couch.

"Deepu, you know I'm team Rohit, mainly because this may be your only chance to be with someone who is that hot and has that many muscles." Mani paused. "Really, I have no idea why he's interested in you."

"Rude, Mani," I said.

"I mean, you wear penguin pajamas and you're *sixteen*. Seriously, this may be your only chance—"

I threw the pillow at her and she dodged easily.

"Let's be real, how many boys are going to be okay with the fact that you color organize your underwear? Or that you made an Excel sheet of our take-out places? That's a lot to love right there."

This time, I got up and made sure the pillow hit her in the face. Ratna burst out laughing and Mani shot her a dirty look.

"Whose team are you on, Ratna?"

Our little sister was dangling her upper body off the couch, which she said helped her think better.

"Team Vik. He's cute, and he's good at *Mario Kart*. Plus, he lets me eat his nachos," Ratna said simply.

"Well, there you go. Hot and muscled, or likes *Mario Kart*," Mani said. "Hard decision."

I groaned.

"But the question is, how do you feel about it?" Mani said.

"I don't know," I said, my voice half a moan. "Wait, that's not true. I do know. I just have no idea what to do about it."

Mani put the remote down, shoved off her blanket, and turned her full attention on me.

"It's Vik, isn't it?" Mani said, looking at me intently. "You did it; you broke up with Rohit."

I took a deep breath and nodded.

She pumped her fist in the air and mouthed "Yes!" silently. Ratna suddenly looked interested.

"And I need to tell him, but he won't talk to me," I said. I sunk my head into one of the couch pillows.

"Well, what are sisters for?" Mani said. "Let's make a plan."

Ratna giggled. "That's such a Deepa thing to say. And do. But I'm down to help."

And for the next two hours, under the auspices of over-the-top gingerbread houses and brightly colored sugar Santa statues on the TV, we plotted. Finally, we had something.

Ratna went to go get us snacks and I collapsed onto the living room floor, staring up at the ceiling fan as it rotated.

My most detailed and difficult plan ever waited ahead of me. The question was, could I pull it off?

28

I was in the middle of making pancakes on Saturday the next week when my phone started going off. Incessantly. We had made it a rule long ago that Saturday mornings were no-phone mornings, which all my close friends knew.

My amamma frowned at my ringing phone as she flipped the pancakes on the griddle. I nudged in and added a sprinkle of walnuts on top, Ratna close behind with the caramelized banana topping we had made earlier.

"That phone is going to ruin my hearing," my grand-mother said. "Why do you all insist on having such shrill ringtones? You should change them to Carnatic music, like I did."

We all nodded absentmindedly. This was a regular refrain from my grandmother, and as of yet, none of us had changed our ringtones.

There was a beat of silence, and then the phone rang again.

"You think that's Lily?" Ratna said, looking up from her spot at the dining table, where she was working on her science project, a plate of pancakes next to her. "Rose's soccer practice is now, isn't it? Maybe she needs your help with something." She gave me a look.

"I think I should pick it up," I said. My grandmother waved me away, muttering about how electronic music was ruining the world. I wiped my hands on the kitchen towel and grabbed my phone.

Our neighborhood group text was blowing up. There were a series of texts, but not from Lily.

> **Vik:** Has Pooja texted any of you?
>
> **Vik:** Hello? Anyone?
>
> **Vik:** Don't make me group call you all.
>
> **Lily:** Sorry, no! Still at Rose's soccer practice! Those Dragon Snouts are SO annoying. Did something happen?
>
> **Vik:** I don't know. The parents are in Maryland for the day and Pooja sent me a cryptic text. Then no response.
>
> **Rohit:** Sorry, man, haven't heard anything
>
> **Vik:** I'll try calling her.

Vik texting the group text must mean something serious. It had been virtually silent since Winterfest, and even now he wasn't texting me. It was Saturday and Pooja was at dance practice. She learned Kuchipudi, an Indian classical dance, from the same teacher I had in middle school. I would have been the right person to text or call, but I guess that's where we were at now.

I sighed and put my phone away, going back to my pancake station.

A few minutes later, Vik texted back.

Vik: Okay, got ahold of her. Never mind.

Finally, I texted.

Deepa: Great! Well, let me know if you need anything. I'm at home babysitting all day (aka the sisters).

Vik didn't respond. Of course.

I tidied up the kitchen and the living room, cleaning up after Ratna's crumbs and piling Mani's magazines back into the corner basket. Ten minutes later, as I was washing the dishes, I saw Vik's car pulling out of the driveway and driving away fast.

Well, guess he hadn't needed my help. But something had gotten him out of there quickly.

I grinned to myself and walked into the garden, where Mani and Pooja sat near the firepit, eating their now-cold pancakes and giggling over their phones.

Especially Pooja, who looked very happy to not be at her Saturday dance class. She may have conveniently forgotten to tell her brother that class had been canceled today. All the better for me.

"How's it going, you two?" I said, taking the seat across from them. A table was laid out in front of us, strewn with papers and props and . . . other prank paraphernalia.

Pooja nearly bounced off her seat. "Perfect. He didn't buy it at first. I called him and was like, 'Bhaiya, my stomach isn't feeling so well,' and he was all, 'Suck it up, P. It's just a stomachache,' so I sent him another text, this time super mysterious, exactly the kind of thing he'd hate. He didn't respond. So then I texted him saying they were checking me for possible appendicitis. That got him moving."

Her phone rang, and she held it up to show Vik's image calling. "See?"

Her smile was a little gleeful, but younger siblings were like that. I winced. I had recruited Pooja and Mani to help me get Vik out of the house, but I wasn't trying to send him into a panic attack.

"Isn't that a little extreme?" I asked. We needed him out of the house, but, well . . .

Pooja shook her head. "Did you forget that time he superglued all your pencils to your desk before that big test in history?"

I *had* forgotten. The terror I had felt at possibly failing that test, however, was still burned in my brain. It had all worked out, but it was a good reminder.

"All's fair in love and war?" I said.

The two girls nodded at me sagely.

"Especially prank wars," Pooja said. She sat back and pressed the ignore button on her phone. "My brother needs a swift kick in the pants, and I'm happy to help you deliver it to him." She cackled evilly, an odd juxtaposition to the bright yellow wool cardigan and floral jumpsuit she wore.

That's exactly what she had said when I had called her a few days earlier. I had barely been able to get her to stop talking long enough to listen to me.

"And I have ideas. What if you hot-glued his phone case to his nightstand? Or put jelly in his baseball hats?" Pooja had sounded a bit too excited at the idea of getting back at her older brother.

"I'm thinking bigger," I had said.

And of course, she had loved that idea. Pooja was the one who had convinced Mani to join. I had been the one to get the rest of the cul-de-sac in on it.

"And he forgot to lock his room door?" I said.

Pooja nodded. "I checked the camera Nikhil installed and Vikram totally booked it out of there. I guess he does love me or something."

Mani and I rolled our eyes. Pooja had Vik wrapped around her finger and everyone knew it. And that's what had inspired me—knowing Vikram. He had never even known that his little "pep talk" would be the start of his downfall.

"You never told me," Pooja said, bringing me back to the present. "That you guys had a fight."

"Mani!" I glared at her. "That was a secret."

Mani shrugged. "Everyone knows now."

I groaned.

Pooja tapped the back of her phone with her nails, looking off into the distance. "So that's why he's been in a weird funk. I thought with all the time you guys had been spending together that you'd finally figured out your whole crush thing. But then he came back home from Winterfest and was in a mood," she said.

"That might have been because of me," I said. "But I'm trying to fix it."

By making him think his sister might have appendicitis, but, well, that was the Oceania Court Drive way. How could you tell someone you cared for them other than by pranking them?

And this one was going to be a good one.

"Do you know how hard it is to get Vik out of the house without locking his room?" I said. "It took me three cappuccinos to come up with this plan, and I've got to see it through."

If Vik was going to keep ignoring me, I'd speak to him the only way we had ever known. Through pranks. And he would have to listen.

Pooja nodded. "He's obsessively careful. This was a good idea."

"Surprised you thought of it," Mani said. "Kidding." I threw a wad of party streamers at her. She caught it and lobbed it back, but it went wide.

"Clock starts in . . . ," I said, looking at my watch. "One minute."

Nikhil had added location sharing to Vik's Google Maps when he wasn't looking, which only confirmed my theory that younger siblings were scary. But useful.

We looked at Pooja's phone with bated breath, watching the little dot on her Google Maps app that showed us where Vik was—and that he was now twenty minutes away, having arrived at Pooja's dance teacher's house.

"Okay, it's go time!" I said.

I immediately fired off a series of texts and then jumped to my feet.

It would take us thirty minutes to get his room and his house ready, so the timing was tight. We were counting on at least five minutes of confusion just due to the parking situation there, and then Pooja was going to send the next text, telling him that she was actually fine and someone had dropped her off at home early. He might want to murder her at that point, but Pooja had decided that was something to worry about later.

"You sure you're okay inviting the wrath of your older brother?" I said, pulling myself to my feet. I checked my phone to a slew of texts as each person on my team reported in. It hadn't been that hard to recruit the others only on the fact that we'd finally be able to take Vikram down for the prank war.

Pooja shrugged. "No sweat. It's literally my job as the youngest. Honestly, if you can pull the rest of this off, I'll vote for you to win the prank war."

But this was more than the prank war. This was more than pulling off one great prank.

If I could pull this off, I might finally get the thing I had actually wished for—a chance with Vik.

Which was all I could hope for right now.

29

We had set up stations throughout the Mehtas' house. Ratna was inside on watch duty, and she was taking it very seriously. She hadn't left her spot near the front-door window for the past ten minutes, her binoculars glued to her face.

Mani and Pooja were working on the living room and Nikhil and Rose were setting up the garden. More like Rose was supervising Nikhil and making sure he didn't just end up playing with the fake cobwebs I had gotten for the next ten minutes. Lily was upstairs with me, in Vik's room. And Rohit, who I was surprised still wanted to help (though I shouldn't have been surprised; he's a great guy) was on outside watch duty, surveying the cul-de-sac for any external threats. And he was picking up the food.

My phone was pinging constantly with updates from everyone, allowing me to keep track of things while putting the finishing touches on my pièce de résistance—Vikram's room. I had already changed into my outfit, the corseted red dress from the boutique. Lily had convinced me to go back and get it when I had mentioned this plan. I owed her for taking the time to convince me to go back—it felt right wearing it.

Like I was finally me. Like I was finally doing the right thing.

This was the largest plan—and prank—I had ever attempted to pull off, and I couldn't help the gnawing worry that everything would tumble down. It wasn't like I had been working on this day and night for a week or anything.

But I had the best team of people, and I knew Vik well. All the elements were in place, and I could only trust.

Deepa: Vik check?

Pooja: He's sending confused texts.

Deepa: Perfect. Deploy "The Call"

Pooja: 😈

It was the signal.

Pooja's voice drifted upstairs. "Yeah, turned out to be a false alarm. I had a queso burrito for lunch and you know what that does to me. Where am I now? Jeez, you don't have to yell. I got dropped off by one of the moms who was leaving early. Why did no one tell you that? I dunno, maybe because you yelled at them, like you're yelling at me. People don't like that, Vikram."

Silence. "He hung up on me," she said.

I smiled.

Exactly where I wanted him. It was actually a lot of fun to see Vik flustered for once.

And when Vik came back, he would realize that I had not only tricked him with the fake Pooja wild-goose chase, but he would walk into a house transformed.

"Time check!" Mani yelled from the foot of the stairs. "He's on the move!"

Lily and I nodded at each other, and I handed her another bag of glitter.

Time to finish this off.

We hustled out of the house as soon as we could, leaving only Nikhil in the house. The rest of us took up our places to watch Vik. He arrived a few minutes after our expected time, his baseball cap askew and looking annoyed as hell. His clothes didn't match at all, and he looked like he had gotten dressed in a hurry, or in the dark.

First part of the plan: the garage door opener wasn't working, courtesy of some switched-out batteries. Vik kept pressing the button, but nothing happened. Now he was forced to go through the front door and our prank house of fun.

He managed to get his keys out and into the front door, only to be greeted by a wall of Saran Wrap. The first stop on the road map of our story together.

The look on his face and the subsequent "Pooja!" was priceless. Picture worthy.

And now step one was done.

Ten minutes later, Vik was annoyed as all hell, a fact I

knew because I had Nikhil watching him and sending me the feed.

So far, Vik had made it through the Saran Wrap door. "Pooja?" This time he sounded a lot more cautious. He was catching on, but I didn't think he was putting the pieces together yet. The bright pink arrows on the floor might help, though.

Vik followed the arrows into the living room, which was covered in books about famous "absolute" monarchs from history. He picked up one of the books, and then another, his look changing from confusion to disbelief.

"Hit it," I whispered to Lily over the phone.

Music blasted through their kitchen. Vik nearly jumped out of his skin, spinning around to face the kitchen. And he finally noticed the kitchen table, where there was a line of Vicky's bubble tea cups and cartons from the places we had visited on our planning day together. Each one had a letter written on it in black Sharpie.

Vik approached the table carefully, his forehead scrunched. "Your . . . move. . . ." He picked up the panda cookie I had placed at the end. I couldn't be totally sure with the slightly grainy feed, but he looked surprised. Recognition lit up his face, like he was putting the pieces together.

We were in the endgame now.

Vik stood there for a little bit, staring at the panda. My anxiety levels hit an all-time high. Was he staring at the panda cookie in a good way? A bad way?

Did he finally get what I was trying to tell him?

Vik turned on his heel and ran up the arrows on the stairs. He would enter his bedroom to find it covered in glitter bombs, similar to our paintball adventure. Real paint would have been too permanent, unfortunately, but multicolored glitter bombs were just annoying enough.

And there, everything would come together . . . or it wouldn't.

I sat back as the feed cut out. Nikhil was supposed to go upstairs now and try to record Vik's reaction, for posterity. I was sure it would be good. I was sure I had pulled off one of the best pranks Oceania Drive had ever seen.

I wasn't sure of anything else.

Finally, Nikhil texted me 😺.

I rushed down the stairs and through our backyard to Vik's, where I had set up everything.

The weather was unseasonably warm for December, but there was still a nip in the air. I pulled my cardigan tighter around me as I waited, trying not to spiral into my worries and thoughts about how Vik would react when he saw me.

The glitter bombs would lead him to the backyard and that's where I stood, under a canopy of stars and icicles reminiscent of Winterfest, and where everything went wrong. I was waiting in the right dress this time, with an apology and an explanation I hoped he would let me get through.

The sound of the backyard door shutting jolted me out

of my thoughts. I quickly fixed my hair and got ready just as Vik walked through.

Vik stopped in his tracks when he saw me. Faint traces of glitter flecked his clothes and the edges of his hair. "Why?"

"To prank you, of course."

Disappointment flickered across his face, briefly. I took it as a sign to approach him. He regarded me warily.

"I heard you ended things with Rohit," he said.

"You did?" I said, surprised.

"He told me. Earlier," he admitted, still watching me with that unreadable, guarded expression. "Good prank. How'd you pull it all off?"

"Thanks. I had help. But that's not the reason I put it all together," I said. "I did it to tell you something."

I stepped closer and grabbed his hands, tugging him toward me. He came easily, letting himself be pulled in, his brown eyes warm but a little wary as they watched me.

I took a deep breath. "It wasn't fake. It was real. What you felt between you and me. I felt it too," I said. "And you were right."

"Wait, can you say that again?" Vik said.

I rolled my eyes. "You were right."

"No," he whispered. "That it wasn't fake."

My words caught in my throat, hope building in my chest at his words.

"It wasn't fake," I said again, my words soft. "Every

moment was real and I wanted to show you that. Welcome to the story of us."

Vik's expression softened. "I noticed. It's a pretty great story."

My stomach flipped, hope rising in my chest. "And I'm sorry."

Vik shook his head. "There's nothing to be sorry for, not really. You didn't do anything wrong."

"I'm sorry that I missed all the signs. And that I was so scared."

Up above us, the fake stars I had strewn across the patio cover blew in the breeze, twinkling dimly as if they were winking at us.

I took a deep breath. "I should've seen it earlier. Or really, I should've not ignored it earlier, because it was there, it has been there for months, maybe even years, and I—"

Vik pulled me into him, his arms encircling me, and then his lips were on mine. Soft and warm and everything I had ever dreamed of.

This was a kiss. Heat rose up my body as I kissed him back, as his hands tangled in my hair.

A cheer went up from behind us. We both paused, pulling back to look at the backyard door and then at each other. All our siblings, and Lily, were lined up, with big grins on their faces. The food had arrived as well. I could see platters of food laid out on the dining table through the windows. They'd been busy.

Lily cheered again, her voice echoing across the backyard. She made a kissy face at the two of us.

"Do you think everyone's known this whole time?" Vik whispered.

"I think so," I whispered back. "I think they knew before both of us."

Vik didn't look embarrassed, or worried. A mischievous smile played at the edge of his lips. So, I smiled back.

I wanted to stay there in his arms, but I knew everyone waiting inside was waiting for us. Plus, Lily wouldn't stop cheering.

"*Finally*," I could hear her saying. "Finally, these two idiots got it together."

"Did she just—"

"Call us idiots?" I said. "Definitely."

We both burst into laughter. Vik stepped back, though he didn't look happy about it, and held out his hand to me.

Lily stopped us. "We have something to address before you go inside. I motion that we give the title of Prank War Winner to Deepa. This was the ultimate."

I shook my head. "I didn't do it alone."

"Okay, true," Nikhil said, leaning against the door frame in a way that was very reminiscent of his older brother. "And I'll totally take like ten percent of the credit, but this idea was initially yours."

"I'd be happy with eight percent," Pooja said. "Because I'm far more generous than my brother."

He made a face at her.

"Either way," Mani said, "Deepa is totally the winner with this prank. Nikhil and I got the whole thing on video. It's going to be an Oceania Court Drive classic."

"That's not fair!" Vik said, an alarmed look on his face. "Isn't there some sort of rule against that?"

"I think it's pretty unanimous," Lily said. She stared at Vik, hands on her hips.

"Fine, fine," Vik said. "I'll concede. This was a thoughtful, beautifully executed prank. While I might debate whether it really fits the boundaries of a prank—"

Lily coughed loudly. "That's up to the prank war council," she said under her breath.

"—it's still the best we've seen this season. Or ever."

Vik bowed out of the way, his eyes twinkling as they caught mine.

"Congratulations, Deepa," he said. "You beat me."

"Sweeter words have never been spoken," I said, accepting his concession with a graceful tilt of my head. With that decided, the others went inside for platters of nachos and pizza. The parents would be arriving soon to join as well. We had forewarned them that prank business would be happening, but that it would end with a party.

Vik and I lingered behind.

"I can think of a few words still left to be said." Vik looked down at me and traced the skin on my palm. "How about . . . I really like you, Deepa. Would you like to go on a date with me?"

I rubbed my chin in mock thought, watching the way Vik's eyes twinkled in the darkening light and wondering how I had missed all of this before.

"I think I just might."

And then he kissed me again. I couldn't believe we had wasted so much time not doing this, when it felt so . . . right. We finally pulled apart, and he moved to rest his forehead against mine.

"Ready to go back in? And face the music?" he said.

I took his hand. "Let's do it."

We stepped inside to the chaos of a neighborhood party.

Ratna had clearly gotten into the trays of doughnuts early, if the doughnut crumbs and quarter-empty tray were any sign. I shook my head, laughing. The door opened, and Rohit walked in, looking a little uncertain. Lily pulled him into the group, where he was immediately accosted by Pooja, who wanted to know where he'd bought his sweater. He glanced over her head and waved at us, a tentative smile on his face.

I waved back and then nudged Vik. "Go to him."

"I'll be just a minute," he said. I looked away, giving them a moment of privacy.

I went for a doughnut myself. The front door swung open and the parents flooded in, looking surprised at the smorgasbord of food the kids had managed to wrangle up. My grandmother bustled toward me, eyeing the doughnut in my hand. I gave it to her and grabbed another for myself.

"So, looks as if your request of the last bloom came true after all, hmm?" my grandmother said. She took a bite of the doughnut and waggled her eyebrows.

"Looks like my wish did come true," I said. "But . . . was it real, Amamma?"

She shrugged. "How are we to say what is real and what is not?"

"A straight answer would be nice," I said with a groan.

"I cannot speak for the magic of the last bloom," my grandmother said. "Except that it is never quite what you think it will be." Her eyes twinkled. "Mani may soon find that out herself."

My grandmother winked at me and left, humming an old song to herself.

When Vik came back, I was watching Mani, who was arguing vehemently with Nikhil about their union bylaws.

"What's going on there? Do you think we should step in?" Vik asked. He clearly had caught sight of the same interaction I had. However, he seemed a lot more concerned, sending darting glances over at the pair of them.

"Don't worry, Mani can take care of herself," I said.

Vik shook his head. "I'm not worried about Mani. I'm worried about Nikhil."

I chuckled at the look on Vik's face.

"By the way, you may not have been able to check your email today—" I said.

"Wonder why."

"—but Mr. Costa sent us an email. Our lock-in proposal was approved early."

Vik whooped, pulling me close again. "We did it!"

"We did," I said.

His hand curled into mine, like it was never meant to be anywhere else, and my heart felt full.

It was funny how things worked out, wasn't it? Somehow, in the last place I ever would've looked, I had found exactly what I needed.

And it was perfect.

Acknowledgments

The idea for this book came to me in the bleak depths of the pandemic, a little while after I had finished up the third book in my fantasy trilogy. I was craving a light story, one that I could sink into and use to escape the world. One that would bring me joy. That's where I found Deepa and the cast of Oceania Court Drive. Hopefully, they've given you some joy too.

Thanks to Mabel Hsu, my brilliant editor, for believing in this story from the start and being a fantastic advocate through the entire process. Also, to the entire team at Katherine Tegen Books, including Julia Johnson, Molly Fehr, Amy Ryan, Taylan Salvati, and all of the wonderful production, marketing, and sales folks who made this book come to life.

Thanks to Kristin Nelson, who has been right by my side along this wild ride that is publishing. It feels great to have you in my corner, no matter what direction I go.

Thanks to my wonderful friends, who supported this book, and me, when I most needed it. To my word warriors, Rosie Brown, June Tan, and Deeba Zargarpur, and my NYC writing buddies, Kat Cho and Meg Kohlmann.

Thanks to my parents and my sisters, who always make me feel like I've achieved the moon with every book. Love you all so much.

And last, but certainly not least, to my husband, Aakash. I choose you every day. Thanks for always believing in me.